KEYFORGE

In the center of the universe hangs the Crucible, an artificial world built from the pieces of countless planets. Over millions of years of new environments and societies being added to the world, cultures have expanded, exploring the possibilities of their interconnected, slowly merging alien biomes: adventuring, surviving – even thriving.

Filled with mysterious devices, lost civilizations, hyper-advanced cities and an incredible array of species, it's a place where fantastical science blends with arcane powers – all made possible by the unique substance known as æmber.

Meanwhile, godlike Archons enlist the other inhabitants to compete in battle and decipher the secrets of the Crucible, gathering the æmber required to forge mystical keys which will unlock the vaults hidden by the planet's legendary creators: the Architects.

BY THE SAME AUTHOR

ANDERSSON DEXTER

Self Made

Act of Will

The Beauty of Our Weapons

Pixels and Flesh

DEVI JONES' LOCKER

Packet Trade

Sea Change

Storm Cloud

Floating Point

Beautiful Red

Children of Arkadia

Modern Love and other stories

The Voyage of the White Cloud

The Martian Job

Retaking Elysium

The Home for Wayward Parrots

KeyForge

The QUBIT ZIRCONIUM

M Darusha Wehm

ACONYTE

First published by Aconyte Books in 2021

ISBN 978 1 83908 066 1

Ebook ISBN 978 1 83908 067 8

Cover art by Natalie Russo
Back cover art by Viko Menezes

Distributed in North America by Simon & Schuster Inc, New York, USA

Printed in the United States of America

9 8 7 6 5 4 3 2 1

asmodee ENTERTAINMENT

ACONYTE BOOKS

An imprint of Asmodee Entertainment Ltd

Mercury House, Shipstones Business Centre

North Gate, Nottingham NG7 7FN, UK

aconytebooks.com // twitter.com/aconytebooks

CHAPTER ONE
Pplimz Climbs a Tree

Wibble hovered cantankerously in the corner, her right flipper grazing the ceiling. She watched as Champion Anaphiel teetered precariously, then fell. Her football-shaped body pulsed with a bioluminescence, the color ranging from lilac to deep royal purple, but otherwise she was completely still. She was quite clearly annoyed.

"Wibble," a patient voice called from the other side of the office. It had only the slightest hint of a mechanical twang. "It's just a game. No, I take that back. It's not even a proper game; no one is keeping score."

"How many have you missed?"

"Well," the voice paused. "None. But that's not the point..."

"I rest my case." She turned slightly, aiming her lower flipper toward the ground. A small, colorful rectangle of cardstock was balanced precariously in three force fingers – extruded sections of her flipper – and she made a couple of tentative flicks toward the ground before flinging the card in earnest. It arced gracefully through the air, sailing toward the upturned felt fedora lying on the floor. Just as it was about to overshoot, the card caught an eddy of breeze and seemed to stop midair, then dropped into the hat where it joined the card emblazoned with the image of Champion Anaphiel and half a deck of its brethren.

"So there!" Wibble shouted in triumph, her body flushing through a pastel rainbow before settling on a smug deep rose as she waggled her tail to descend toward the hat. "I told you I could make that shot!"

"Indeed you did," Pplimz said, extending a mechanical arm to collect their hat. As their arm retracted to where they were seated at a large wooden desk, the rectangular screen that displayed the face they were currently wearing looked mildly amused. They dumped the cards onto the desk and said, "I am deeply unconvinced that tossing cards into a hat is a sensible or enjoyable activity to pass the time."

"You're only saying that because I won," Wibble said.

"There are no rules, and therefore no method of determining a winner," Pplimz argued, neatly collecting the cards with three appendages extruded from their sleek, dark body, ordering the cards with blinding speed, then placing them back in the box.

"I'd like to see you make that shot."

"When I learn how to float," Pplimz said, drily, "I will attempt it."

"You *should* learn to float," Wibble said, hovering over the desk directly in front of Pplimz's screen head. "It's delightful!" She bobbed up and down as a demonstration.

"Wibble," Pplimz said, exasperation plain in their voice. "Will you please get off the desk?"

"Why?" Wibble said, although she slowly flowed off to the

side. "There is absolutely nothing whatsoever going on right now."

"I'm afraid you're mistaken," Pplimz said, their limbs reconfiguring to a more humanoid appearance – two matching arms, one on each side of their thin torso. "We're getting a call."

The desktop illuminated and a shimmering screen popped into view. A jerky video feed appeared, an out-of-focus face more or less centered in the frame.

"Oh dear," Pplimz said, recognizing the caller.

"Ooh, goody!" Wibble exclaimed as she floated over to Pplimz's side. "This doesn't look boring at all!"

Pplimz sighed and flicked open the communicator.

"Tailor the Taupe?" Pplimz said. "Is that you?"

The video feed was of extremely poor quality and there was a distinctive lag. He must be calling from a cave or tunnel. Every type of terrain imaginable was found on the enormous planet, so that didn't exactly narrow down his location.

"I always thought it was Taupe the Tailor," Wibble said in a whisper.

"Be quiet, Wibble! Tailor? Are you there?"

The video resolved, and a pale blue face with luminously glowing eyes appeared. And it seemed particularly worried.

"I don't have long," the elf said, glancing behind himself nervously. "I'm in trouble."

"Again," Pplimz said, not entirely unkindly.

"Yes, again," Tailor admitted. "But it's not my fault. I didn't do anything wrong, but no one wants to hear what I have to say. I've had to make a run for it and I'd better not stay in one place too long." His amber eyes widened as he stared into the camera. "If I send you coordinates will you meet me?"

Pplimz turned their screen face toward Wibble, arching a

pixelated eyebrow. Wibble wiggled midair, her tail undulating excitedly.

"Please? Come on, Pplimz, just hear me out."

"Send us the coordinates," Wibble said.

"Thank you, Wibble!" Tailor said, relief flooding his face. "I knew I could count on you."

"We haven't agreed to anything," Pplimz reminded him. "But we'll think about it."

"That's the best I can hope for, I guess," Tailor said, then startled at a sound behind him. "Got to go," he whispered. "I'll be in touch." The video blacked out and Pplimz turned to Wibble.

"You'll say yes to anything, won't you?"

"Of course not," she said. "Well, probably not, anyway. Besides, it's this or more games of toss the card into the hat, and we all know you don't want to lose another round."

Pplimz said nothing, shaking their screen head in disbelief. A tiny smile played on their simulated lips, though. They picked up the dark charcoal hat and placed it gingerly atop their head. Defying all laws of gravity, and most senses of aesthetics, it stayed put. They shrugged on a muted gray and black plaid double-breasted suit coat, which matched the slim cuffed trousers that hid their lower appendages. Their nimble carbon-fiber fingers buttoned up the coat and they gracefully waved an arm toward the frosted smartglass door of the office. The glass displayed several glyphs rendered by a system which automatically detected a visitor's species, then displayed in the languages they might be expected to read: *Wibble and Pplimz, Investigators for Hire.*

"After you."

• • •

"Honestly, Wibble," Pplimz said, settling into a plush armchair in the passengers' section down below on the ship, "could you have possibly found a more conspicuous form of conveyance on the entire Crucible?"

Wibble jiggled thoughtfully. "I'm sure I could have. And I'll have you know that this ship is very stealthy for a night voyage." Indeed, with its pitch-black hull made of a lightabsorbing polymer, in the dark it would have been near undetectable. Not a soul would have seen its two protruding articulated tentacles thrusting from the bow, its enormous batwing rudder extending from the underside of the hull, or its eleven-legged cephalopod captain scuttling across the decks.

"Too bad it's the middle of a bright summer afternoon, then," Pplimz said, as the ship's rudderwing swung back and forth, propelling it forward and up into the air from the landing pad at the Hub City transport terminal. They rose over the gleaming spirescrapers of the central metropolis, joining traffic bound for all corners of the impossible world of the Crucible. They passed over the city's Central Stadium, where a team of mech-assisted giants trained for an upcoming spikeball tournament, then over the Martian Enclave, with its heavily fortified green-tinted saucer-shaped structures.

"There's no reason to sneak around," Wibble said. "Lots of beings are heading off for a holiday in the Plains. No reason we can't be two of them. After all, there's nothing more suspicious than looking suspicious."

"Thank you for that profound insight," Pplimz said, but they knew Wibble was right. They were among several passengers on this flight to Floating Pines Resort, which wasn't far from the coordinates Tailor the Taupe had sent them. It was a perfectly good cover story. Not to mention that the resort had an excellent mechanic on staff. Pplimz secretly hoped that they might get a quick spa treatment in before they had to return home. The actuator on their fifth upper manipulator had been stiff for a while.

"Besides," Wibble said, interrupting Pplimz's train of thought, "Captain Flurrbitz owed me a favor."

At the sound of her name, the skipper of the vessel undulated down the companionway into the passenger compartment. Her shiny skin was as black as the ship's hull, only two pale yellow eyes marring the complete darkness of her body. Her tentacles writhed incessantly as she slithered toward the passengers, and didn't stop wriggling even once she'd reached them.

"Welcome aboard the *Black Star*." A kindly voice came from the captain as she addressed the passengers. "I know you have many transportation options, and I'm pleased you chose to travel with us. If there is anything we can do to make your voyage more comfortable, please don't hesitate to input your request to the serving bots." She raised a tentacle to indicate the glowing terminals embedded in the ornately carved bulkheads. "Refreshments are now served at the galley port. Please help yourselves, and we'll have you to Floating Pines in no time."

A few of the other passengers rose and headed toward the snacks, and the captain slithered toward Wibble.

"Thanks for the last-minute berths," Wibble said.

"Black Star Tours is always happy to help," the captain said, cheerfully. Then quietly added, "If there's anything else you need..."

"Well–"

"No, thank you," Pplimz interrupted, glaring at Wibble.

"Whatever debt you think you owe us is fully repaid. We deeply appreciate your help."

A slight crimson tone flashed briefly across the captain's body, then she returned to her natural hue. "As I said, I'm always happy to help. Please, enjoy the hospitality on your way to the resort." She wriggled up the companionway ladder and disappeared onto the deck.

"Now look what you've done," Wibble said.

"We can afford to pay for passage," Pplimz said. "There's no need to extort favors from anyone."

"It was not extortion!" Wibble said, indignantly. "I offered to pay for this trip but she wouldn't hear of it. Flurrbitz comes from a people with a strong belief in the balance of the universe. I helped her out with a minor miscommunication with a dry dock when the *Black Star* needed a refit, and ever since then she won't stop asking to repay me. She feels beholden, and I fear that a couple of free tickets isn't going to be sufficient."

"I see," Pplimz said, ashamed to have assumed the worst of their partner. "Well, I wish you'd told me that before."

"Hmm," Wibble said, her body flashing a pale blue. "So do I." She rolled over lazily, then said, "It is a beautiful ship, isn't it?"

Pplimz looked around at the ornately carved compartments, the velvety seating, all in various shades of black.

"Not exactly your style, is it?" they asked, eyeing Wibble's pastel-hued body, emitting a low bioluminescence.

"I appreciate many aesthetics," she said quietly, rolling away from Pplimz's view. They caught a glimpse of themself in the refection of a porthole, their own noir-toned body and clothes blending in perfectly with the ship's decor.

"Right. Well, uh, why don't we go see about those refreshments?" Pplimz changed the subject abruptly, then stood, carefully balancing on their two lower limbs in time to the ship's roll.

"Since when do you eat food?" Wibble asked.

"Who said anything about eating?" Pplimz countered, and gingerly picked their way to the galley window.

The ship docked at the Floating Pines Resort and Spa precisely on time, and they disembarked with the other passengers. As the majority of the guests turned left toward the reception area of the resort, Pplimz and Wibble slipped away from the group and veered right, toward a poorly lit path among the eponymous floating pines. The forest appeared to be composed of perfectly ordinary pine trees, save for the fact that their roots grew into the air instead of soil, and ended no less than four inches above the ground.

"Aren't these trees lovely?" Wibble said, bobbing up and down to investigate a rather large pine from bottom to top.

"I'm sure they are," Pplimz said, rapidly extending two of their upper appendages to help them navigate in the severely reduced gravity. "I'd rather not investigate them quite so closely," they added, as they tripped and narrowly avoided crashing into a ball of roots.

"Let me help you," Wibble said, coming down to hover next to Pplimz and offering them a flipper. They took it gratefully and let Wibble steady them as they half walked, half hopped along the forest path. While the trees' branches were still in full bush, the path was blanketed by many-colored needles – most were some shade of green, but there were yellows, blues, and purples liberally strewn among the litter. As they followed the path, needles dropped slowly and steadily from the branches, like multi-colored falling rain.

"It really is lovely in here," Pplimz said, finally getting the hang of moving through the lighter gravity that was endemic to the area. The engineered world of the Crucible contained habitats of wildly varied types, suitable for life of all forms – some places suitable to no life at all. Pplimz had visited several locations with unusual environments, but it always took them a little time to adapt.

"Well, don't get too enraptured with the view," Wibble said. "We need to start looking for those coordinates."

"I'm on it," Pplimz said, and they were. Part of their mechanical augmentation was multiple sensory systems, which allowed them to see the forest both in its natural beauty, and separately as a map with the trail to the coordinates Tailor the Taupe had sent them. "We should take a left after that rock."

There was nothing obvious to see on the other side of the rock, but a few yards in, one of the taller trees had a well-disguised rope dangling among its roots.

"After you," Pplimz said, transforming their hands into climbing cams to better grip the rope.

"See you there," Wibble said, and began to float up toward the canopy. Pplimz fed the rope through their new ascenders and began to pull themself up the tree. The lighter gravity made it easy and they quickly caught up to Wibble, who was taking her time.

"Any chance we're walking into a trap?" Wibble asked, gleefully. "That would be exciting!"

"No one is walking into anything," Pplimz said, then paused

for a beat before gesturing at their feet dangling into empty space.

"Very funny," Wibble said. "You knew what I meant."

"We are rather a good distance from any pockets of what I'd call civilization," Pplimz said, continuing to hand-to-hand their way up the rope. "If I were looking for a good spot for an ambush, this would do rather nicely."

"Shall I scoot up and do a little reconnaissance?" Wibble suggested, her body losing its characteristic coloration and taking on a decidedly translucent appearance.

"No," Pplimz said. "I'd rather we stuck together. It's not as if Tailor the Taupe doesn't know what you're capable of."

Wibble sniffed. "I don't think even you know everything I'm capable of."

"Perhaps not," Pplimz said, "but even if you can be nearly invisible, neither of us has been exactly inaudible. I don't think we're sneaking up on anyone right now."

With that, they were vindicated, as a voice from above called down, "Wibble. Pplimz. Am I ever glad to see the two of you!"

CHAPTER TWO
Wibble Gets Stuck

"Come in, come in!" the voice called from the entrance to a platform built atop a nest of branches, and Wibble floated up to peer inside. She tipped sideways in confusion, then reached a flipper down to help Pplimz onto the platform. They clambered up to the treehouse, which was small, rustic, and completely devoid of elves.

"Can I offer you anything from my humble refuge?" The voice came from a small communicator sitting on a shelf that was laden with bottled water and packages of ready-made meals.

"No, thank you," Wibble said, floating around the space and very obviously inspecting the decor of the hidden shelter.

"We rather expected to meet you in person," Pplimz said, inspecting the communicator, then searching the treehouse for surveillance devices. There was nothing readily apparent to the eye, but they felt some faint electromagnetic pulses near the doorway. Pplimz reformed their hands from rope-climbing cams into precise EM sensors and felt around the doorjamb. A pair of tiny cameras and an infrared device were secreted in natural-looking notches in the wood. Very clever.

"Sorry about that." The voice that came from the tinny communicator didn't sound sorry at all. "Can't be too careful."

"Fine," Pplimz replied, vaguely annoyed but also impressed by Tailor's commitment to security. "Now, I understand time is of the essence. Perhaps you should tell us what's going on." Pplimz turned back into the small treehouse and perched themself on a large sawn-off tree branch that functioned as a chair, then swiveled their head sharply. "Wibble! Get out of there!"

Wibble's front end was buried deep in a rough sack sitting on the floor of the treehouse, her tail waggling out its mouth. She tried to turn over in the bag, but her side flippers got caught in the opening and for a moment it looked as if the sack had come to life as she squirmed about inside it. Eventually, there was a muffled *pop* and she floated out of the bag, a sheepish orangey-blue tint to her now perfectly spherical body.

Pplimz blinked slowly twice, then turned back to the communicator, ostentatiously ignoring Wibble. For her part, she popped back to her normal ovoid shape and wafted over to them.

"I have found myself in rather a delicate predicament," Tailor said. "It seems that the Star Alliance has issued a writ of detainment with my face on it."

"Ooh, that's not good," Wibble said, her tone sounding as if it were, in fact, rather good indeed.

"I've been accused of stealing a rather valuable piece of jewelry from a Star Alliance officer," Tailor continued.

"Oh dear," Pplimz said. They wouldn't put theft of anything

past Tailor, but the newest arrivals on the Crucible were still a bit of an unknown quantity.

When the *SAV Quantum*, one of the finest exploration ships in the Grand Star Alliance fleet, crashed into the Crucible not long ago, it had made waves all across the enormous world. Not literally, of course. It had crashed into an arid area in the East, far from any of the many oceans and seas in this small corner of the Crucible. But beings far and wide heard the news of the giant starship and its mostly but not entirely human crew, with their lofty ideals and killer technology.

"I didn't take it!" Tailor said. "But..." he paused briefly, "I was in the neighborhood when the tiara disappeared. And you know how humans are – a lot of elves happen to be thieves, so when something goes missing and there's an elf nearby, well, obviously that's who they're going to suspect."

"I don't know about that," Pplimz said, frowning. "I've never heard of a Star Alliance officer who jumped to conclusions. They tend to assume the best of beings... unless proven otherwise."

"Look, I admit that I've ended up in the middle of bad situations more often than chance would allow," Tailor said, "but have you ever known me to actually steal anything?"

Pplimz looked over at Wibble, who pulsed with a thoughtful yellow light and was uncharacteristically still.

The first time they'd encountered Tailor the Taupe was during an investigation into a weapons-smuggling ring on the edges of Saurian Republic territory. Tailor had been working with one of the compsognathus scribes on a scheme to open a restaurant, when it turned out that the scribe had also been running a sideline in creating false custom sword orders for the local blacksmith. The elf had nothing to do with the weapons business, but because of the partnership had ended up in the middle of the mess. Tailor hadn't been welcome in any of the saurian city-states since.

"Tell us what you know," Wibble said.

"Honestly," Tailor said, "not a lot. I'd been working on a perfectly above-board and entirely legitimate project in that marketplace near Quantum City when out of nowhere there's a writ of detainment out for me."

New beings arrived in the Crucible all the time, drawn there by inexplicable forces of the universe, and equally inexplicably none were ever able to leave. But the Star Alliance ship Quantum contained the single largest group of new inhabitants anyone in the area could remember, and its well-trained, enthusiastic, and unusually broad-minded crew upset the uneasy balance among the many species and factions. Of course, the more enterprising – and mercenary – beings saw the new arrivals as an opportunity, and a bustling marketplace built up around the downed starship.

It was nothing like Hub City, with its spirescrapers, aircars, and well-defined enclaves. But the enterprising crew and the other beings who'd moved into the area were building a township on the site of the wreckage of the *Quantum*, and while the Star Alliance personnel still referred to it as Camp One, everyone else called it Quantum City.

"What could I do?" Tailor said, miserably. "I went underground."

Wibble poked her front end out the door of the treehouse. "More like way above ground."

"You know what I mean," Tailor said. "As soon as I heard they were looking for me I made a run for it, and I've been burning through my safe houses ever since."

"A sensible, if slightly suspicious, mode of operation," Pplimz said. "So why call us?"

"I'm running out of boltholes," Tailor explained. "And apparently the Star Alliance has no shortage of resources to come after me. I swear, I had absolutely nothing to do with that tiara going missing."

"Did it occur to you to perhaps tell the authorities that?" Pplimz asked.

"Since when is the word of a pointy-eared small-time grifter going to be believed over that of a Star Alliance officer?" Tailor said, angrily.

"Did someone in the Alliance call you that?" Wibble demanded, her body flushing deep purple.

"Not to my face," Tailor admitted, "but you hear things."

"You shouldn't believe everything that you hear," Pplimz admonished, but their voice was gentle. "So, how can we help?"

"I don't really know," Tailor said. "I mean, if you could find out who really did steal the tiara, that would probably do the job. But let's be honest. Things disappear all the time. Tracking down this tiara isn't going to be easy and something tells me there won't be any reward in it. The Star Alliance as an organization isn't big on commerce and I'm not exactly in a position to offer much."

Pplimz looked over at Wibble, and the face on their screen head disappeared. In its place, a series of symbols flashed rapidly, the text in a language that they and Wibble had created precisely for those moments when they wished to communicate silently and privately.

"Agreed," Wibble said aloud when she'd finished reading. "Tailor, can the communication device you're using handle level ten superposition encryption?"

"Sure," Tailor said, "but you'd need a special receiver. There isn't one in the treehouse."

"That won't be a problem," Pplimz said, extruding a data connector from their chest and hooking it into a port on the communicator. A fuzzy sound briefly emanated from the device and then it was silent, the now encrypted data transferred directly from Tailor's location to Pplimz's implanted circuits. "Let's set up a channel where we know we can talk freely."

Several minutes later, Pplimz carefully disconnected from the communicator, then stowed the device in their suit jacket pocket.

"No point leaving this here," they said. "I don't think there's any way to trace it back to Tailor, but why take the chance?"

"And it's not going to get any use in here," Wibble said, taking a slow tour of the small space. Tailor had obviously left in a hurry; a few days' provisions were still laid out on the shelf, not to mention the bag of gear in which Wibble had been briefly trapped.

She floated back in its direction and Pplimz said, "Not that again."

"Hush," she said and, much more carefully this time, poked her front end into the bag. "There's something in here."

Pplimz walked over and waved Wibble away. They pulled open the bag and reached inside. "Feels like a change of clothes," they said.

"Looks like it, too," Wibble confirmed. "Because that's exactly what's in the bag. But there's something else. I think it's sewn into the lining. It's very small, I bet you can't even feel it, but I sensed it when I was in there."

That explained why she got herself all tangled up in the bag. Wibble's echolocation allowed her to see things that even Pplimz couldn't, so they followed her directions to locate the hidden object she'd identified.

"A little to the left. Down. No, the other down. Just little more… there! Don't move, that's it, right where your sixth digit is."

Pplimz couldn't feel anything out of the ordinary about the bag, but they made a tiny incision in the interior fabric with a thin blade that sprung from their hand. The lining came away to reveal a small silver square that appeared to have been printed on the inside of the material.

"It's a data pattern," they said, magnifying their vision to peer at the square.

"Can you read it?"

Pplimz shook their head. "Encrypted. I'll need the mainframe in the office to decode this."

"Let's just take the whole thing with us," Wibble said. "Tailor isn't coming back here anytime soon."

Pplimz nodded and quickly resealed the lining with a molecular thread, careful not to touch the data pattern. Then they tossed the food and water into the bag, and slung it over their shoulder, securing it with a secondary manipulator.

"No point leaving good provisions to go to waste."

They shimmied down the rope to the forest floor, tucking it back in amongst the tree's roots and branches. When they were done, Wibble floated down, poking the rope in here and there to hide it even more thoroughly.

"If we hurry, we ought to be able to make the return trip on the *Black Star*," she said.

Pplimz sighed. "I'd been so looking forward to a visit to the spa at Floating Pines," they said, wistfully.

"We could get some other transport back to the city in the morning," Wibble suggested. "I'm sure Floating Pines would find a room for us if we asked."

Pplimz thought about it for several microseconds, but eventually said, "No. Work comes first, Wibble. We need to start looking into this missing tiara before the trail grows cold. The spa will still be here when the case has been solved."

"Suit yourself," Wibble said, brightly. "We'd better get a move on if we're going to make the late sailing." She swished her tail back and forth a few times to punctuate her point, then sped along the path toward the resort. Pplimz was grateful for having grown accustomed to the reduced gravity, and bounded along in her wake.

Wibble and Pplimz were the only passengers on a same-day return trip back to Hub City, but Captain Flurrbitz made no comment on their unusually quick excursion. It was late in the day when they made landfall at the transport terminal, but there was no shortage of beings bustling about the area. Hub City was busy at all times with representatives of every species which had found itself bound by the impossible world of the Crucible.

Giants and goblins mixed with sapient plants, crystalline entities, and descendants of dinosaurs, while ethereal spirit creatures and cyborg demons carried out their mysterious errands. Pplimz hailed a passing aircar, and gave the automated driver an address after they and Wibble piled in. The car shot upward as soon as the door irised shut, expertly dodging the other flyers in the city's airspace. Only a few minutes and a few more Æmbits later, they alighted outside the front door to their office building.

It was a strange-looking construction – rectangular, five stories tall, with evenly spaced glass windows along each edge and an ornate metal-grated door to the main entrance. It didn't fit in at all with the multi-colored domed apartments next door, or the thickly vined jungle-mall across the street, but the rent was cheap. Pplimz climbed the three flights of stairs to the floor where they kept their offices while Wibble floated at their left shoulder.

The door to their office was primarily made of what appeared to be dead trees, inset with a pane of smartglass etched with translationscript. Wibble unlocked the door with a complex series of taps with her flipper, and, contrary to what one might expect from its appearance, the door slurped open wetly. The building was actually a single, organic structure, grown rather than built by its phyll designer in an homage to an ancient human architecture. Unfortunately for the developer, while most humans found the appearance familiar, they were unsettled by the living nature of the structure. Other beings tended to think it was simply hideously ugly. And thus was created an excellent bargain for a large office in the middle of the city.

Pplimz shut and locked the door behind them, then took the bag they'd taken from Tailor's hideout to the large desk. They cleared off the deck of cards and other assorted detritus, and carefully reopened the seam they'd made in the inside of the sack. They removed a section of the lining, then placed the data pattern under a camera lens, which they connected to a small but powerful computer core built into the desk. They sent a series of instructions wirelessly to the computer, then sat in the overstuffed rolling chair at the desk.

"This might take some time," Pplimz said to Wibble, who was hovering impatiently right over the desk. "We'll need to decode the encryption before we can even see what's on here. And who knows if it's even going to be relevant? This could just be Tailor's plans for opening a Star Alliance teashop."

Wibble turned a slow somersault above the desk and faced Pplimz. "I like tea," she said, after a moment. "It feels tingly on my skin!"

"Thank you for sharing that profoundly useful tidbit of information, Wibble," Pplimz said, concealing a smile by opening a cupboard and extracting a suitcase.

"Planning a trip to Quantum City?" Wibble asked.

"Of course," Pplimz said, opening up their closet to reveal a large selection of extremely similar yet entirely unique suits. "That's where the trail begins. I'm sure they won't mind a couple of professionals barging in and asking questions."

CHAPTER THREE
Pplimz Admires a Hat

Pplimz had selected then dismissed half a dozen suits, and in the end had stowed three outfits, complete with matching hats, in the suitcase by the time the computer sounded a chime.

"Finally!" Wibble said, drifting down from her usual resting place in the upper corner of the room. "What have we got?"

Pplimz disengaged the camera and brought up a screen projection on the desktop. Rough hand-drawn notes in Svarr, a common elvish script, appeared along with a holographic three-dimensional image. It was a small silver crown, open at the back, with elaborate thin filigree along the edge. In its center an iridescent gem was set, about the size of a goblin's fist. It appeared to glow slightly, but that could have been an artifact of the holography.

"Very pretty," Pplimz said, admiring the image.

"You think so?" Wibble asked. "It's a bit ostentatious, isn't it? I mean, where would you wear something like that?"

"Wherever you'd like, I imagine," Pplimz said. "After all, it's just a fancy hat."

"I suppose so," Wibble said. "But it's a *very* fancy hat. It has a name and everything." She gestured at the script under the holo, which labeled it as *The Qubit Zirconium*.

"Fancy enough for someone to want to steal it," Pplimz agreed. "And fancy enough for Tailor the Taupe to lie to us about it. He said he didn't have anything to do with the tiara, but here's a whole file of notes he's made about it, on a data pattern he hid very carefully in his things."

"There's more going on here than we know," Wibble said, as an emerald hue came over her body. "I love it when there's more going on than we know!"

The next morning they were back at the main transportation terminal, Pplimz attired in yet another black and gray suit, this time in a jaunty houndstooth pattern. They'd topped it off with a wide-brimmed fedora and floor-length coat.

"For the cargo capacity," they'd explained, showing off deep interior pockets in the coat. Wibble, as usual, carried nothing. She liked to travel light.

"Ooh, let's take the SkyBounder!" Wibble pointed at a garish sign offering two-for-one deals on an upstart zeppelin service. "I haven't been on a blimp in forever."

"For a being who is naturally less dense than the atmosphere nearly everywhere on this world, you have a remarkably odd obsession with air travel."

Wibble grabbed Pplimz's hand with her flipper and began dragging them toward the SkyBounder booth. "Blimps are wonderful! So round and ponderous. It's a magnificent way to travel."

"And, at least today, economical," Pplimz said, peering at the tariff posted at the automated ticket machine. "Which is good, since I'm not sure we're going to be compensated for this job. Tailor's right that the Star Alliance is unlikely to offer a financial reward, and he's skint as always."

"There's more to life than currency," Wibble said, bobbing up and down with excitement. "Make sure you get us spots in the observation lounge."

Once aboard the dirigible, it became obvious why the tickets were so cheap. SkyBounder was a brand-new service that had clearly sprung up when its proprietors found themselves in possession of a very old, very basic, but apparently functional airship. The observation lounge was less a comfortable parlor and more of a repurposed cargo hold with an open grille along the exterior bulkhead. Wibble didn't seem to mind, and pressed herself right up against the rusty screen.

Pplimz hung on tightly to the fraying strap dangling from the ceiling as the ship lurched and juddered. A colorful insectoid krxix fell into them, apologized, then took the unusual step of dropping to all sixes to scuttle away, joining the rest of her party clinging to a post on the other side of the so-called lounge. Once they'd ascended to cruising altitude, though, the ride became much more even, and most of the passengers tentatively moved to the edges of the space to enjoy the scenery.

"Look at this view!" Wibble shouted over the sound of the engines, which were just aft of the open-air compartment. The vista was spectacular, Pplimz had to admit. They were entering the Eclipse Valley, with its two towering mountain ranges on either side. There was something both unnerving and breathtaking about flying in line with the summits of the smaller peaks, looking down on the winding river and lush meadows below as they followed the path of the valley.

Pplimz was almost getting used to the ride when a terrible grinding sound assaulted their audio inputs, before a merciful quiet descended. It would have been quite a relief if it hadn't meant that one of the engines had sputtered out.

"Nothing to worry about, folks," a gruff voice came over the loudspeaker. "But I'm going to have to ask everyone to move over to the port side of the ship. Thanks, that would really be great." The PA clicked off, and alarmed passengers milled around until a harried-looking spirit draped in a pair of cargo shorts and a pale green SkyBounder-branded polo shirt with a tag that read "Passenger Liaison" swept into the compartment.

The spirit waved their incorporeal arms toward the left side of the room, herding the passengers over to the far wall, while a team of goggled and helmeted maintenance workers opened a hatch on the starboard side. The giant leading the crew clipped a sturdy tether to a D-ring welded to the floor, then confirmed that the other ends were well secured to the chest harnesses of the other staffers. She then led them out to an access walkway which connected to the engine bay.

"Well, this *is* exciting," Wibble said, floating above the passengers to get a better look at the repair crew.

The team moved with confidence along the walkway, and had reached the dead engine in a few seconds. The giant issued instructions, and the crew soon had a hatch open in the side of the engine compartment and were busily tinkering with the components inside. It would have inspired quite a bit of confidence, if the airship hadn't been drifting closer and closer to the side of a mountain, which happened to have rather jagged obsidian cliffs aimed at them like an oversize demon's blades of pain.

One of the krxix released a sweet-smelling chemical in fear, and a goblin dressed in expensive traders' robes pulled out a handheld communicator and began rapidly making calls. Pplimz locked their hand onto a solid metal railing and calculated the terminal velocity of a nattily dressed cyborg in the local gravity.

"Please, everyone," the spirit in the SkyBounder t-shirt intoned, their voice inherently calming with its ethereal quality, "I'm sure we'll be just fine. The mountain face appears much closer than it really is, I assure you."

That might have been enough to calm the passengers' nerves, if it weren't for a gust of wind from the north which buffeted the airship and drove it even closer to the mountain. Someone outside hit something very hard with a hammer. Someone inside the airship screamed. Wibble turned green, which proved she really was enjoying the excitement.

The sound of an engine turning over filled the air, and the maintenance crew scurried back inside, the leader the last one in the line. The engine was still roaring to life, but the airship was listing closer and closer to a razor-sharp rock.

"Hang on, everyone!" the giant called from her perch on the outer walkway. She grabbed hold of the rail with her enormous, gloved hands, then swung her body out parallel to the ground like a gymnast. Her large, booted feet made contact with the side of the mountain, and she deeply flexed her knees, absorbing the shock of the impact. Then she grunted and kicked off, just as the now fixed engine fully engaged. The airship slewed away from the mountain, as the giant hand-over-handed her way back into the passenger compartment.

A stunned silence came over the entire group, then erupted into a cheer as the giant got to her feet. Her teammates closed up the access hatch, then helped her toward the door back to the main cabin. Her broad face was bright red – from exhaustion or modesty or both – as the passengers thanked her and slapped her back.

"See what I mean?" Wibble said. "Isn't airship travel terribly exciting?"

"Wibble," Pplimz said drily, "next time we are taking a train."

The rest of the trip passed without incident. Once the other members of the maintenance crew convinced her to join them, Gadorgga, the giant who had saved them all with her strength and quick thinking, spent the remainder of the trip being celebrated by the passengers. At first she was shy and kept trying to tell everyone that she hadn't done anything special, but eventually the reality of the situation sunk in and she admitted that at the very least she'd been in the right place at the right time. Soon the passengers had pooled the snacks they'd brought along for the trip into a potluck picnic, and everyone was sharing their perspectives on the experience.

"You'll want to keep those boots," one of the passengers dressed in a deep blue cloak from head to tail said. "As a souvenir."

"How so?" Gadorgga asked.

"Look!" a small sylicate covered in bright orange crystals pointed at the sole of her left boot. Gadorgga grabbed her enormous foot and pulled it on to her lap in a demonstration of remarkable flexibility as she examined her boot. There was a deep, rough gouge clean through the sole of her boot where the rock had cut into it.

"Whoa," she breathed, her eyes wide. "That was a close one."

"Indeed it was," a deep voice from the doorway said. Everyone turned to see a willowy saurian wearing faded robes emblazoned with a brand-new patch that read "SkyBounder." "On behalf of SkyBounder Transport Industries, I'd like to thank Gadorgga and the entire maintenance team for their excellent work. It is a testament to our extensive training and exemplary hiring practices that we have such a dedicated and competent crew aboard the airship. Mechanical issues happen to every ship, and I am proud to say that here at SkyBounder, we have the personnel to deal with them in a timely and safe manner."

Everyone was silent, and confused looks were exchanged among the passengers. Someone coughed, and then the passenger liaison wafted over to the saurian and whispered something in their ear.

"Yes, well, I trust you will all enjoy the rest of the voyage." The saurian swept out of the room and as soon as the door closed, Wibble burst into laughter.

"Already trying to spin this into a positive story," she said, once she'd stopped giggling. "I have to admire their audacity."

"Audacity indeed," Pplimz said, "to pass this bucket of bolts off as a sky-worthy vehicle."

"I'm sure we'll get there in one piece," Wibble said, peering out through the grating toward the mooring mast near Quantum City.

"The trip isn't over yet," Pplimz countered.

They did, in fact, arrive safely and were all given SkyBounder loyalty cards, with an extra hole punched for their trouble.

"Ninth flight free," Wibble read. "We're a quarter of the way there!"

"Honestly, Wibble." Pplimz sighed and reviewed the notes

they'd made. "Can we please at least try to track down the officer whose tiara was stolen without some madcap antics getting in the way?"

"Where's your sense of adventure?" Wibble asked, extending a nearly invisible section of her body in a hook to pick up Pplimz's suitcase and tow it underneath her as she floated toward the exit.

"The same place as your sense of self-preservation, I expect," Pplimz murmured, smoothing the lapels of their suit jacket.

Compared to the bustle Wibble and Pplimz were accustomed to, the Quantum City terminus was quiet, with only a few merchants and itinerant wanderers waiting for the next transport. Outside, instead of the aircars and trams and hired carts all vying for a traveler's time that one would find in Hub City, there was a single dusty road that led to the sprawling Horizon – the area just outside the secure zone surrounding the downed ship *Quantum*.

"It's not exactly a booming metropolis," Pplimz said, as a gust of wind blew a patch of dust down the road.

"Calling this Quantum City must be an example of their aspirational worldview," Wibble said, floating up to get a better view, then called down to Pplimz.

"Come on, let's get the lay of the land!"

It was a short walk – or in Wibble's case, hover – to the first sign of civilization: Cynthala's Inn and Watering Hole. Not much more than a series of rough shacks, Cynthala's was a popular place for new visitors to the area to use as a base, both to rest and for information. Wibble floated into the tavern, looking for all the world as if she were riding the suitcase, but none of the occupants of the bar even took a second glance. Beings of all kinds were welcome here, so long as they didn't make any trouble and they paid their bill on time.

"Welcome travelers. What can Cynthala offer you today?" The being behind the bar appeared to be a large, winged serpent dressed in a robe of muted colors, with mechanical arms strapped to his body. He was polishing a ceramic mug with two hands, while wiping the countertop with another.

Pplimz had consulted a guidebook for the area, and learned that whichever staff member was on duty at the time was referred to as Cynthala, and used he/him pronouns. The real Cynthala, if such a being had ever even existed, was lost to time.

Pplimz casually dropped a couple of gleaming Æmbits on the bar. "We need to speak to someone in Star Alliance security. And we'd like a room, if you have one available."

"With electricity, if possible," Wibble added, taking in Pplimz's slightly dimming screen.

"The room will not be a problem," Cynthala said, his tail sweeping up from behind the bar to curl around the coins. "Electricity will be billed by the joule."

"That will be fine," Pplimz said.

"Do you require resting facilities? We have hammocks, sludge tubs, hanging rafters, beds, floor mats ..."

"Does it have a ceiling?" Wibble asked. Cynthala nodded, and Wibble said, "Then we won't need anything special."

Cynthala handed Pplimz a pair of metal keys imprinted with flakes of Æmber. "Very well. You'll be in the green circle room. Turn left at the door and it's about halfway down the track."

"Thank you," Wibble said. "What about Star Alliance security?"

"Security," Cynthala hissed, "will be more of a challenge." He curled an articulated finger in a gesture for them to come closer. Pplimz hopped up onto one of the stools at the bar, and Wibble floated up to hover just above the bar itself.

"The perimeter of the Star Alliance territory, even the outer Bivouac, is heavily guarded and fortified by an impenetrable force fence. But while the Alliance may be somewhat paranoid, they are not isolationists. Many beings cross in and out each day. It is not impossible to gain access if you have the right credentials, or…" Cynthala flicked his forked tongue in and out quickly, "if you have something they want."

"And what is it that they want?" Wibble asked.

"The thing they want most is a means to repair their ship, and escape the Crucible back into open space," Cynthala said, then laughed, a surprisingly melodic giggle. "Of course, we all know that is not something any being can truthfully provide. If one does not mind offering false hope, however…"

Pplimz frowned. "I'm afraid that's not our way," they said. "We shall have to prevail upon our history and hope that they will see us as legitimate professionals with whom they are willing to confer."

"Suit yourselves," Cynthala said, sibilantly. "Please see me if there is anything else Cynthala can provide." He turned back to his cleaning and left Wibble and Pplimz with the keys to their room.

CHAPTER FOUR
Wibble Has a Nap

Wibble and Pplimz found the door marked with a large green circle easily. The room was small, but there were several electrical ports at various currencies and voltages, as well as a large workdesk for them to use. Pplimz turned the desk on, projecting a screen over the far wall. They plugged into a port on the desk and beamed their notes to the screen, taking care to ensure that the desk was not surreptitiously copying any of the data. Cynthala's was not known for grifting its customers, but one could never be too secure.

Wibble set the suitcase down in an out-of-the-way corner, then allowed her body to naturally float up to rest against the ceiling.

"Tired?" Pplimz asked.

"I'm fine," Wibble replied, though both her voice and skin were noticeably less bright than usual.

"The Star Alliance crew are mostly humans," Pplimz said, scrolling through their research. They'd consulted news and gossip sources from across the Crucible, as well as asked around their informal networks in order to create a reasonable dossier on the newcomers. "I understand that they usually sleep at night, and find conducting business during the dark hours to be an imposition. I think we will have more success if we wait until the morning to approach the checkpoints. I intend to recharge, and I dare say you could stand to do the same."

"If you like," Wibble said. "First, let's check in with Tailor."

"Agreed." Pplimz opened an encrypted communications channel to the endpoint they'd pre-arranged with Tailor and waited for the elf to respond.

Nothing happened.

Wibble floated down to rest near Pplimz's shoulder. "Is something wrong with the crypto?"

"I don't think so. I'll try again."

Pplimz reset the system and set the urgency protocol to high. Still nothing.

"I don't like this," Pplimz said, calculating the probabilities of various unpleasant scenarios, even as they didn't want to contemplate them.

"Maybe Tailor is busy?" Wibble suggested. "Or sleeping. Elves do that too, you know."

"Or maybe something has gone wrong," Pplimz countered. "We agreed to keep in touch every day, and I can't see any reason why Tailor would abandon that plan. Even if he can't speak to us, he could send us a respond code. But there's nothing. No sign that the signal is even getting through." Pplimz turned to face their partner, now glowing a faint indigo. "I really don't like this, Wibble."

Wibble laid a flipper on her partner's shoulder, creating a slight calming electromagnetic flow down Pplimz's arm.

"I know," she said. "But there's nothing we can do about it from here, so let's rest tonight and see what the morning brings."

Pplimz nodded, and disconnected from the desk. They removed their suit, hanging it carefully on the wardrobe rack. Their thin body was mostly covered in layers of dark metal, silicon, and polymer, but organic tissue could be seen in the spaces between the overlapping plates. They unspooled a thick power cable from a hatch in their torso and plugged the end into an appropriate power point. They sunk into a chair and their screen face flickered.

"Good night, Wibble."

She floated back up to the corner, her flippers and tail drooping and her body translucent.

"Good night, Pplimz. Sweet dreams."

Whether their dreams were sweet, sour, or even if they dreamed at all, Pplimz had nothing to say on the matter. Instead, when the sky began to illuminate with the single warm yellow sun that appeared in this area, Pplimz disconnected from the room's power supply, picked out a fresh suit, and packed up their things. When Wibble finally stirred from her perch in the corner of the ceiling, their rented room was as neat and tidy as it had been when they'd first entered.

"Ready to go?" Pplimz asked as Wibble descended.

"I was born ready!" she exclaimed.

"Were you now?" Pplimz asked, hefting the suitcase with seemingly no effort into the room's small closet. "Born, I mean. I always guessed that you appeared fully formed from the fever dream of a starsick interstellar traveler knocked off course and lost in space."

"Well," Wibble said, genially, "that's a kind of birth, isn't it? Come on, let's go. I've never met anyone from the Star Alliance before. From what I've heard, they sound deliciously innocent."

They left the room and Pplimz locked up behind them.

"Now, Wibble, it's not nice to make assumptions," Pplimz said. "Just because their philosophy is remarkably unprejudiced, that doesn't necessarily make them all naïve."

"We won't know until we meet them," Wibble said, squeezing past Pplimz on the way to the road, "so let's go meet them!"

Pplimz stopped into the tavern to pay the Cynthala on duty, then hurried to catch up with Wibble, who was well on her way down the track toward the Bivouac proper. They passed several other hostels and rooms for let, a few large operations of varying levels of respectability, and many independent merchants selling food and drink, trinkets, and "Mysterious Artifacts of the Star Alliance." Most of the latter appeared to be nothing more mysterious than generic robot hardware, but that didn't seem to stop some of the tourists from purchasing them as souvenirs. The crash of the *Quantum* was the largest influx of new beings to the Crucible at one time in as long as anyone could remember, and curiosity had gotten the better of many.

The hawkers advertising their wares with hovering laser signs, carved placards, handwritten notices, and good old-fashioned shouting didn't catch Wibble's attention, even though she was the most naturally curious being Pplimz had ever encountered. She was single-minded in her determination to get to the force fence which protected the perimeter of Star Alliance territory, though Pplimz didn't fail to notice that she kept to the winding road rather than aiming directly for the checkpoint.

When they arrived, a squat, silver robot greeted them.

"Designations?" it asked in a mechanical voice.

"What language is that?" Wibble asked. She understood most of the languages used on the Crucible, and when she encountered one she didn't know she was able to tap into the translator in Pplimz's hardware. The translator appeared to have managed perfectly well, but the sounds coming from the robot were decidedly alien to her.

"Something called 'Earth Standard,'" Pplimz explained, consulting the readout from the translator. "I've never heard of it."

"Designations," the robot repeated, and Wibble tilted her body side to side in her version of a shrug.

"My name is Wibble and this is Pplimz," she said. "What's your name?"

The robot beeped and a few lights on its upper casing flashed in what looked rather like confusion. Then it said, "I am PR0T3K-TR, serial number 5649819874. State your intentions, please."

"We are investigators for hire from Hub City," Pplimz said, "and we'd like to talk to Star Alliance security about an item that has gone missing from one of the officers: the Qubit Zirconium tiara."

This led to quite a lot of flashing lights and beeps from PR0T3K-TR, which then spun around on its circular base three times before moving very quickly into a small housing with an opening that fit its body with little room to spare.

"I think we scared it," Wibble said, her body turning a pale blue.

"That seems implausible," Pplimz said, even though it had

appeared startled. But surely the drone was accustomed to all manner of strange visitors. Regardless, the little robot emerged from the enclosure after only a brief interval.

"Your credentials have been confirmed," it said, a drawer sliding open from its casing. Two small badges in the shape of a four-pointed star lay inside. "These visitors' passes will allow you limited access to Star Alliance facilities. They are equipped with a location beacon and are keyed to your individual vital signs, so do remember to wear the one assigned to you. Please affix them to your…" It stopped speaking and a lens emerged from near the center of its rounded top, which swung back and forth between the two detectives. "Are you each wearing garments?"

"I'll have you know that this suit is bespoke from the finest of haberdasheries in Jur," Pplimz said, defensively, stroking the fabric.

"Now, Pplimz, I'm sure this robot has simply never seen such a splendid outfit before," Wibble said, smoothly. "And while I do not wear garments as a rule, I am happy to do so if the local custom requires it. Otherwise, I'm quite certain I can get this badge to stick to me." She extended a flipper and scooped up her badge, which she affixed to her side with a deep slurping sound. She shimmied vigorously to demonstrate that the badge would, indeed, stay put.

"This is acceptable," the robot said, and swiveled back to aim the drawer at Pplimz. They took the badge and carefully threaded its clasp through the buttonhole of the jacket's lapel. Both badges illuminated briefly, then the force fence in front of them flickered. Wibble shot through to the other side and flipped over to face Pplimz, who stepped forward gingerly.

"Welcome to the Star Alliance Bivouac," the robot said, then unceremoniously rolled back into its hut, a door sliding shut behind it.

A uniformed human glided overhead wearing a powered jetpack, as a team of what appeared to be new recruits performed coordinated exercises in a marked clearing near to the road. The barking of their instructor was clearly audible even from several yards away.

"Well, this is different," Wibble said, as she looped around in circles trying to see it all.

"For an organization that believes that all sapient beings are equal, and honors the rights of all to coexist in harmony, they do have a rather militaristic approach, don't they?" Pplimz said.

"Now, Pplimz, it's not nice to make assumptions," Wibble echoed back Pplimz's own words to them, then shot up into the sky before they could retort. She scanned the area from her elevated vantage point, then floated back down and extended a flipper to the left. "I think that's a security station just over there."

They passed more officers and recruits, all wearing the form-fitting Star Alliance uniform, blindingly white with orange and gold accents. Most were human, but there were several krxix, as well as the occasional representative of other species. Robots of several configurations bustled about the compound, most transporting cargo and supplies. A few of the crew eyed Wibble and Pplimz as they passed, but seeing the Star Alliance insignia on their visitors' badges, no one questioned them. A couple of the humans even said hello.

They reached a clearly prefabricated outbuilding that was festooned with glyphs that Wibble didn't recognize, but then as

Pplimz caught up to her, their communication system projected a head-up-display which superimposed the words translated into their shared private script: Star Alliance Security Outpost 4.

A brown-skinned human with long gray hair plaited into a pair of braids stepped out of the building and aimed a wrist-mounted scanner at the badges Wibble and Pplimz had been given. Pplimz took the opportunity to read the frequency and protocol of the transceiver, and sent a matching signal toward the officer's own badge, which dutifully sent back basic details: this was Security Officer Class 2 Paulie Barros, she/her, human, member of the original *Quantum* crew.

"Wibble, Pplimz," Officer Barros said, turning to each of them in turn. "What brings you to the Star Alliance today?"

She spoke rudimentary but comprehensible New Saurian. It made sense that this was the local language they learned, since the *Quantum* had crashed near three saurian city-states and the members of the Republic were undoubtedly the first beings the crew of the ship would have encountered. However, Pplimz set their translator to respond in Earth Standard, as it would make for superior communication, and hopefully put the officer at ease.

"We are investigating the disappearance of an item of jewelry belonging to one of your officers," Pplimz said. "We'd like to speak with him, if possible."

Barros frowned and consulted a pad that looked remarkably similar to Pplimz's head. "The only missing property report is from Officer Zoarr, for a..." she scrolled for a moment, "silver tiara. I see here that a writ of detainment has already been issued for a suspect. Do you have additional information on this matter?"

"Not as such," Wibble said. "But we are acquainted with the being who has been accused, and we aren't convinced that he had anything to do with the disappearance. We'd like to take a look, if you don't mind. Feel free to check our references, if that helps."

Pplimz handed Barros a datatab, and after a moment's hesitation the officer scanned it with her wrist com. She turned to the pad and read through the extracts of Wibble and Pplimz's previous cases, her eyebrows raising on occasion.

"Impressive," she said, when she'd finished. "You appear to have helped people all over this world – there are several species names here that I've never even heard of before. However, your credentials don't transfer to your client. We do find it rather telling that this..." she consulted the pad again, "Tailor Taupe chose to run rather than help us with our enquiries." She gave Wibble and Pplimz the hard look that security officers on all worlds seem to cultivate.

"You really haven't been on the Crucible long," Wibble said. "It's hard to know who to trust around here, and many's the being who avoided a nasty end by being fleet of foot rather than cooperative. Safety first, that's what I always say!"

"Surely everyone knows that it's safe to trust the Star Alliance," Barros said, haughtily. "Justice and integrity are the founding principles of the Alliance!"

Pplimz shrugged. "So you say. But you can't blame a being for erring on the side of caution."

Wibble floated a little closer to Barros, lowering her voice conspiratorially. "If you haven't noticed, there's an adversarial nature to quite a lot of encounters here on the Crucible. It's easy to run afoul of someone who has the backing of a larger, much more powerful group. There are more factions and splinter groups on this world than there are stars in the Alwaysnight sky."

"I don't think Officer Barros knows where Alwaysnight is," Pplimz said, seeing the confusion on the human's face.

"Ooh, you must visit!" Wibble said to Barros. "It's a bit tricky to get to, you have to traverse the acid plains of Skrr, but it's worth it in the end – assuming you survive, of course. Such lovely constellations!"

"Wibble," Pplimz said, "perhaps we should offer travel tips another time?"

"Look," Barros said, "I really don't know what you think you're going to find here, but the Star Alliance has nothing to hide. We welcome any help you might be able to offer. I'm sure Officer Zoarr would be happy to talk to you. I'll update your badges to allow you passage into the officers' quarters." She pointed to a small tower across the training ground then tapped something into her pad, connecting her wrist com to it with a thick cable. Then she aimed it at their badges and pressed a button. Nothing obvious happened, but when Pplimz took a reading they saw that their clearances had been increased.

Perhaps the Star Alliance was just as objective as they claimed after all.

Given the general cobbled-together state of the rest of the Bivouac, Wibble had expected barracks – bunk beds, shared latrines, a complete and utter lack of creature comforts. She was taken aback when they entered the large officers' quarters building to discover what felt more like a pleasant apartment block. There was a directory near the front entrance, and it appeared that most Star Alliance officers had their own individual living spaces, although some appeared to be couples, triples, or quartets, and there were a few families as well.

"This seems nice," Pplimz said, as they scanned the directory for Zoarr's quarters. They were located on the lower deck, near the back of the building, down a short corridor from the main entrance. Not the finest of locations, but still. Better than a bunk in a drafty prefab.

Wibble pressed the call button next to the door, and a frightful crash emanated from inside the room.

"It sounds like a herd of Kelifi Dragons rampaging in there," Wibble said. "That's a bit odd, isn't it?"

Before either of them could investigate further – or run away – the door cycled open. An enormous mountain of a being stood before them, over nine feet tall with a long flowing black beard and bright tattoos cascading down heavily muscled exposed forearms. A huge, scarred battle-ax lay as if it were weightless in their left hand, and their ruddy face scowled at the detectives above the collar of a fuzzy orange bathrobe. Pplimz wondered if it was standard issue – the color was right.

"Can I help you?" the giant asked, in a deep rumbling voice.

"We're looking for Officer Zoarr," Pplimz said.

"Well, you've found him," the giant said, scanning their visitor's badges then stepping aside to let them enter the apartment. "I apologize for my attire, I'm off duty until the mid-shift. Won't you come in?"

CHAPTER FIVE
Pplimz Multitasks

"I had no idea there were giants in the Star Alliance," Wibble said, once she and Pplimz had entered Zoarr's quarters, been offered and declined a hot drink, and perched themselves on a plush sofa.

"There weren't," Zoarr said, cinching the bathrobe tighter against his solid body, "until me." He grinned with obvious pride. "And I'm the first of many, I'm sure."

"How long have you been part of this organization?" Pplimz asked.

"As soon as I heard about the interstellar exploration ship that crashed in the desert, I knew I wanted to know more," Zoarr said. "I was born here, on the Crucible, but I've always been fascinated by what lies beyond the boundary. My kinfolk are brobnar, and nearly everyone in our clan spends their lives either preparing, fighting, or recovering from an Æmber raid. We boast two Vaultwarriors in my immediate family."

Wibble thought that there was a mixture of pride and sadness in his voice. "That was not the path that called to you?" she suggested.

The giant shook his head. "I enjoy a good brawl as much as the next person," he said, "but fighting for shards of Æmber on behalf of some mysterious Archon brings me no joy. I want to know things!" He slammed a fist on the arm of the sturdy oversize chair in which he sat, then gestured toward the sky. "Things about the universe outside of this world. The Crucible may be larger than a planetary system, but it is still too small for me."

"I can imagine that an entire ship of beings who could tell stories of worlds beyond the boundary would be appealing," Pplimz said.

The giant nodded vigorously. "I left my clan's traveling camp as soon as I heard about the *Quantum*. I will admit that when I arrived, I did not expect to be welcomed by the crew. As you can imagine, most beings encountering a brobnar giant tend to be, shall we say, less than inviting. And I won't pretend that when I arrived I was immediately accepted without concern. The crew had obviously encountered brobnar clans before." He chuckled at the memory. "But once I explained that I shared their goals, and proved that I was more than willing to undergo the training regime for new recruits, they were more than willing to allow me to join. The captain herself activated my wrist module when my induction was complete." He extended a meaty hand to show off the communicator strapped to his wrist. On his oversize body, it looked more like a delicate bracelet than a chunky piece of alien technology. That thought reminded Pplimz of the reason they were having this conversation.

"We understand that you recently filed a missing property report. A silver tiara?"

Zoarr snorted loudly. "Not missing. Stolen! That elven suit maker took it, I know it."

"Suit maker?" Pplimz said.

"Oh, Tailor!" Wibble said. "I didn't know he was an actual tailor. Is he? Well, that would certainly explain that stylish jerkin and boots ensemble he was sporting that one time–"

"Wibble, not now," Pplimz said, glancing toward the rather angry giant now towering over them with hands balled into fists.

"Ever since I first acquired it, he was sniffing around after the jewel," Zoarr said. "I saw him sneaking around the officers' quarters the night it went missing. There's no doubt in my mind that he stole the tiara."

"Well, we're here to help determine that," Pplimz said, keeping their true intention – and the identity of their client – out of the conversation for now.

Zoarr took a few deep breaths, then lowered himself back into the chair. It creaked ominously under his weight, but held firm.

"Yes, your IDs indicate that you are well-regarded investigators," he said, gesturing at their visitor's badges. "I'm grateful for any help you can offer in retrieving it."

"Can you tell us why you had it?" Wibble asked. "I've seen a holo-image. It's very… ornate."

Zoarr looked at her quizzically. "I'm a giant," he said, as if that alone explained it. "I like pretty things."

"Of course," Pplimz said. "I'm sure the holo doesn't do it justice. Was it quite valuable?"

"The amount of Æmber I traded for it is not significant," Zoarr said, "but the tiara is priceless to me. Please, help me get it back."

Wibble tipped forward and shimmered a light gold. Material

objects had never been especially interesting to her, but she understood that some other beings felt strongly about certain things. "We will do our best."

"We need to talk to Tailor," Wibble said, once they were well past the officers' quarters and Zoarr's oversize ears.

"I agree," Pplimz said, "but there's a slight problem with that."

"Oh?"

"I've been trying to raise him on the encrypted communicator all morning, and there's still no sign that he's connected."

"All morning?" Wibble confirmed, though she knew Pplimz was not inclined to exaggerate. She was developing a distinctly bad feeling about Tailor.

"Yes, I've been trying the entire time we were talking with Zoarr," Pplimz said. "I'm trying now, on all the possible frequencies he could be using. There's nothing, nothing at all. I hate to admit it, Wibble, but I'm starting to think that it's most likely that something has happened to Tailor. Something... unpleasant."

Wibble flushed a deep indigo. "I hope not," she said. In the times they'd worked with Tailor the Taupe, she'd become fond of the elf and his schemes. "But I think it's time to see if there's anyone around here who had any dealings with him. I feel like there's more going on than we've been led to believe."

"Tailor told us he was working in the Horizon when this all happened. He's not the type to keep to himself. Surely some beings remember him. Perhaps one of them knows something useful."

"Agreed," Wibble said, as she bobbed above the path back toward the perimeter. She stopped suddenly, then floated up quickly to hover next to Pplimz's head. "Although I don't think we're quite finished here yet." She gestured toward the security hut they'd visited earlier.

"Zoarr did mention that Tailor had been seen here, inside the secure area of the Bivouac," Pplimz said. "Which means that there's probably a record of the visit."

"It's not entirely impossible that Tailor got here by not entirely above-board means," Wibble pointed out.

"Sure, but given everything that happened, there would still be a record," Pplimz said. "In Zoarr's missing property report at the very least."

"Right. Let's go talk to security again."

Security Officer Class 2 Paulie Barros was still on duty when they returned.

"How can I help you?" she asked, genially.

"Officer Zoarr was very free with his time," Pplimz said, "and has agreed to help us with the investigation. I was wondering if you have any records of the suspect's movements here in the secure zone?"

Barros frowned. "There's nothing in the report."

"You may have had a bit of trouble with the name," Wibble said. "Earlier, you called him Tailor Taupe, but his proper name is Tailor *the* Taupe. Or it could be Taupe the Tailor. Either way, maybe if you tried those in your system?"

"Sure, why not?" Barros entered some commands into the terminal in the security outpost and her eyebrows shot up. "Well, what do you know? Tailor *the* Taupe was issued a visitor's badge with limited access to the Bivouac. Quite some time ago, in fact."

She turned the screen toward the detectives and they read the logs. The elf had been sponsored by a Star Alliance officer called So, and had been working as a runner between the Bivouac and the Horizon.

"Tailor was working as a delivery clerk?" Pplimz asked.

"So it appears," Barros confirmed. "According to the logs he had free access through the checkpoints to take orders and make deliveries." She looked slightly sheepish. "We are not finished rebuilding our systems after the crash, and there are still many items we find it easier to get from the markets than to manufacture ourselves. There's a good trade to be had out there, and it doesn't hurt to have a local making sure we don't get completely fleeced."

"Of course," Wibble said. "Very sensible."

"Do you have a record of the last time Tailor crossed the checkpoint?" Pplimz asked.

"Sure." Barros scrolled the terminal screen. "It was the day that Zoarr reported the tiara missing."

Wibble and Pplimz exchanged glances. That confirmed what Zoarr had told them, but it didn't prove anything.

"Do you have the badge that was issued to Tailor?" Pplimz asked.

"No, according to the records, he still has it."

"Wait a minute!" Wibble said. "The cute little robot who gave us our badges said they have location beacons. Can't you just look up where Tailor is that way?"

Barros shook her head. "The location data is only broadcast when inside Star Alliance territory. For privacy reasons, you understand."

Pplimz nodded. "Of course. But what about the other

information it sends? Is there any chance you can still read the badge Tailor was issued?"

Barros consulted the terminal. "The range is quite impressive, if I may say so myself. The badges report basic data, such as whether or not they are being worn by the person to whom they were issued, that sort of thing. They also report if that person is in distress, or…" She gasped and looked up at Wibble and Pplimz with genuine concern. "According to these readings, there are no vital signs being detected by Tailor's badge."

"Surely he removed it before he left," Wibble said. "I certainly wouldn't go on the lam wearing a tracking device belonging to the very people I'm avoiding."

Barros shook her head. "It's an entirely different signal when the badge is removed. This is a particular pattern. According to these readings, Tailor the Taupe is wearing his badge. And is dead."

"We can't be certain of anything at this point, Pplimz."

The detectives had left Officer Barros and returned to Cynthala's to regroup. They took up a small booth in a dark corner in exchange for a few Æmbits passed to the spry old goblin now working behind the bar. He'd offered food, drink, a sunlamp, or electricity, but they declined all nourishment. They only needed a quiet spot to think – and worry.

"I know, Wibble," Pplimz said, sounding miserable, "but we have to accept the evidence we have. There's a very good chance that Tailor is gone, and I find it hard to fathom that it could be a coincidence."

"All we have is what Officer Barros told us. While she appeared to be telling the truth, I don't have enough experience with humans to be sure. And for all we know these badges aren't able to properly compensate for all the differences among us anyway. You really think this little toy is going to understand your physiology? Or mine?" Wibble tossed her visitor's badge on the table. In the absence of concrete evidence to the contrary, she was going to assume an explanation other than Tailor's demise. There would be time to grieve later if things turned out badly, and, in the meantime, she needed to be able to focus.

"I know you're trying to give me hope," Pplimz said, "and it's working. I'm still sending Tailor a signal and I don't intend to stop. But I think we have to proceed under the assumption that something has happened to him, and that changes how we approach this problem. It's not just a simple theft any more."

Wibble bobbed up and down slowly in agreement. "I'm starting to think it never was."

"Let's take a look at those notes he made," Pplimz said, and projected a screen onto the tabletop. The holo-image of the tiara rotated above the table, the gem in the center subtly shifting in shape and hue.

"It looks like a list of people and places," Wibble said, reading the handwritten notes. "I think these are trade prices." She gestured at a series of scribbles with a flipper.

"If Tailor was acting as procurement agent for Star Alliance officers, this makes perfect sense," Pplimz said. "I think this might be the results of negotiations for the tiara." They looked up at Wibble. "Do you think Tailor was the go-between for Zoarr's acquisition of the jewelry?"

"That might explain why Zoarr immediately thought Tailor was the thief," she said. "But there are a lot of names here. If you were just doing the shopping for someone, wouldn't this be a single source and a price? Why all the extra noise?"

"Maybe it wasn't a simple transaction?" Pplimz suggested. "If Zoarr was looking for something specific, something he didn't know how to acquire, then this might be the result."

"You know what I want to do?" Wibble said, floating out of the booth and heading toward the door of the tavern. "I'd like to see how a giant wears a Star Alliance uniform."

They found Zoarr among a group of other new officers on the training ground in the Bivouac, largely missing the target with the hand blaster he was learning to fire. If they'd given him a stone mace – or even a pointed stick – he'd surely have outclassed them all easily. But the ray pistol was tiny and awkward in his hand and his instructor was patiently showing him how to aim, fire, and recharge. Wibble and Pplimz waited until the trainees took a break before approaching the giant in his form-fitting white, orange, and gold one-piece uniform suit.

"Have you found something already?" he asked.

"Not exactly," Pplimz said. "Can you tell us how you acquired the tiara? Was it just a lucky find in a merchant's cart?"

Zoarr blinked a few times, as if trying to decide how to answer. "I'd heard about it from other bijoux enthusiasts. It's an interest of mine; we're a small community and we share interesting items as we come across them."

Wibble looked him up and down. Aside from his wrist com and Star Alliance badge, his outfit was entirely unaccessorized. "Funny, you don't seem to be much of a jewelry wearer."

"Regulations," he said, sadly. "The uniform regulations only allow for a certain amount of personal adornment, and my tattoos fill the allotment."

"So, you sought out the tiara specifically," Pplimz confirmed. "And did you use an agent to help you find it?"

Zoarr sighed. "Yes, it was that elf, of course. I should have known he was up to no good."

"He was trusted by Star Alliance security, though," Wibble said. "He helped many of your officers make trades in the Bivouac."

Zoarr grunted. "They should know better than to trust elves," he said under his breath, but that was still more than loud enough for his instructor to hear. She jerked her head to look at them, a disappointed expression on her lined face. She strode over to them, briskly moving her wiry compact body.

"Officer Zoarr," she said, warning in her tone, "as you in particular well know, we do not judge anyone based on their background. Are you talking about Taupe, the local who helped with provisioning and such?"

"Tailor the Taupe, yes," Pplimz said. "You knew him?"

"Sure," the instructor said. "Most of us did. He was very useful in finding things we needed from the area. He often could source material and supplies from beyond the Bivouac. I find it hard to imagine that he'd ruin such a good working relationship by stealing something from one of us."

"Especially after he'd already delivered it," Wibble added. "I mean, if it were me, I'd just have said I couldn't find it, then kept it for myself. Much simpler that way."

"Wibble," Pplimz said, in a warning tone.

"You know, *hypothetically*," she added.

Zoarr looked like he wanted to argue, but glanced at his instructor and kept quiet.

"Well, Officer…" Pplimz scanned the instructor's badge,

"Officer Levesque, I'm afraid that we may have some unpleasant news. It appears that Tailor's Star Alliance badge is reporting no vital signs from its wearer."

Her eyes widened and her hand flew up to her mouth. "Oh no…"

"I don't suppose you know anything about that?" Wibble asked Zoarr, brightly.

"Of course I don't," he blustered. "What are you insinuating?"

"Oh, nothing," Wibble said, "I'm just investigating. We're investigators. Questions are what we ask, answers are what we seek."

"Well, perhaps you ought to be seeking those answers elsewhere," Zoarr said, then stormed off in the direction of the mess hall.

CHAPTER SIX
Wibble Weaves Wordplay

"That wasn't entirely unsuspicious," Wibble said, as she and Pplimz headed away from the training ground toward the checkpoint.

"It also isn't an unreasonable response from someone who's the victim here," Pplimz countered.

"You think Zoarr is an innocent victim?"

"There's no evidence to the contrary," Pplimz said.

They carried on in silence for a moment before Wibble said, "You're being rather careful to avoid actually offering an opinion, Pplimz."

"I am, aren't I?" they answered, and elaborated no further. Typical Pplimz – they might be analytical but they did have feelings and irrational prejudices just like any other being. They simply tried very hard not to jump to conclusions. It was one of the things Wibble valued about her partner, but it could make them a dull conversationalist when there wasn't much to go on.

"You're right," Wibble said, as if Pplimz had explained their thinking in full. "It's far too soon to make any assumptions. We need more information, so at least we can agree with Zoarr on one thing: we need to ask more beings more questions."

Finding someone in the Bivouac who'd known Tailor the Taupe was as hard as finding a cybernetically enhanced mutant in a Logos enclave, which is to say, not even remotely difficult. As a Star Alliance acquisition agent, Tailor had transacted with most every merchant at some point, and, according to the beings they spoke to, he had a good working relationship with them all. Unfortunately, none of them were particularly close relationships, and no one had any idea where Tailor might have gone.

"I. Hope. That. He is. All. Right," Ranick, a sylicate seller of entertainment data chips slowly ground out. "Tailor. The. Taupe. Was very. Adept. At finding. A. Good. Match. For the. Humans." There was an excruciatingly long pause as the merchant shifted their stone body to gesture toward the racks of chips with brightly colored teasers of the subject matter projected above them. "He. Brought. Me. Many. Repeat. Customers."

"Did you ever hear of any of the *Quantum*'s crew having a problem with Tailor?" Pplimz asked. "Any unhappy customers, personal issues?"

Ranick ponderously shook their head.

"There was a particular item of interest that Tailor was looking for–" Wibble began but was interrupted by Ranick.

"You. Must. Mean the. Qubit. Zirconium."

"Yes!" Wibble said, wobbling in excitement. "What can you tell us about it?"

Quite a long time later, Wibble and Pplimz left the merchant with a name. It was quite a small amount of new information for the time it took to acquire, but it *was* new information, and both the detectives had rather loose experiences of linear time anyway.

It was getting close to the end of the day, and most of the stallholders were packing up their wares, but Wibble and Pplimz managed to catch Sassert, a heavily ornamented hybrid who looked like a cross between a furry mammal and a small floral bush, just as the shutters were coming down on the display case of shiny trinkets.

"Excuse me," Wibble said, hovering over to the bustling little being.

"I am closing for the day." A melodious voice emanated from the ring-tipped fronds along the being's muzzle. "However, if you already know what you would like, I could reopen the case."

Pplimz shook his screen head. "We'd just like to talk, if you have a little time."

"Talk is not as expensive as jewels, but it is not free, either. Perhaps a meal at Orry's?" The merchant extended a bloom-paw and gestured toward a nearby eatery.

"A reasonable trade. I'll get us a table," Wibble said, and floated toward the door of the restaurant. Pplimz waited for Sassert to close up the stall, then followed as the being loped toward the smell of something organic being grilled.

They watched as the jeweler tore into a hunk of blackened something, then, once the chewing had slowed, Wibble said, "We understand that you sold a tiara to a Star Alliance officer called Zoarr. Do you remember the trade?"

"Of course," Sassert said, wiping dripping juice with a leafy appendage. "The Qubit Zirconium. One of my finer pieces, if I may say so myself."

"You made it?" Pplimz asked.

Sassert nodded with pride. "I smithed the tiara and set the stone. A lovely, delicate setting for such a remarkably bright gem. Have you seen it?"

"Only in holos," Wibble said.

"A shame," Sassert said. "Perhaps the officer will show it to you, if you ask."

"I'm afraid Zoarr no longer has the tiara," Pplimz said. "He says it was stolen."

"Oh my!" Sassert said, appearing to suppress a belch. "Stolen? I..." Sassert rubbed two forepaws together in thought. "I admit that I am fond of my work, but I must inform you that the item is not worth a particularly great deal. The gem is unusual, yes, but it is nothing more than a pretty bauble. I daresay the silver of the setting is worth more than the stone."

"Hmm." Wibble thought. "What about the buyer, Zoarr? Do you have any impressions of him?"

"I never met him," Sassert said. "Until you told me, I didn't even know the name of the buyer. All the negotiations went through Tailor the Taupe. He managed many deals for Star Alliance beings. But I have not seen him for several sun cycles."

"No one has," Pplimz said. "Zoarr accused Tailor of stealing the tiara, and now Tailor has gone missing. It seems that this bauble of yours has caused a great deal of disturbance."

"Now see here," Sassert stood on four short trunk-like legs. "My jewelry is not responsible for any of this! If it was stolen, then it's the thief's responsibility, not mine. And as for Tailor, I can't see how anything that happened to him is my fault!"

"No one is blaming you," Wibble said, "we just want to find out what happened."

"Well, I don't know anything about any of this. I appreciate the meal, but I must be going now." Wibble hurried to catch up as Sassert quickly made for the door.

"One last thing before you go," she called out. "Where did you get the stone?"

"From Tailor the Taupe," Sassert said.

"What?"

Sassert nodded. "He sold it to me in trade for some earrings on behalf of someone from the *Quantum*. Levay or Rebeck, some funny name like that." Then Sassert was out the door and off at a trot into the night, the scent of flowers and meat trailing behind.

"Could that be Officer Levesque?" Pplimz asked.

"Anything is possible," Wibble said. "Including that Tailor the Taupe is mixed up in the middle of this after all."

"He has always been somewhat sparing with the truth," Pplimz said, disappointed but unsurprised at the nature of their client. "I suppose it's back to the Bivouac in the morning, then."

Training Officer Helene Levesque sat at an outdoor table near the parade grounds, a mug of some dark steaming liquid in front of her. She took a sip, closing her eyes and savoring the taste. Wibble thought it smelled like dirt, but kept the observation to herself.

"We understand you sold a gemstone to Sassert, the jeweler in Horizon," Pplimz said.

"I wouldn't call it a gemstone," Levesque said. "At least, it's like no precious stone I've ever seen before. But I suppose it was pretty enough. Gems aren't really my thing."

"No?" Wibble asked. "Sassert said you traded the stone for earrings."

Levesque nodded, and brushed her long hair behind one ear to reveal a series of polished metal studs and plugs running up her ear. "I like jewelry, just not gems."

"Then why did you have the stone in the first place?" Pplimz asked.

Levesque sighed. "I feel a little foolish telling you this," she said. "It's one of the reasons we ended up using Taupe for so many of our transactions lately."

"Go on," Wibble said, her body flushing a light green in excitement.

"We have no interest in shaming anyone," Pplimz assured the Star Alliance officer. "But there has been a theft, and, of course, Tailor the Taupe is now missing, maybe worse."

"Of course," Levesque said, clearing her throat. "I'll give you any help I can. I don't know how much you understand about our experience here…"

"Let's assume we know nothing," Wibble said.

"All right. The *Quantum* is the flagship of the Star Alliance. We were on a long-range exploration mission when we encountered a spacial anomaly. Or perhaps it was a temporal or even dimensional anomaly – our sensor systems were knocked out as soon as we made contact with it. All I know is that we had been in clear space one minute and then we found ourselves trapped in a gravity well and unable to escape. There was an atmosphere and a planet, or planet-like structure, hurtling toward us. Of course, we crashed. Here." She gestured toward the remains of the starship, half buried at an odd angle in the desert at the base of a small mountain.

"We are all lucky to be alive, and luckier still that many of the ship's systems were able to be repaired," she went on. "But our engines are still down. While we are, of course, taking this opportunity to learn about all the incredible people and places on this world, our primary mission must be to repair the engines, and return to our greater mission in the galaxy beyond the bounds of this world."

"You intend to leave the Crucible," Pplimz said evenly.

"If any of the crew wish to stay and make their homes here, that would be their choice," she said, "but yes. Once the ship has been repaired, we will leave and continue our mission."

"You are aware that no one has ever left this world," Wibble said, not unkindly. "It is believed to be impossible."

"Nothing is impossible for a well-trained and motivated crew," Levesque said.

"A fine philosophy," Pplimz said, diplomatically. "But what does this have to do with the stone you had?"

"That's the embarrassing part. I'm afraid to admit that in my eagerness to help find a solution to the engine problems, I was a little too willing to believe it when I thought I'd found something I very much wanted to acquire."

"Oh?"

"There was one of those itinerant merchants in the Horizon," Levesque explained. "From one of those operations that specializes in that strange substance everyone calls Æmber. They had a selection of artifacts – everything from what looked like rough lava rock to brilliant diamonds. But this one stone seemed to be different, and when I asked about it, the merchant told me that it had demonstrated unusual properties. I was curious, so I scanned it and was amazed to see that it appeared to be a source of an isotope very much like tritium, which we need to power our fusion engines. I didn't even haggle, I just paid the merchant and took the stone back to our engineers." She paused for a moment, staring out toward the remains of the downed ship. "I really believed for a moment that I had done it, that I had found the one missing piece we needed to get back out there. But no."

"No tritium, then?" Wibble asked.

"No. And when the engineering team scanned the stone, there was no indication of anything even remotely like tritium. I must have misinterpreted the readings. I'd completely wasted their time and got everyone's hopes up over nothing more than a shiny rock." She looked miserable. "I feel like such a fool."

"Ah, but how much more foolish would it have been to ignore a possible solution?" Pplimz said. "There is never anything wrong with trying something, even if it does not work as one hopes. If we never try, we can never succeed."

"Thank you," Levesque said. "You're right. But I did get fleeced by that rock seller, and we all agreed that utilizing a little local knowledge was the right thing to do in the future." She stared off into the distance. "I do hope that nothing has happened to him."

"As do we all," Pplimz said. "So when you learned that the stone you had was not what you'd thought, what happened?"

"Once Taupe had been recruited to help us with our transactions, I asked him to see if he could trade it for something. Honestly, I just didn't want it around any more," Levesque said. "It was a constant reminder of my failure. And of the fact that we seem to be stuck here."

"Well, we're all stuck here," Wibble said, brightly. "It's not so bad once you get used to it."

"I have no intention of getting used to it," the officer said. "And I can't understand why so many people here just accept that they are trapped!"

Wibble and Pplimz shared a glance.

"For most of history, planet-dwelling beings have been confined to their home worlds," Pplimz pointed out, gently. "No one knows why the Architects of the Crucible created it to be inescapable, but that does appear to be the nature of this place. Perhaps it is meant to be a reminder of those older times, when our ancestors could only dream of the stars."

"Well, I for one intend to do more than dream," Levesque said. "And I'm sure I'm not the only one."

"Fair enough," Wibble said. Plenty of beings on the Crucible hoped to leave the world someday. Even Wibble herself had, long ago, numbered among them. She understood. "So can you tell us more about the merchant who sold you the stone? A name, species, anything?"

"I have the bill of sale, if that helps," Levesque said.

"Anything helps at this point."

The officer tapped on her wrist console and then turned to Pplimz, taking in their many implants and augments. "I don't want to make assumptions based on what you look like," she said. "Do you have some kind of interface we can use to transfer this data?"

"I do," Pplimz replied, and unspooled a thin cable from one of their fingers. Levesque took it and connected the end to her console.

"This is written in Kaakorlin, one of the goblin languages," Pplimz said, once the transfer was complete.

"Yes, the *Quantum*'s translator software has done a reasonably good job with that one," Levesque said. "I can't even blame this on a communication failure."

"It says here that the seller, one Honest Harb, operates a wholesale outlet from a warehouse near The Pit of This Pair."

"That's halfway to Nitrogen Falls from here," Wibble said. "We'll need a flyer to get there."

"Well, part of the sales pitch they gave me was that they were just passing through the area," Levesque said. "The limited time offer was made pretty clear."

"Don't get too excited, Wibble. We can get in touch with them remotely." Pplimz brought up a scan of the document, which was more advertisement than invoice. There were communicator codes for half a dozen different systems listed.

"Well, I suppose it's time to get Honest Harb on the horn," Wibble said. "Who will be hopefully helpful in honing a history for her hustled hasty harvest." She gestured at Levesque with a rosy flipper.

"Stop it, Wibble," Pplimz said, but Levesque couldn't repress a giggle. Pplimz turned to the chuckling officer. "Please don't encourage her or it will be like this all night. Come on, Wibble, let's go."

"Good luck with your mission," Wibble said, delighting in Pplimz's feigned annoyance. "I hope to hear you have healed hardware henceforth!"

"Honestly!" Pplimz exclaimed, and Levesque burst into peals of laughter as the detectives took their leave.

CHAPTER SEVEN
Pplimz Explains Anatomy

"I assure you that under no circumstances whatsoever did I promise or imply that the item in question conferred any particular power or that it contained any specific characteristics of any kind."

Honest Harb had been more than happy to take a holocall with Wibble and Pplimz when zie'd thought they were getting in touch as potential customers. When it became apparent that they were interested in discussing an item that had already been sold, however, zir tone changed abruptly.

"All our merchandise is traded on a strictly as-is basis," zie added. "There are no guarantees in life, or at my shop, and no returns or exchanges can be offered."

"We aren't interested in returning the stone," Wibble explained, hoping that assuring the merchant that zie'd get to keep the fee would increase zir willingness to talk. "We'd simply like to know more about it. Can you tell us where you got it?"

Harb's demeanor changed again, perhaps catching the sniff of a sales opportunity here after all. "I'm afraid I don't know of any other stones exactly like it, however I do have a few lovely Æmbercrafted items which might have a comparable aesthetic feel." Zie switched the visual to a catalog page showing several items of very little similarity other than being encrusted with gems.

"Thank you, but no," Pplimz said. "It's the history of that particular stone we're interested in."

"Very well," Harb said, the holo-image filling with zir pale green face again. "When I acquired it, the stone was part of a jeweled goblet. The setting was, frankly, rather amateurish, and the other stones were mostly worthless. I'd never seen anything quite like that particular gem, though, and thought it might be appealing to someone who likes novelty."

"Did you do a full analysis of the jewel?" Wibble asked, pleased that they were finally getting somewhere.

"Of course," Harb said. "Or, rather, I tried. As I said, it's like nothing I'd ever seen before. I compared it to the records of all known gems previously seen on the Crucible and it didn't match any of them. My instruments did not detect any significant technological or magical properties, other than a slight trace of Æmber. Of course, very little in this world has no contact with that substance. My professional appraisal was that at best it might possibly be unique, but otherwise it was of no more than aesthetic value."

"Can you tell us anything about the history of the goblet?" Pplimz asked.

Harb shook zir head. "Nothing useful, I expect. It was part of a reclamation bin from a Logos macro-research facility. You know, those crates full of odd ends of wire and broken switches, but they are easy to acquire and once in a while there's something interesting to be found. The goblet wasn't the kind of item I was expecting, but you never know with those logotarians. They'll study anything once."

"You said the goblet was, shall we say, not the highest quality crafting?" Wibble asked.

Harb laughed. "That's generous. It reminded me of a saurian hatchling playtime project. The gems were affixed with glue. Can you imagine it, glue!"

"Can you tell us which facility it came from?" Pplimz asked.

"Sure," Harb said, and a note popped up on the display. "Now, are you absolutely certain I can't tempt you into something from my collection?" The display changed to a catalog page again. "I just received a shipment of proper Æmbercrafted pieces from an artisan in the Everfire. The stones are imbued with real fragments of the inferno."

Even knowing nothing about jewelry, Pplimz could tell that these were indeed much finer pieces. There were pins, earrings, tail spirals, and more, each neatly engraved and adorned with a gem that did indeed seem to contain a tiny living flame. They had to admit, the pieces were stunning.

"Ooh, that necklace is lovely," Wibble said, pointing with a flipper.

"Wibble, you don't have a neck," Pplimz reminded her. "It would just fall off you."

"I don't need a neck to admire it," she said. "Let me think about it, Harb. I'll get back to you."

Pplimz sighed. "Thank you for your time," they said to the merchant, then cut off the connection before Wibble could buy anything. "I suppose technically we learned something there," Wibble said. "It doesn't seem terribly useful, though."

"Every piece of data gives us more to work with," Pplimz reminded her primly, then admitted, "it really wasn't much, though. Half the objects on the Crucible have passed through a dozen owners. There's nothing unique about that."

"Well, perhaps those Logos researchers have something more illuminating – and less mercenary – to share with us," Wibble suggested. "At a very minimum, they'll be sure to have data."

At first the ethereal spirit clad in a bronze goggled and geared containment suit who answered their call said he had no time to talk to them, but when they offered to allow him to take a holo of Pplimz's five-dimensional elbow rotator, the spirit miraculously found a few spare minutes. After consulting several colleagues, he finally was able to tell them that the goblet had been found in a dumping site not far from the Dead Range.

"Seems like an odd place for logotarians to be out wandering," Wibble said.

"We have found several useful and interesting items in that location, so it's a regular spot on our collector drone's route. Many beings use the area as a place to offload things for which they no longer have a use," the spirit said, shaking his head. "Just because nothing living can survive there, that doesn't mean it should be used as a garbage dump."

"If nothing living can survive there, how does anyone manage to drop off their junk?" Wibble asked.

The spirit shrugged. "Matter transporter, probably. A remote drone could do it, obviously. Or maybe it was one of my brethren. We aren't, you know, technically alive from a purely biological perspective."

"So this goblet was just thrown away?" Pplimz confirmed. "Then you sent it on for reclamation too?"

"It wasn't very nice," the spirit admitted with a grimace. "Just a cheap cup with some sparklies stuck to it. Nowhere near as interesting as this!" He brandished half a circuit board with what looked like a very old, very ripe foxberry peel stuck to it.

"Hrphm." Pplimz made a judgmental grunt, then thanked the spirit for his time.

"Oh, it's not *my* time," he said, cryptically. "I still have to use the same time as everyone else. But maybe one day I'll succeed in making my own. Wouldn't that truly be a breakthrough?!" With that, he broke the connection.

"It's hard to believe that something that was chucked out as trash – twice! – is now so valuable that it's been stolen," Wibble said.

"And possibly led to something much worse," Pplimz said, darkly. "I still can't get any connection whatsoever to Tailor. I'm starting to become rather worried, Wibble."

Wibble was unusually quiet for a moment, her body pulsing with shades of indigo. "Whether that stone is valuable or not, a being's life is more important," she said, finally. "I'm afraid that we're wasting our time chasing the history of this gem when we should be trying to find Tailor."

"I know," Pplimz said, "but whatever has happened to Tailor the Taupe, it's overwhelmingly likely to be related to this missing jewel."

"I think we need to expand our search area," Wibble said.

"Whoever has the tiara could be nearly anywhere by now."

"I agree," Pplimz said. "I'll get in touch with the usual informants and have them be on the lookout for any information about the crown."

"Best to describe the gem itself as well," Wibble said. "After all, it does seem to have a history of being taken out and put into something new."

"Do you think there's something special about the gem after all?" Pplimz wondered. "Like Officer Levesque thought?"

"Could be," Wibble said, dubious. "Or it could just be that it took until it got to Sassert for an artisan to set it properly. The tiara is certainly the nicest setting it's been in by a long shot."

Pplimz nodded and began preparing a file to send out, with the holo-image of the tiara and a written description of the gem based on the information they'd been given. While they were busy creating the dossier, Wibble hovered out the door to visit the front desk.

The pair had taken a retainer on the green circle room at Cynthala's to use as a base near Quantum City, which gave them access to communications, storage, and other sundries. She stopped by the office to chat with today's Cynthala, a petite compound-eyed multi-limbed being, with slavering jaws and razor-sharp appendages. He was wearing a gleaming headset with a laser magnifier while soldering a complicated-looking device on the countertop.

"Ooh, what are you making?" she asked.

Cynthala looked up, just barely catching a neon green drop of drool with a handkerchief. He tossed the hanky into a nearby clay pot, where it promptly burst into flames.

"It's a toy for my babies," he said, poking the device with a claw.

It sprung up into a ball with an audible whirr, then sprouted legs and began scuttling across the counter. "They do like to chase at this age."

"How fun!" Wibble extended an invisible force finger and prodded at the device. A pair of sharp pincers extruded and began snapping at her. She giggled. "I'm sure your kids will have a wonderful time with it."

"I hope so," Cynthala said, removing the headset. "How can I help you today?"

"You wouldn't happen to have a spare communicator I can use?"

"Of course," Cynthala said, antennae wiggling. "Is there a problem with the system in your room? I can have a technician take a look."

"Oh no, it's fine," Wibble said, then hovered closer even though they were alone in the office. "My partner is busy working in there and ... I have a private message I'd like to send, that's all." That and making sure her partner who was busy working didn't know about the message. But she didn't need to mention that.

"I understand." Cynthala bent down and handed her a small wireless device. "There's a soundproof studio just through there." He gestured at a small door.

"Not necessary," Wibble said, calling up Honest Harb's catalog, then tapping at the device with her flippers quickly. "All done! Thanks again." She handed the device back, then tilted her front end down to get closer to the toy. Without warning its pincers flew out in a flash, slicing and snapping well past the outer boundary of her body.

"Eeee!"

"Oh no!" Cynthala shouted, grabbing at the spherical device, which skittered out of range of his claws.

"Eeee," Wibble continued shrieking, "it tickles!" She shimmied away from the unit's continued attacks, and Cynthala managed to contain it by impaling it with one of his serrated claws. He looked up at her with concern, but her body appeared to be utterly unscathed by the experience.

"Your kids are lucky to have such an attentive parent." She waggled a flipper in his general direction. "Toodle-oo!"

She floated out of the office as Cynthala breathed a deep sigh, then carefully switched the device into safe mode.

Pplimz was sending out the last of the messages when Wibble returned to the room.

"Was that you I heard making such a mighty racket?"

Wibble told Pplimz about Cynthala's toy, casually omitting the actual reason for her visit to the front desk.

"You probably terrified the poor thing!" Pplimz chided. "Most beings who are not obviously armored would have been injured. They have this substance called *skin,* remember – it's quite delicate and easily ruptured. You really must take more care, Wibble."

"But it tickled," she said in justification. "And it is truly a terribly cute little toy."

"I'm sure it is," Pplimz said, then a small yellow light illuminated on their wrist casing, indicating an incoming transmission to their public communications channel. "Well, that's a surprise. I only just sent those messages out." They opened the channel and an unfamiliar human face appeared on the holoscreen.

"Hello?" the voice tentatively said. "I'm trying to reach the detectives Wibble and Pplimz?"

"Yes, that's us!" Wibble said, floating into the view of Pplimz's camera lens. "What information can you give us about this strange gemstone we're looking for?"

The human's face scrunched up, the head rotating back and forth slightly. Wibble had seen other humans make that gesture and thought it was a type of non-verbal communication indicating a negative response. "Gemstone? No. I'm..." The human paused, then went on, much more quietly. "Look, can we meet? I understand you are based in the Horizon. I could come to you. I'm in the area."

"Of course," Pplimz said. "Are you familiar with Cynthala's?"

"I'm afraid not."

"Not to worry," Wibble said. "Once you leave the Bivouac you follow the road all the way past the market that sells those delightful flying spiders on a stick, then turn left at the boiling lava baths. If you make it all the way to where those itinerant verpy-traders are set up, you've gone too far."

"They're *itinerant,* Wibble," Pplimz said. "There's no reason to believe they are still in the same place."

"Oh, I suppose there isn't, is there?" Wibble said. "That may be a bit of a problem, then."

Pplimz sighed. "Cynthala's is the inn closest to the transportation hub," they explained.

"Oh," the human said, "I'm sure I'll be able find it." They set up a time to meet in the tavern the next day, and then the human broke the connection.

"Well, that was strange," Wibble said.

"Your directions were strange," Pplimz muttered.

"They were entirely accurate," Wibble retorted. "Aside from

the bit about the traders. Although now that I think of it, I'm not entirely certain it's the *traders* who are the nomads. For all we know, they are permanently based here in the Horizon and are offering the services of itinerant verpies."

"Surely an itinerant verpy would never allow itself to become domesticated for use as a beast of burden, Wibble."

"What do you know about verpies?" she asked. "Have you ever ridden one?"

"I most certainly have not," Pplimz said. "And I know at least as much about them as you do."

"Exactly!" she said triumphantly. "Almost nothing."

"Wibble," Pplimz said, deftly changing the subject, "did you get the impression that this human was somewhat distressed?"

"Now that you mention it, I did," Wibble said. "And I also got the impression that this meeting is not in response to your messages about the stone at all."

"The only humans I've been in contact with are *Quantum* crew, and I didn't send any messages to anyone in the Star Alliance today," Pplimz confirmed. "After all, they already know as much about this as we do."

"Well, at least that's what they've been saying," Wibble reminded her partner. "That's no guarantee that we have been given the whole story. You can't take everyone at their word, Pplimz."

"Indeed not. Some beings do have a tendency to dissemble, don't they?" Pplimz sounded disappointed.

"It's an occupational hazard, my dear," Wibble said. "In our line of work we often see beings at their worst. However, I for one am pleased to see that you haven't completely given up on your faith in others. It's good to be trusting. Just not *too* trusting."

"Well, that makes everything completely clear," Pplimz said. "Say, what were you talking with Cynthala about anyway? We are all paid up, aren't we?"

"Oh yes," Wibble said, "we have the room as long as we need it. Nothing to worry about there. I was just getting a change of scenery. It can get a little dull in here sometimes, don't you think?"

"Not really."

"Hmph. Say, Pplimz, what do you think riding a verpy is like? All that fur looks comfy and soft but I don't know about those horns all over. And wouldn't the second set of wings get in the way?"

"Wibble, if you are contemplating hiring us a pair of verpies, let me make it absolutely clear that I am not interested!"

Wibble lazily turned over to float on her back, her tail swishing up and down. "Well, all right," she said. "But I really don't think we'll both fit on one."

CHAPTER EIGHT
Wibble Opens a Box

The human walked into Cynthala's tavern precisely on time and appeared to recognize Wibble and Pplimz easily.

"Thank you for meeting me. My name is Véronique So, my pronouns are she/her."

"I'm Wibble, she, and this is Pplimz, they."

So slipped into the bench seat across the table. She gave off an air of professional detachment, but her left index finger tapped a pattern where she rested her hands on the tabletop. Unlike the few other humans in the bar, she was not dressed in a Star Alliance uniform, but rather wore a cream tunic under a blocky tan blazer not entirely dissimilar in cut to Pplimz's own suit jacket.

The tavern's server appeared at the table, literally materializing out of thin air. "Might I offer you any refreshment?"

"Yes, thank you, a magnaflower tea if you have it," So said.

"Of course," the server replied. "For either of you?"

"No, thank you," Pplimz answered. The server disappeared

and they sat in silence for another moment.

"How can we help you today?" Pplimz asked, eventually.

"Honestly, I don't know," So said.

"Well, how about you start with what brings you to Quantum City?" Wibble asked.

"I live here. I'm an engineer grade two in the Star Alliance," So said, a look of confusion on her face, then she seemed to understand, gesturing at her outfit. "Oh, the uniform. I'm off duty now. I know many of the others wear theirs all the time, but that seems strange to me. I didn't arrive on the *Quantum*. I used to live in Hub City, but when I heard that there was a whole shipful of humans who'd just arrived, I knew I wanted to join them. I've been here since they began taking on local recruits."

"I see," Pplimz said. "Was it much of an adjustment?"

So laughed. "Was it ever! Don't get me wrong, I don't regret signing up for a minute, but the uniform is restrictive in a lot of different ways. All the original crew have been in the Alliance for a long time, and of course life on an intergalactic exploration ship is, by its very nature, going to be regimented. They all live, work, and play with their crewmates, and there have to be rules and a chain of command. Now that they are stuck here, they all have to learn how to operate in this new environment." So leaned back, seeming to be more at ease as she talked.

"Between us," she said, "I sometimes wonder if the adjustment has been harder for the original crew than for those of us who joined later. For me, it's exciting to find more people like me, and the work gives me a sense of purpose. For them, it's a life they specifically didn't choose. Every single crew member of the *Quantum* signed up to travel the stars, not to be bound to one place, and yet here they are. It's no wonder they are so focused on trying to get back out there."

"What do you think about that?" Wibble asked.

So shook her head. "I was born here, on the Crucible. But my parents were newcomers. They were part of a rockhopper team that fell into an uncharted wormhole on a cargo run and found themselves transported to the edge of Hub City." She made an expansive gesture with her hands. "Of course, they tried to leave, as so many newcomers do, but you know how it is." Pplimz nodded. "By the time I was born they'd made a new life here, and I grew up knowing that no one leaves this place."

The server materialized with So's tea, and she held the steaming cup up to her nose. "I feel for the original crew of the *Quantum*, I really do, but I know they'll all be much better off as soon as they accept the reality of their situation. There's so much to explore and learn here, more than enough to fill a thousand lifetimes. You don't need to travel the stars to investigate unusual realms, meet new cultures and people, or explore previously undiscovered areas."

"That has certainly been our experience," Wibble said.

So nodded. "I remember hearing about you, back in Hub City," she said. "I know you've helped a lot of people."

"We do our best," Pplimz said, modestly, but the glow of their screen face illuminated slightly.

So took a deep draught of her tea, closing her eyes as she swallowed. She breathed out a plume of magenta vapor, the distinctive aftereffect of an infusion of genuine magnaflower leaves. "I know you're here because of Tailor the Taupe," she said. "And I knew I had to get in touch with you, because it's my fault that he got caught up in this. It's my fault that he…"

She trailed off, and cleared her throat. "Tailor did broker the exchange for the Qubit Zirconium tiara, but it wasn't on behalf of Zoarr. It was for me."

"If it's actually yours, why did Zoarr report it missing?" Pplimz asked, once the initial shock of So's revelation had worn off, which was essentially immediately to anyone who didn't have a technologically enhanced sense of the passage of time.

"Zoarr did have the tiara," So explained. "And it is missing. But he stole it first."

"Well, that's certainly unexpected," Wibble said. "I thought there was some kind of documentation showing that Zoarr was the tiara's rightful owner."

So nodded. "There is, and that's part of the problem. You know how I mentioned that the Star Alliance is, shall we say, very keen on following protocol? Well, it's a big part of their culture. Every Alliance trade that goes on in the Horizon has forms and processes that have to be followed, even for personal items. I'd gone through the proper procedure and requested a procurement order for the tiara. It was passed on to Tailor the Taupe as the purchasing agent, who completed it and filed it with the quartermaster after he'd collected the item. But somehow between the time that Tailor submitted it and it was processed, I guess the order had been altered to show Zoarr's name instead of mine as the buyer. When the tiara was delivered, it went to Zoarr."

"But if Tailor knew the tiara was meant for you, why did he give it to Zoarr?" Pplimz asked.

"Protocol," So repeated. "All trades are delivered to the Procurement Office, who confirm the order, then pass the item on to its final destination. Neither Tailor nor I had any idea that something had gone wrong with the documentation until I never got the delivery. I didn't even know Zoarr had stolen it until he reported it missing."

"You're sure it wasn't just a clerical error?" Wibble asked.

"Zoarr did imply to us that he'd asked Tailor the Taupe specifically for the tiara," Pplimz reminded her. "He said he'd been looking for it in particular."

Wibble shimmered. "He did, didn't he?"

So shrugged. "With all the documentation to back him up, there's no reason for him to tell a different story," she said. "All the proof indicates that what he told you is accurate. It's my word – and Tailor's – against his. But Tailor isn't here to back me up."

"And you think the authorities would believe Zoarr over you?" Wibble asked. "I mean, you are a fellow human, after all."

"No, people in the Star Alliance don't think like that," So said. "Both Zoarr and I are new recruits, so we have equal standing. And to be completely honest, I haven't really fitted in as well as he has." She looked down at her non-uniform clothes. "Add that to a database trail that clearly shows him as the rightful owner, well… I'm not sure even I would believe me."

"Then why should we believe you, Engineer So?"

"You probably shouldn't," she said, miserably. "But it happens to be the truth."

"Something being improbable but true is less uncommon than many beings think," Pplimz said.

"And Zoarr was rather quick to accuse Tailor of the theft," Wibble pointed out. "That struck me as odd at the time. Sure, there are a lot of thieves who are elves, but there are a great many more giants who aren't Star Alliance officers, and you'd think

Zoarr of all beings would know not to make assumptions. But if Zoarr orchestrated a change to the database, Tailor would have known that the manifest was faked, so throwing suspicion onto him would be an excellent move to distract from Zoarr's own involvement."

"Are you certain that Zoarr altered the records?" Pplimz asked.

"I'm not certain of anything," So said. "But the database shows him as the originator of the procurement order, not me, and he's the one who benefits. It seems awfully likely that he did it. Not to mention that his specialization is in cryptography and applied communications operations."

"He's a spy?" Wibble blurted.

"Of course not, there are no spies in the Star Alliance," So said, hiding a slight smile behind her teacup. "But he would possess the skills to alter a database record, and he has access to the main computer."

"It's far from conclusive," Pplimz said.

"But it's something," Wibble added. "Like a loose thread on a bag that's hard to open. It might not be the way the maker intended you to get in, but if you pull on it hard enough, you might create a hole. And even if you don't, you might unravel the stitching enough to see where the opening really is."

"Or you might just ruin a perfectly good bag because you couldn't be patient enough to find the clasp," Pplimz said. "I'm not sure that analogy really applies here."

"That's the trouble with metaphors, Pplimz," Wibble said. "If you think too hard about them, they stop making sense."

"Are you absolutely certain it's the metaphors that stop making sense, Wibble?" Pplimz said, archly.

Véronique So was staring at them, her eyes wide and a look of bemused concern on her face.

"Don't worry, this is all part of the process," Wibble said, brightly. "Come on, let's go tug on some strings."

On their way back to their room, the on-duty Cynthala swooped out of the office, gliding on wing-like skin flaps which extended from his outstretched forelimbs. He was very small, with pale green scales all over his body and tail, and he alighted on the wall next to Pplimz, tiny feet sticking to it as easily as if he were wearing gravity boots. He flicked his tongue out a couple of times, then said, "There is a package for you at the front desk."

"That's odd," Pplimz said, as Wibble floated toward the office door.

"I'll take care of it," she said, and shooed Pplimz toward their room.

"Don't open it if it smells like explosives," they said, but left Wibble to deal with the mystery parcel. They suspected Wibble was up to something, but experience had told them it was best to let her play out her schemes. They scanned their messages in the hopes of something new from their enquiries about the gem, but it was nothing but a handful of obvious grifters offering vague promises of non-specific information in exchange for "a reasonable fee."

They were composing polite but firm responses to their erstwhile scammers that essentially said, "Go away," when the door dissolved. Wibble floated in, a bright shade of pink, with a small velveteen box perched on her back.

"I couldn't help myself," she confessed, slapping her tail in the air and causing the box to flip off her back and land on the desktop next to where Pplimz was plugged into the console.

"What's this?"

Wibble opened the lid of the box to reveal one of the stones Honest Harb had tried – and apparently succeeded – to sell them. It was a small dewdrop shape of a smoky crystal with a pale blue flame dancing in its heart, set against a bar of engraved metal.

"It's a..." Wibble consulted the small card nestled inside the box, "tie-clip!"

"Wibble," Pplimz sighed. "You don't wear a necktie. You don't wear anything! Honestly, what in the universe do you plan to do with a piece of jewelry like this..." they inspected the stone, "even if it is exquisite?"

"I don't wear a necktie," Wibble said, plucking the item from its box and hovering over the desktop facing Pplimz. "But you do." She affixed the clip carefully to Pplimz's slate gray and black tie, where it sat as if it had been made just for them. The blue of the flame perfectly matched the glow from their screen face.

"I don't understand," Pplimz said.

"Don't you know what day it is?" Wibble asked.

Pplimz said nothing.

"It's the forty-third of Garuum!"

"No one follows the Scytherian ephemeris any more," Pplimz said, gruffly, though they felt a rush of electricity in their chest.

"What calendar we use isn't important," Wibble said. "What's important is that we first opened our office together on the last forty-third of Garuum, and I wanted to get you something to celebrate."

"Sometimes you can be unpredictably sentimental," Pplimz said.

"I suppose I can," Wibble agreed, bobbing up and down and fiddling with the jewelry box nervously.

Pplimz looked down at the tie-clip, its tiny blue flame flickering right where their core power supply was located deep inside their body.

"It's magnificent," they said, softly. "And so are y–"

"What's this?" Wibble interrupted, fishing a rolled-up note from where it had been concealed underneath the packing inside the box. She unfurled it on the desktop and a holomessage began to play.

Honest Harb's face appeared in the tiny projection. "After you so generously put in this order I, er, remembered something about that gem you are looking for," zie said in the recording. "Before I put it on the market, I ran it through the Jewelry Guild database. A typical precaution in case of items that might not entirely be of the provenance supplied by the seller. As it happens, the database returned rather a lot of positive results. Far too many positive results, in fact. From what I could tell, that stone has been seen in dozens of different places all over the Crucible, from the height of the canopy web in the Wooden City to well beyond the Æginne Ocean. Some of the entries even made it look like the gem was in multiple places at once. Clearly it is either one of a set, or there was an error in the logs, but either way, no one ever seemed to keep it longer than a few days. Obviously, there could be only one logical conclusion: the stone is cursed. So, I got rid of it as soon as I could. And I recommend you stay as far away from it as possible. Thank you for doing business with Honest Harb and I hope you will trust us again with your next jewelry purchase."

The message ended and the holo-image dissipated.

"Cursed?" Wibble repeated. "I didn't think goblins were superstitious."

"Perhaps that one is," Pplimz said, thinking of Harb's genuine skittishness over the gem. Zie had to have been truly concerned to have gotten rid of otherwise perfectly good merchandise. "And you know, one being's curse is another's enchantment. Maybe there's more to this Qubit Zirconium than just being a pretty stone." Pplimz looked down at Wibble's gift flickering on their chest. "Not that there is anything whatsoever wrong with a pretty stone. Thank you, Wibble."

"I'm so glad you like it," she said, unusually shyly. "Now, shall we go bother a giant?"

CHAPTER NINE
Pplimz Draws a Line in the Sand

"So, what's the plan?" Wibble asked, as she and Pplimz crossed the border into the Bivouac. They passed through the force fence as if it wasn't there, and the little security robot didn't even bother to pop out of its hutch to check their credentials.

"I'll play the heavy and you can be the sympathetic one? I've never tried to wrestle a giant before. I bet it's loads of fun."

"Wibble, no," Pplimz said. "There's no need to intimidate anyone. We'll just ask some questions and see what he says. Perhaps Zoarr will tell us something new. And if he sticks to his story it either means that he is lying or that Véronique is lying. Either way, that's useful information."

"Something tells me that asking for a favor is unlikely to be successful when we're about to accuse him of theft," Pplimz said, "but don't let that stop you."

"It's all a matter of forcing an overcorrection in the offensive stance," Wibble mused.

"Please try to keep any offensive stances to your imaginary wrestling bout, Wibble," Pplimz said. "This is going to be a delicate conversation."

"I can be delicate," Wibble said. "Probably."

They found Zoarr in his quarters in between training exercises.

"Have you got any leads on the tiara?" he asked when they entered.

"Possibly," Wibble said. "Can you tell us exactly how you went about the process of acquiring it?"

"I don't see how that is likely to help you find it now," Zoarr said gruffly.

"Humor us?"

Zoarr sighed deeply, the sound very nearly causing the entire room to vibrate. "There is a requisition form to complete for personal items," he explained. "Then a local agent – Tailor the Taupe, in this case – is dispatched to make the actual trade. Now, I don't mean to cast aspersions on any of my fellow officers, but I have heard that some of the newer recruits go ahead and make their own negotiations with the merchants in the Horizon. I believe in following the regulations," he said, with more than a hint of superiority in his voice. "Even if the rules are somewhat overbearing. But if you take a look at the quartermaster's records, you'll find that my requisition is entirely in order."

"You don't mind if we examine the records?" Pplimz confirmed.

"Of course not," Zoarr said, haughtily, and tapped his wrist com, sending them a copy of the requisition code. He obviously knew they would find that he was, indeed, listed as the tiara's owner.

"Speaking of examinations," Wibble said, and Pplimz glared at her silently, terrified that the next thing she would say might have something to do with Zoarr's body mass. "Would it be possible for us to take a look around your quarters? For any indication of how the thief got access to the tiara."

"Star Alliance security has already conducted an investigation," Zoarr said. "They found no evidence that the door lock had been tampered with, and I can confirm that, aside from the missing tiara, nothing else had been disturbed."

"Did they perform a complete molecular scan of the area?" Wibble asked.

Zoarr shook his head. "I'm afraid not. It's just a personal item, after all."

"I'd like to take a full sweep of your quarters," Pplimz said. "There is always a remote possibility that we might find something they missed. At the very least, surely you'd appreciate a second opinion." Pplimz arranged their face into a genial appearance.

"Of course," Zoarr said, after a moment's pause. "Anything you can do to help me get my property back is most appreciated." He gestured widely with an arm indicating that they should proceed.

Pplimz carefully removed their suit jacket, draping it over a chair back, then undid their left cufflink. Pocketing the item, they rolled up the sleeve of their silky black shirt, revealing a thin arm of what looked like braided heavy gauge wire, which glowed with a faint blue light. One of the strands uncurled itself in an almost organic movement, and its tip expanded to create a wedge shape. A wide-angled scanning beam shot out and Pplimz methodically waved it over the room in a neat, even grid, covering every surface.

"The results will take some time to come in," Pplimz said when they were finished and were resetting their outfit back to its usual impeccable standard. "We'll let you know if we find anything."

"Please do," Zoarr said, showing them briskly to the door.

"One more thing," Wibble asked, as she hovered out into the hall. "Does the Star Alliance have a wrestling squad?"

Zoarr stared at her, confused.

"Never mind that," Pplimz said to him, dragging their partner along by the flipper as they moved quickly away from the giant. "Honestly, Wibble, read the room."

They were greeted at the desk of the Procurement Office by Assistant Quartermaster Third Grade Piten, a krxix who was putting all of their limbs to use. One gloved hand gave them a friendly wave while they tapped at their wrist com with another, and sorted boxes and packets with two more.

"What can we do for you today?" they asked cheerily, scanning the detectives' badges with their waving hand. "Pplimz and Wibble. Lovely to meet you both! It's always nice to have visitors from other parts of this world, not that many come down to see us here in the PO. After all, we're more or less an internal department that rarely has any need for outsiders, not directly at any rate. Please don't mind me if I keep sorting while we talk. I have quite a lot to get through, as you can see."

There was, indeed, a large pile of incoming packages to their left, all awaiting scanning and categorizing.

"Please don't let us interrupt you," Pplimz said. "We're helping to locate an item that may have been stolen from Officer Zoarr."

"Oh, yes," Piten said, antennae twitching, "the giant! I remember hearing about that, terrible business. It's hard to imagine that even here in the Bivouac one has to be concerned about theft." They shook their head sadly. "I confess that I truly hope it is merely some kind of misunderstanding. I hate to think that someone would actually take something that didn't belong to them. Of course, it couldn't be one of the original crew. That's beyond belief!"

"Aren't you also a new recruit?" Wibble asked, then immediately regretted giving the krxix an opening for more conversation.

"Oh, no, I was on the *Quantum* when it crashed," Piten obliged. "People don't realize that the Star Alliance is not just a human organization, but is a true alliance of multiple species, including the krxix. There are many of my people in the Alliance and several of us were stationed aboard the *Quantum*. Imagine our surprise when we landed on this world and discovered so many of our home species already here."

"Indeed," Pplimz said, as the krxix paused for breath. "Back to that stolen item, would it be possible to see the procurement record? Zoarr gave us the requisition code." They projected a copy of the requisition code Zoarr had provided, and Piten scanned the glyph.

"Ooh, that is pretty," Piten said as the procurement order shimmered into view. It showed a holo of the tiara, along with the data which clearly showed that Zoarr was the purchaser of an item which was sourced from Sassert the jeweler and brokered by Tailor the Taupe.

"May we take a copy?" Wibble asked.

"Of course, of course," Piten said, scanning and sorting

several boxes while they talked. "Anything to help."

The quartermaster sent a coded, read-only file to Wibble's security badge, which Pplimz copied to their own system for detailed examination.

"Thank you for your time," Pplimz said. "We'll let you get back to your duties."

"Oh, no need to leave on my account," Piten said, with only a hint of desperation. "I can work and chat at the same time, no problem."

"I'm afraid we're needed elsewhere," Wibble said, hovering quickly toward the door.

"Perhaps another time," Pplimz added diplomatically.

"That would be delightful," Piten called after them as they left. "I'm here every day."

"You get the feeling Piten is a bit lonely in that position?" Pplimz asked, after they were out of earshot of the Procurement Office.

"It does seem like tiresome work," Wibble said, "but we'd have been stuck in that office until the heat death of the universe if we stayed as long as they were willing to talk."

"It was nice to speak with someone who actually wanted to answer our questions for a change," Pplimz said, "but you're not wrong. That's a difficult job for a being who so obviously prefers company."

They carried on toward their room at Cynthala's, when Pplimz broke the companionable silence.

"I've finished analyzing that database record, and, from what I can tell, if it was altered it was a professional job. There's no sign of tampering that I can see."

"Perhaps Zoarr is rather good at being a not-spy," Wibble suggested.

"Could be," Pplimz conceded. "I have no doubt that it's possible for someone with the right skills and access to change a record without leaving a trace. But why? It would have been a lot of work, and if he were caught that would certainly be the end of Zoarr's career in the Star Alliance. And all for nothing more than a sparkly trinket."

Wibble flushed yellow. "According to what Honest Harb told us, the stone can't have been all that valuable, since no one has hung on to it. And while Sassert's work was lovely enough, I can't see that it increased the value of the piece that substantially."

"It does seem like an awful lot of trouble to go through," Pplimz agreed.

"You think that Zoarr was telling the truth?" Wibble suggested.

"If he was, then Véronique So must not have been, and she sought us out with her story," Pplimz mused. "Which implies that she's trying to get a hold of the tiara herself, and is hoping to use our investigation to her own advantage."

"There's something we're missing here," Wibble said. "I'm starting to wonder if Officer Levesque wasn't as foolish as she thought."

"What do you mean? Do you think that the Star Alliance engineers misread the composition of the stone?"

"No," Wibble said. "Their technological skill is too far advanced to make that kind of error. I don't think it really was a possible power source for them. But what if it is something else? It could be more than just a stone after all.

Harb said it contained traces of Æmber, which isn't meaningful in itself, but could indicate that some clever Æmbercrafter has created something powerful but disguised it in a nondescript package."

Pplimz called up the image of the tiara and displayed it on their screen face. "This isn't exactly nondescript, Wibble."

"Fine," she said, "but you know what I mean! It looks like it's only jewelry, but what if it's actually some kind of powerful tool? Or a data store full of secrets? Or a terrible weapon?"

Pplimz set their screen back to its usual depiction of a face. "That would explain why so many beings are now trying to claim the tiara for themselves," they said.

"Maybe the stone wasn't changing hands so much because beings no longer wanted it," Wibble suggested, "but because others wanted it more?"

The rendering of Pplimz's face froze on the screen, then reanimated. And it reanimated quite significantly, their eyes wide and mouth taking on a startled O shape.

"You might be onto something," they said.

"Of course I might!" Wibble retorted. "You don't need to sound so surprised."

Pplimz completely ignored Wibble's attempt at alliteration, instead silently bringing up a projection showing a complex graph of the readings they'd taken of Zoarr's quarters.

"Look at this!" They pointed at a listing of trace elements the scan had identified.

"Xylocarbonate-zeta," Wibble read aloud. "Along with zyphoric acid? I've only ever seen that combination in martian technology."

"Exactly!" Pplimz said. "And not just any martian technology, either. Wibble, that's the residue left behind when a matter discombobulator-recombinator has been used."

"An MDR," Wibble said. "The martian transporter. I always assumed that was just martian war propaganda, not actual functioning technology. But you're saying it's real?"

"Very real," Pplimz said, "and very hard to come by. The Martian Empire keeps a tungsten grip on all its technology, but the MDR-2000X is probably their most closely guarded. I've only ever seen readings like this once before, and that was in Zyypzyar."

"When were you in the capital city of Mars?" Wibble demanded.

Pplimz waved a hand as if to waft the question away. "Another lifetime," they said, "before I met you."

Wibble knew that she wasn't likely to get anything further out of Pplimz. They both kept most of the details of their lives before they met to themselves. The ever-changing nature of the Crucible made it easy for a being to reinvent oneself, and they both believed that who one was now was more important than anything they may have done – or been – in the past.

"Well," she said, smoothly changing the subject, "that would certainly explain how someone stole the tiara without breaking in. But is an MDR precise enough to target a single item like that?"

"I have no idea," Pplimz said. "I have seen the effects of an MDR before, Wibble, not taken one apart and determined its complete capabilities."

"Fair enough," Wibble said. "You are the closest thing to an expert we have, though."

"The one thing I do know is that they have limited range," Pplimz said. "That's why the martians haven't been able to use them to transport their saucers beyond the influence of the Crucible's boundary. Not for lack of trying, from what I've heard."

"The martians are keen to send their saucers back into space."

"They certainly are," Pplimz agreed.

"The martian outpost Zyvax isn't that far from here," Wibble said. "It's probably the best place to make our enquiries."

"We'd probably have better luck interrogating this patch of dirt," Pplimz said, dragging a foot across the dusty road.

"Dirt can tell you a lot," Wibble said, dipping a flipper into the dust and feeling through the particles for the taste of different elements. "For one thing, there's been quite a lot of heavy drone traffic through here lately. Some poor overloaded robot lost its wheel."

"You're right, of course," Pplimz said. "I shouldn't be so negative. Even if the martians aren't likely to be entirely forthcoming that doesn't mean we shouldn't try to learn what we can. Very well. Let's see if we can find some kind of passage to Outpost Zyvax." Pplimz paused and stared at Wibble intently. "Land transport this time."

"Oh, Pplimz, you really should get that sense of adventure personality expansion pack I keep suggesting," Wibble chided. "Or at least a set of wings. Flying really is the most marvelous way to travel!"

"It's not flying I have a problem with," Pplimz said. "It's the dodgy cut-rate transport operators that put me off. And if we're going to Mars, I don't think we can entirely avoid those, so I'd rather keep whatever rattletrap conveyance we end up booking passage aboard as close to the ground as possible. I'd like to be able to simply jump off if the need arises."

Wibble shimmered a rosy glow. "A nice set of custom carbonite wings would solve that problem," she said, breezily. "Just saying."

"I'll augment myself – or not – how I like, thank you very much," Pplimz said, primly. "Now let's go find a ride to Mars."

CHAPTER TEN
Wibble Gets Taken for a Ride

All the beings on the Crucible originally came from somewhere else. It is a diaspora world of immigrants, stowaways, and lost souls. Most societies created new homes there, some forged otherwise impossible alliances, many sought a means to escape the locked-in world and return to their original homelands, and plenty of individuals used the opportunity to chart a different course for themselves. The Martian Empire, however, had a novel experience.

When martians first arrived on the Crucible, it wasn't on a downed spaceship like the *Quantum*, nor were they individual groups of travelers mysteriously drawn to the enormous world. Rather, a large portion of the planet was miraculously transported to the Crucible intact – landscape, cities, inhabitants, and all. They didn't have to recreate Mars on the Crucible; Mars – or a part of it, anyway – was already there.

Another civilization might have panicked, cowed by whatever terrible power could kidnap an entire section of a planet.

Martians, however, feared no one. Undeterred in their belief in their own martial superiority, the martian regiments who found themselves stranded on this new world saw only an opportunity to conquer more territory and beings. The fact that they were significantly outnumbered, and, in some cases, severely underpowered in comparison to their new neighbors only made them more determined to play a long game. The Martian Empire may lose a few battles, but they intended to win the war.

That most of their "enemies" failed to acknowledge that such a war even existed was utterly beside the point.

However, it did mean that one did not simply walk into Mars. The purloined terrain, officially called Nova Hellas, was guarded by several outposts of elite soldiers, and access was heavily restricted. The martian border made the checkpoints at the Star Alliance Bivouac look like a welcoming committee offering two-for-one cocktails and a free hat.

Wibble and Pplimz had encountered martians before, and knew that access to the main cities would be a challenge. But the traveling outposts existed as a buffer between Mars and the rest of the Crucible, and it was possible to talk with some of the more open-minded martian elders there. Of course, that only meant that there was a chance they might not shoot on sight. There was a limit to how friendly a martian could be.

"I suppose we have our answer," Wibble said, as she surveyed the open lot near the Horizon's transportation hub where independent operators sought to drum up business. "It was the traders who were itinerant after all, not the verpies."

Pplimz looked around and saw that Wibble was right – there were a few flitters for hire, a pedal-powered cart, and some rickety looking autocars, but there was not a single verpy in sight. They would have breathed a sigh of relief, if they'd had lungs.

"No chance of proper transport to Zyvax, is there?" they asked hopefully, downloading the schedule from the transportation hub. As expected, though, none of the comfortable passenger liners were traveling to Martian territory.

"I'm afraid we're going to have to rough it," Wibble said with delight. "I'd really hoped to get to ride a verpy."

"I'm not sorry at all to disappoint," Pplimz said. "However, would this do as a reasonable alternative?" They stepped aside to reveal a gleaming chrome and bone two-wheeled machine, its Æmber-injected engine purring quietly. Neon racing stripes along its side wriggled organically, and its tendon shocks flexed slightly as if it were eager to get going. Wibble squealed in a register that half the beings nearby couldn't even hear and which caused the other half to plug their auditory receptors.

"Have you ever driven one of these things?" she asked, zooming over to the vehicle. She moved so quickly that she appeared to pop in and out of phase as she inspected its handlebars, headlights, tires, seat, and sidecar.

"Of course not," Pplimz said. "But it has a computer. I have a computer. We speak each other's language." They swung a leg over the seat, which instantly conformed to the shape of Pplimz's hip joints, and then settled their feet into grooves close to the front wheel. A tendril of filament snaked out of each trouser leg to interface directly with ports in the osteocycle. Pplimz credited the rental company a not-insubstantial deposit and the engine roared to life briefly, the skull-lamp blinking on and off as Pplimz settled their hands on the knobby bone handlebars.

They jerked their head toward the sidecar. "Get in, Wibble."

She shimmered a deep emerald green and settled into the small round extension attached to the left of the cycle. A force shield popped up to cover the top of the sidecar and Wibble prodded it experimentally with a flipper once it had gone transparent.

"Flexible and strong," she said, approvingly.

"Safety first," Pplimz said, then leaned forward and the cycle maneuvered slowly through the maze of other vehicles toward the open road beyond the transportation hub.

"Hold on," Pplimz said, sliding a pair of goggles incongruously over their screen face.

"To what–" Wibble began, but the rest of her question was cut off by the sound of engine and wind as Pplimz opened the throttle and she was thrown against the plush back of the seat as they tore off down the dusty road.

They'd made it past the Pollus Doctrian bypass and were tearing toward the Eclipse Valley when Pplimz noticed the cycle making a high-pitched keening noise. They were in the middle of nowhere, and a breakdown would be terribly inconvenient, but it was prudent to determine if there was an issue before it became a catastrophe. They slowed to a stop to investigate the problem, but the sound continued. They turned to Wibble, and realized the noise was coming from her.

"Are you all right?" they asked, dismounting.

"Eeeee!" Wibble said, her voice lowering until she was quiet. "What? Oh yes, I'm fine. Better than fine, I'm fantastic! Why have we stopped? Is there a problem?"

"Well, you were screaming," Pplimz said.

"Was I?"

Pplimz nodded.

"Sorry about that," Wibble said. "I guess it just came out. I have to say, Pplimz, I think this is probably an even better way to travel than on verpyback. Faster, certainly."

"We are about halfway there," Pplimz agreed. "Outpost Zyvax is unusually northward for this seasonal time. It's this side of Macis Swamp."

"That bodes well for us," Wibble said. "Usually when the martians are further from home that means they are more inclined to trade. I do hope we won't have to barter with Susan here."

"Susan?"

"Yes, it's what I've named the osteocycle. It just feels like a Susan, don't you think? Oh..." She paused and flushed a pale blue. "Have I been terribly rude? Do you think it already has a name?"

"I don't think so," Pplimz said. "It hasn't introduced itself at any rate. It's sometimes hard to tell if something is entirely alive, especially if it doesn't communicate in a way we can easily understand. But from what I can tell, having interfaced with it, I don't think it's sapient."

"Well, either way I hope we don't have to trade Susan for information," Wibble said. "I'd hate to think of some martian technomancer dissecting it for spare parts."

"Not to mention that if we don't return it in a few days, we'll lose our deposit."

"Hmph," Wibble snorted disapprovingly, although she knew that Pplimz would go to any lengths to protect a fellow cyborg, whether it was sapient or not.

Pplimz mounted the cycle again and its engine started with a hum. "Shall we be off?"

"Yes, please!" Wibble prodded the force shield to make sure it was engaged. "And you can go faster if you like."

"Anything for you, Wibble," Pplimz said with a sly grin, and gunned the engine.

A short time later they pulled into Outpost Zyvax, which for a martian settlement was positively crawling with aliens. Indeed, for every twenty small, green martians there was some foreign being, trying to engage with the soldiers and elders from Mars. For all its insular societies and wildly variable landscapes, the Crucible was a remarkably interdependent place. In order to survive, beings relied on the skills, technologies, and supplies each other could offer. Even xenophobic Mars had to accept that. And so there were the outposts, the closest things they had to zones for open exchange.

Pplimz stowed Susan in a lot at the perimeter which already held a few carts and gyrocopters. They set a strong cryptographic lock on the wheels and engine, just in case someone happened to think that they might make an easy, off the books trade-in. Then they and Wibble walked over to the well-marked border control station.

"What do you bring to Mars?" demanded the martian dressed in the silver and blue uniform of a loyal soldier staffing the checkpoint. They brandished a blaster aimed at Pplimz, who noticed that the safety switch was still engaged. So it was to be a friendly welcome.

"I am Wibble and this is Pplimz," Wibble said, hovering a judicious distance from the soldier. "We are investigators from

Hub City, and we–" She was cut off as the soldier's attention was drawn away from them to the communicator embedded in their uniform's collar.

"Not again," they said, angling their round green head into their shoulder. "I'm on my way." They turned back to the detectives. "No touching, no tasting, no holos," they said. "All transactions must be approved by Commanding Elder Zaalyl."

"Understood," Pplimz said, as the soldier snapped to attention then scurried away toward the set of saucer-shaped prefabricated buildings which dominated the center of the outpost.

"Well, that was efficient," Wibble said.

"Usually there are waivers to sign and promises of dire consequences for any transgression," Pplimz noted. "I highly doubt that this outpost has merely chosen to dispense with the protocols."

Wibble floated up to get a skydweller's view of the scene. Several uniformed soldiers were massing toward one of the central saucers, where they all disappeared into the building.

"Something is going on," she said.

"Well, touching and tasting are out, but they didn't say anything about wandering around or looking," Pplimz said. "Let's see what's up."

They followed the soldier – at a respectable distance, of course – toward the building, but were stopped at the entrance by two heavily modified bioengineered guards. They were the size and shape of a standard martian solider, coming up only to Pplimz's shoulder, but with ray guns for hands and a springy antenna coming out of the backs of their heads. Their gun hands were pointed downward at their sides, at least.

"Access denied," the one on the left intoned. "This area is for martians only."

"No problem," Wibble said. "And what is this area, exactly? So we know where we can't go."

"Access denied," the guard on the right replied. "This information is for martians only."

"I see," she said. "Well, that's very illuminating, thank you."

"I don't think these two are going to be fruitful sources of enquiry," Pplimz said. "Let's see if anyone else knows what's going on."

They left the guards to their duties and Wibble spotted a bedraggled-looking singa lounging under a parked saucer. It appeared to be fast asleep, but its right ear twitched as they approached.

"Greetings, hunter," Pplimz said, and the creature's eyes opened to slits. "This seems an unlikely place to find a herd of yakalope."

The singa yawned prodigiously, exposing razor-sharp canine teeth and a long, pink tongue. It stretched, two front paws extending out toward them, claws glinting in the low light. Slowly, it padded out on all fours from under the saucer, then stood up on its two back legs and eyed the detectives.

"It's an unlikely place for anyone who isn't a martian," the singa said. "But we all have to trade where we can."

"How true," Wibble agreed. "Have you been here long?"

The singa shook its head, its matted mane swaying. "I'm meeting a team for a vault raid near here. Are you part of that group?"

"No, we're after information, not Æmber," Pplimz said, and the singa frowned, as if puzzled by the very notion that anyone could be uninterested in Æmber. Pplimz pointed toward the saucer building. "Any idea what's going on in there?"

The singa's tail swished against the ground. "The command center is off-limits to visitors," it said. "But something isn't right. I have never seen martian soldiers behaving like this before." It looked around as if making sure no one was listening. "Earlier today I heard some of them … singing."

"Singing?" Wibble echoed. Maybe martians weren't as joyless as she'd been led to believe.

"And I found one of them hiding out near the perimeter, weeping."

"Did you talk to them?" Pplimz asked, concerned by the unusual behavior. They hoped it was not contagious.

The singa shook its head. "No," it said, "that did not seem prudent. However, I can tell you that I didn't smell anything. No illness or intoxicants. It is all very strange."

"Agreed," Pplimz said. Just then, they were approached by a huge lizard with an impressive set of antlers, and a tiny glowing blue-feathered sprite who was riding on the lizard's shoulder.

"That's my team," the singa said, dropping to all fours and loping toward them. "May your information hunt be swift and merciful."

"Thank you," Wibble said, "and good luck with your hunt as well."

The three made for the edge of the outpost and Pplimz said, "I've never heard of martians showing emotions other than anger or annoyance. Certainly not in front of outsiders."

"Do you think this might be the curse?" Wibble asked.

"The curse?"

"The curse that Honest Harb mentioned," she explained. "That causes beings to get rid of the stone that's now set into the Qubit Zirconium. Maybe the tiara is here at Zyvax after all, and it's what's causing these strange reactions."

"If the stone does have a psychoactive effect, I hardly think that makes it cursed," Pplimz said.

"Perhaps not, but some beings might think it is." She waggled a flipper toward the martian compound, where a soldier was now leaning out of a porthole, giggling wildly, and apparently flying their uniform pants as a kite. "They might, for example."

"I feel ridiculous." The muffled voice that came from the large, boxy cleaning drone was barely audible, but Wibble's excellent hearing had no trouble making it out.

"You look fine," she assured Pplimz. "I mean, I wouldn't recommend going in for a maintenance check, and I think the sweepers might be a fraction too narrow, but you've done an excellent job. Besides, no one ever pays any attention to the cleaners."

While Pplimz maintained a roughly humanoid appearance as a rule – two arms, two legs, a torso and a head – their many augments allowed them to reshape their body significantly. They'd found an unattended maintenance outbuilding and changed out of their suit, handing the carefully folded clothes to Wibble to stow in Susan's capacious panniers. Then they'd reshaped their body into the blocky shape of the martian service drones, extruding bristles, cloths, and sweepers to mimic the appearance of a cleaning bot. The rolling bucket they'd snagged from the outbuilding and hooked to a clip on their side completed the ensemble.

"We should be able to move about the outpost freely now," Wibble said.

"Well, I should," Pplimz countered. "You're still rather obviously an alien."

"True. But that's only relevant if someone sees me," Wibble said, lowering herself into the bucket and piling oily rags over the top of herself. "See! I'm undercover!"

Pplimz groaned.

"Now, let's see if we can find some dirty little secrets," she added.

"Wibble, please." Pplimz rolled forward in the zig zag pattern they'd seen the other cleaning bots perform.

"It's time to clean up this place!"

"Keep that up and I'll find something absolutely vile and throw it right into that bucket."

"Now you're getting into character," Wibble said. "Excellent!"

CHAPTER ELEVEN
Pplimz Cleans Up

Mimicking the movements of a cleaning drone meant that they couldn't make straight for the main buildings, but it also gave them an opportunity to eavesdrop on the few foreigners who were loitering at the edges of the outpost. A pair of traders with a truckload of self-securing blaster bolts utterly failed to pay them any attention as Pplimz swept the dirt behind their stack of crates.

"This was a waste of time, Chimble," the large, chitinous, five-legged creature said to her companion, her twenty-three bright pink eyes flashing.

"We don't know that yet," Chimble replied, rubbing his hairy front forelimbs together. "Zaalyl said that they want these blaster bolts and we both know there's no one east of Bone Island that has this quantity. I know it's not easy, Tazzer, but we just have to be patient."

"We've been here for five days!" Tazzer complained, pacing back and forth, her many feet skittering in the dust. "First we had to wait for the scout patrol to return, and then, once they did, all ordinary business completely dried up. That human we passed on our way in was the last being to get anything out of these green monsters."

"Now, Tazzer, there's no call to be rude. I'm sure we look as strange to the martians as they look to us. It's probably just some administrative delay," Chimble said, fluttering his dark leathery wings. "We'll offload these bolts, I'm sure of it. With the amount of honeyblood they've offered in trade, it's worth waiting for. Then we can get back to the hive, and we'll be set for the brood season."

"I hope you're right," Tazzer said, then turned toward where Pplimz was going around in circles. They trundled away and left the bolt sellers to their fretting.

"We should find out more about this patrol," Wibble said quietly. "Let's see if we can get into the main compound."

"We won't be able to get access to the buildings," Pplimz said. "They have internal maintenance systems. But we may not need to."

A small group of martian soldiers was huddled around something in the clearing between two of the larger saucer buildings. They were laughing and slapping each other on the back, as one of them kicked the small object in the middle of their circle.

"Oh no," Wibble said, "are they hurting some being?"

Pplimz rolled forward to see what was going on, and tried not to laugh. "They appear to be kicking a ball back and forth."

"They're *playing*?"

"So it would appear."

A tall, thin, regal martian elder appeared from inside the

compound, and rushed over to angrily try and break up the game.

"This is conduct unbecoming to a loyal servant of Mars!" they shouted at the group, who were still deeply engaged in their game of kickball. "I will be forced to report this to your squad commander, Xyzzyl, and I have no doubt that there will be swift and severe consequences for all of y– Oof!" The elder doubled over as the ball was driven hard into their midsection by one of the players. The soldier who had delivered the shot approached the elder sheepishly to retrieve the ball and the elder's black ovoid eyes grew nearly spherical in surprise. "Xyzzyl?!"

"Sorry about that," Xyzzyl said, without any of the usual obsequious language martian soldiers used when speaking to their betters. "I'm just having a bit of fun with the crew, you know?"

"I most certainly do not know!" sputtered the elder, who brushed themself off and stalked away, speaking rapidly into their collar communicator.

"It's affecting Xyzzyl's entire squad," they said as they bustled toward the compound. "Yes, the sergeant as well. We need to contain this before it spreads to the rest of the platoon." They disappeared into a building as the squad continued to punt the ball between them, shrieks and giggles of enjoyment filling the air.

Something had clearly happened to the squad. Pplimz concluded that if the gem they were looking for had a psychoactive effect, that would explain everything – including why Mars would want to get their little green hands on it. It wasn't proof, but it was a solid lead.

"We need to talk to these soldiers," they said, "and find out if they've come into contact with the tiara."

"I have an idea," Wibble said, floating up out of the bucket, then shaking herself vigorously, rags flying in all directions off her back.

"What are you doing?!" Pplimz hissed. "They're going to see you!"

"That's rather the point," she said, hovering over to join the soldiers. "Mind if I tag in?" she said as she entered the circle of martians. They stopped playing for a moment, all staring at her in surprise.

Then one of them said, "Sure, why not?" and they tossed her the ball. She caught it deftly, balancing it on her front end, then arched her back, tossing the ball high up into the air. As it was descending, she flipped forward and smacked it with the flat of her tail, sending the ball shooting forward to the martian furthest from her. They connected with their foot and the game was on.

As they passed the ball back and forth, Wibble said, "Say, I don't suppose you folks have happened to come across a cute little tiara, have you? Silver crown, neat little jewel in the center?"

"No, I've never seen anything like that," one of the soldiers said as they head-butted a high ball back across the circle.

"Anyone else?" Wibble asked, lobbing the ball toward Sergeant Xyzzyl. A whole series of green heads shook "no."

"It sounds lovely, though," one of them said, dreamily.

"So, what have you all been doing?" Wibble asked casually. "You know, before you got back here to the outpost, when was it... ?" She thought back to the conversation she'd overheard earlier, "Two days ago?"

"Nothing remotely interesting," one of them complained.

"Now, Yrxyx," their neighbor said, "it certainly would have been interesting if we'd found a shard of anti-psionic Æmber after all."

"But we didn't," Yrxyx said. "And we had to walk all the way though the Great Glass Desert and then back again, and it was hot. And bright. And *slippery*."

"It was hot," another martian agreed sullenly.

"You said you went all the way through the Great Glass Desert?" Wibble confirmed.

"And beyond," Xyzzyl said. "Between you and me, I'm starting to think that there's no such thing as psionic Æmber."

"Well, thanks for the game," Wibble said, hovering quickly back to her bucket as another group of angry and confused martians were coming out of the building toward the squad. She settled atop the rags and whispered, "Let's get out of here," to Pplimz before they could see her.

"Have you ever been south of the Great Glass Desert?" Wibble asked when they were back at the perimeter and Pplimz had returned to their usual body form.

"Never had the pleasure," they replied.

Wibble shimmered. "Interesting choice of words," she said. "For many beings it is a real pleasure, indeed, but for others that part of the Crucible is nothing but pain. You won't know what you'll experience until you're there, and by then it's too late."

"That sounds ominous," Pplimz said.

"I've heard it called the Emotional Landscape," Wibble explained. "Something in the geography causes significant psychological upheavals in the visitors. It affects everyone differently, and no one knows exactly why one being has a positive experience while another doesn't. Some beings feel euphoria, others great sadness, and everything in between. All of it heightened and all of it overwhelming."

"And you?" Pplimz asked gently.

Wibble's body pulsed all the colors of the rainbow, settling in the blue range. "I did not find the episode overly pleasant, and I have no desire to ever return there. I understand that some beings return, seeking to repeat their previous encounters, but find themselves undergoing an entirely different effect. Even so, I'm not taking any chances if I can help it."

"I'm sorry you had a negative experience," Pplimz said. "How did you ameliorate the effects?"

"I didn't, really," Wibble said casually. "It wears off after a few days once you've left the area. There doesn't seem to be anything one can do to speed it up – or make the effects last, if that's the preference."

"So you think our martian friends are going to be back to normal soon?" Pplimz asked, having put it all together.

"Very soon, I'd imagine," Wibble said.

"The elders will be happy about that," Pplimz said, then smiled. "Well, I suppose not happy exactly, since apparently it takes a visit to the Emotional Landscape for that."

"Oh, I'm sure they are happy sometimes," Wibble said, "even if they don't know how to express it ordinarily. After a particularly delicious victory, perhaps."

"Perhaps," Pplimz said, dubious.

"So, what now?" Wibble asked. "I think it's safe to say the tiara has nothing to do with how the martian squad is behaving, and there's no actual evidence that anyone here stole it."

"I agree," Pplimz said. "The squad wasn't even at this outpost when it was stolen, and the elders don't seem like the types to get their white gloves dirty."

"Just because the MDR-2000X is martian technology that doesn't mean it was necessarily a martian who used it," Wibble said, and looked around. "This is a trading outpost, after all. Perhaps it was sold."

"Martians aren't generally in favor of open accounting methods," Pplimz pointed out. "It's not like they're just going to tell us to whom they sold a device that's banned in ten out of eleven jurisdictions."

"And they aren't generally up for an afternoon of ball juggling with an alien stranger, either, but here we are."

"You're suggesting we ask the soldiers," Pplimz said. "Find out if one of them has developed a tendency toward oversharing as part of their new personality."

"It might be worth a try. We need information and it's not like the martians are going to volunteer it otherwise."

Pplimz frowned, then leaned against Susan. "Wibble, when you're under the effects of the Emotional Landscape, would you say that you were not entirely yourself?"

"I… don't really like to think about it," she said, after a moment's pause.

"No, I suppose that's fair," Pplimz said. "But you should think about it, quite seriously, if you're contemplating taking advantage of the situation the martian squad is in."

Wibble was quiet for a moment, her body rippling through different colors.

"I wasn't 'not myself,'" she said, finally. "What I experienced were aspects of my mind that don't often come to the fore, but I wasn't some other being or anything."

"All right..." Pplimz said, but trailed off, as if expecting her to continue.

"But that's not entirely correct either," she said, eventually. "I wasn't in control. If someone had... taken advantage of those effects, I wouldn't have been able to react the way I would normally. It wouldn't have been fair. And I suppose that means it's not fair now."

"No, I don't think it is," Pplimz said. "Even if those martian soldiers could tell us everything we need to know, we have no right to use this situation to get that information."

"We aren't even sure that they know anything," Wibble said. "Fine, you've convinced me. But what now? It feels like a waste to just abandon this lead, especially as we came all this way."

"You didn't seem to mind the trip," Pplimz reminded her with a wry smile.

"That's not the point," Wibble said defensively, then she softened. "I really thought we were on to something with that transporter."

"It's not as if we are entirely out of options," Pplimz said, gesturing toward the small group of non-martians who were still camped out by the perimeter.

"You're sure that everything is going to go back to normal soon?" Gorp, a jittery piscine being encased in a translucent landsuit, said through the communicator on his suit as he swam around in nervous circles.

"The effects will likely be wearing off already," Wibble assured him. "What the martians do next will be up to them, but if they want these goods, they'll probably come and trade for them once the crisis is over."

"That doesn't look like a crisis to me," grumbled Karn, a small, furry, six-legged engineer who had been waiting to help repair a gravity pump for several days. "Looks more like a party."

"Well, to the martian elders, a party is a crisis," Pplimz said, to a few chuckles from the other traders.

"There's a reason most beings don't want to trade with Mars," Tazzer complained.

"They aren't terribly reliable?" Wibble asked.

"No, that's not usually the problem," Tazzer said, "but they like to pretend they don't need anything from anyone, and that whenever they trade with you, they are doing you some immense favor. But a good trade means both parties come out ahead. They don't like to acknowledge that."

"They don't have to in order for it to be a good trade," her partner Chimble reminded her. "They have something surplus that we think is useful. We have something they need. It's good for everyone. They'll see that eventually."

There were bubbles and tail-swishes of agreement among the merchants, but it was obvious that they were all frustrated. The outskirts of a martian outpost were not known for their creature comforts.

"When was the last time they came out to trade?" Pplimz asked.

"Not since I've been here," Karn said. "I arrived just before the squad returned."

"No idea," Gorp said. "I swam in after Karn."

"When we got here, someone was just leaving," Chimble said. "I don't know how to read human expressions very well, but they did not seem upset. And they were carrying a large, empty sack, so I assumed they'd offloaded whatever it was they brought."

"I don't imagine they'd have left empty-handed," Tazzer added. "Those Sun Confederacy members always seem to get what they came for."

Pplimz glanced at Wibble. "Sun Confederacy? Do you mean Star Alliance?"

"Yes, that's it," Tazzer said. "I can never get that name right."

"How did you know the human was a member of the Star Alliance?" Wibble asked. "Was it the uniform?"

"No, they weren't wearing a uniform," Chimble said, his mandibles clicking in thought. "It was the bag! It had the symbol on it. You know, that four-pointed yellow star with the orange ring."

"Could you describe this human?" Pplimz asked.

"Oh, sure," Chimble said. "Four limbs, the anterior ones much chunkier than the front legs. No visible skeleton and very little fur. Somewhere between three and six feet in length. Oh! And they had a bunch of tools on their belt."

"I bet that was what they traded for," Tazzer said, her hairy feet tapping a pattern in the dust.

"Weapons?" Wibble asked.

Tazzer shook her head. "Martians refuse to trade their blasters and ray guns. But they'll part with some of their other handheld devices. They have long since worked out how to harness Æmber as a power source for their simple printers, and creating a new bolt driver is easy for them. It makes for a good trade ratio."

"Thanks for your help," Pplimz said, and turned to Wibble. "Looks like we're going to have to try to get some information out of the martians after all."

CHAPTER TWELVE
Wibble Is In the Soup

"Well, that was a fruitful conversation after all," Pplimz said as they headed back to the checkpoint at the martian border. "I have a fairly good guess as to who that human was."

"Really? That description covers literally the entire species," Wibble said. "And probably a hundred other ones. Chimble might as well have been describing you!"

"True enough," Pplimz said. "But who do we know who fits the description of a person with access to Star Alliance materiel, but who doesn't always wear the uniform, and might be in the market for a martian tool which could be used to try to acquire an item she very clearly desires?"

Wibble stopped and hovered very still. Then she said, "Véronique So."

Pplimz nodded. "We only have her word that Zoarr changed the procurement manifest, and none of the evidence backs up her story."

"If she's the thief, why would she seek us out?" Wibble asked. "Why not just lie low and stay quiet until it all blows over?"

"Maybe she thought we were close to finding her on our own," Pplimz hypothesized. "She might have been trying to send us in another direction while she makes a getaway."

"Or maybe she isn't the thief," Wibble suggested. "We don't know that the MDR was used to steal the tiara. She could be hoping that when we find it, we believe her story and hand it over to her."

"Either way," Pplimz said, "I'm starting to become more inclined to think she didn't tell us the whole truth."

Wibble gestured toward the checkpoint. "Let's hope we get something useful here, then."

A different martian soldier was on duty. They scowled at Wibble and Pplimz as they approached from within the perimeter.

"What do you want?" they demanded.

"Your colleague informed us that all trades must be authorized by Elder Zaalyl," Pplimz said.

"That's right."

"How would we go about speaking with them?"

"You wouldn't," the soldier said brusquely. "You enter your trades into the daily log, and on the third watch the approved transactions are posted to the list." They gestured at a flickering green screen mounted to a pole near the area where the merchants were congregated.

"Thank you, you've been very helpful," Pplimz said, turning away and heading toward the screen.

"Please don't tell anyone," a voice came from behind them. Pplimz turned back to see the soldier looking at them plaintively. "I'm sorry, but I'll get in a lot of trouble if they find out I've been helpful."

"Are you a member of Xyzzyl's squad?" Wibble asked. "The ones who had the mission to the Great Glass Desert?"

The soldier nodded miserably.

"It will pass," Wibble said, gently. "I've been there. I know it can feel like you have no control over your emotions, but I assure you that you will be yourself again soon."

The soldier nodded again, then said in a small voice, "Maybe I like this version of myself better?"

Wibble laid a flipper on the martian's shoulder, and they didn't flinch away. "Then that's a decision you get to make," she said, "when you are free to make the choice."

The soldier sniffed loudly, then drew themself back up to attention. "Your business here is complete," they said, and it wasn't a question.

"Of course," Wibble said and hovered back toward Pplimz and the screen, which was a dumb terminal, only showing the most recent approved trades as per Elder Zaalyl's decree.

"At least it looks like Tazzer and Chimble managed to offload those blaster bolts," Wibble said, as they scanned the list. "Too bad this data doesn't go back further. You think we can sneak into an office and get the rest of it?"

"Wibble, that would be stealing!" Pplimz said, aghast. "And besides, there's no need." They peered at the edges of the screen. "What we can view here is just a limit of the screen. See here, when new trades appear at the bottom, everything simply shifts up. I don't think it's a new list each day that replaces the previous day, but rather it's a rolling feed of all the trades."

"Great," Wibble said, "but I don't see how that helps us see the trades for five days ago."

"Oh, that's a simple fix," Pplimz said. "We just need a bigger screen." They unspooled a slim cable from the collar of their shirt and surreptitiously attached it to an edge of the screen.

"You're not going to interface with that, are you?" Concern tinged Wibble's voice. Martian hardware was well known for its robust tamper detection and its high voltage zap-first-don't-even-bother-with-questions protocols.

"No need," Pplimz said, breezily. "This appears to be an ancient emissive electroluminescent film screen, but that's just for aesthetics. It's really a regular boxed constraint projection. All I need to do is give the constraints a little more space..." They flicked the cable like a whip and the edges of the screen shimmered, then began to expand. "And voilà!"

The screen grew to the size of a cinematic display and hundreds of trades were now clearly visible. A few of the nearby merchants looked over at the now huge display, but luckily the soldier at the checkpoint was still too wrapped up in their emotional issues to notice. Wibble hovered over to look for anything around the time the imps said they'd seen the human.

"Here it is!" she said, drawing a flipper under a record. "The final trade before a period of five days with nothing, just like Tazzer said. One gross of offline print entertainment matter in exchange for a discontinued MultiTool-ZX."

"Books?"

"Yup!" Wibble said. "About enough books to fill a Star Alliance branded sack. No doubt a being would need something to read on those long shifts at a remote outpost." She checked the screen again. "There's no record of the seller in any of these trades, but I'd bet my tail that this is our human. What's a MultiTool-ZX?"

"I'm not sure," Pplimz said, disconnecting from the screen, which shrunk back to its usual size. "Let me look it up."

They brought up a projection and logged into a comprehensive Crucible-wide equipment database they'd downloaded before leaving Hub City. They ran a search for the item's name along with the keyword "Mars," and an extensive record popped up.

"It's a handheld device that incorporates stripped-down versions of several common martian technologies," Pplimz read out. "There's a mini bolt driver of course, a laser saw, a small sonic knife, tweezers, a toothpick, and…" They magnified the image of the slim, matte khaki-colored device and pointed at a small button along its side. "An MDR-2000X. The portable version of the martian transporter."

As Pplimz was unlocking Susan, Chimble and Tazzer rolled by in their now significantly lighter truck, waving as they passed.

"Hold up!" Wibble shouted and zoomed over to hover just outside the driver's side window. "Hey, Pplimz!" They walked Susan over to the truck. "Do you have a holo of Véronique So?"

"Sure." Pplimz pulled up the Star Alliance's public roster, and found So's official identification holo.

"Is this the human you saw?" Wibble asked.

Tazzer blinked a dozen eyes quickly and worked her mandible. "Maybe?" she said finally.

Pplimz flipped to a group shot of several human Star Alliance officers. "How about one of these?"

Chimble crawled across his partner to squint at the holo. "These are all different beings?" he asked.

"Very different," Pplimz confirmed.

Tazzer shook her head. "Sorry," she said. "It could have been the first one you showed me," she added. "I mean, it definitely wasn't this one." She pointed at a figure in the group photo.

"That's a tree," Wibble said.

"See," Tazzer said to Chimble with no shortage of pride, "I'm getting much better at humans!" She clicked her jaw and the two set off down the dusty road.

"Did you really expect to get anything useful out of those two?" Pplimz asked.

"Hope springs eternal," Wibble said, settling into the sidecar. "I suppose it's back to Quantum City for us, then."

"Shall we take the scenic route?" Pplimz suggested, gesturing to the winding mountain road ahead.

"Have you ever once known me to decline the incline?" Wibble said, flashing green.

"No, but have you ever known me to presume continued consent based on past experiences?"

"Nope," Wibble said. "Now that we've established that neither of us has visited the Emotional Landscape in recent memory, let's go already!"

Over the twin ranges that bordered the Eclipse Valley was the most direct route back to Quantum City as the volatusaur flies, but the mountain pass road was a winding track of switchbacks and steep grades. Susan and Pplimz handled it expertly, but there were several moments when Wibble's sidecar was airborne as they took a particularly tight turn. The howling of the wind at altitude sometimes managed to drown out her excited shrieks.

At the summit of the first ridge, Pplimz stopped and dismounted.

"Susan needs a break," they announced.

"Is everything all right?" Wibble asked.

Pplimz nodded. "No mechanical or medical issues," they confirmed. "Just a good time to stop and enjoy the view." They could see all the way across the lush pink and purple valley to the next range over to the north, which shimmered as light bounced off its glassy peaks. Toward the south, they could still make out the transplanted craters and hills of Mars at Nova Hellas.

"It is a beautiful part of the world," Wibble said, then yelped.

"What's wrong?" Pplimz asked.

"Nothing," Wibble said. "It's just that it's snowing." Another fat, orange flake landed on her back, the heat of it diffusing across her skin. The snowflakes here were all colors and temperatures – the redder the flakes, the warmer they were. It made for a disconcerting experience as some flakes were as cold as ice and others warm as a bath.

"We should probably head off, then," Pplimz said. "I don't want to get caught in a rainbow blizzard."

They took the initial descent slowly, but soon enough were below the snow line. They encountered no other travelers along the twisting road, which was for the best as there were points where the road narrowed so much that the osteocycle and sidecar filled the complete width. Once they reached the bottom, though, the road led to a small, automated township next to the creek which flowed through the valley. It was an incongruous sight, the technologically advanced smartpods and molecular sustenance spray booths nestled among the wilds of the valley.

Wibble looked up at the darkening sky. "It's almost time," she said. The valley's eponymous eclipse happened regularly every 63.2 hours, which meant that soon it would be too dark to drive.

"We'll wait it out here," Pplimz said, looking around at the services available at the roadside town. It obviously catered to travelers like them, as well as those few tourists who came to view the spectacular eclipse.

"How's your power level?" Wibble asked.

"I'll make it back to Quantum City," Pplimz said, "but if there's a charging station I'll top up here."

"How about Susan?" Wibble asked. "Does it need power?"

Pplimz shook their head. "If that restaurant has a protein shake or something like that it would probably be a good idea, though." They handed Wibble a small bag of coins.

"I'll check." Wibble went over to the automated solid nourishment dispenser next to the spray booths and scrolled through the options. As an aerosynthesizer, Wibble neither ate nor drank, but she'd seen beings ingest all manner of interesting concoctions, and had an academic familiarity with most common foods. She found a likely option – liquid, high in protein and lipids. She made the selection and dropped a couple of Æmbits into the payment slot. A self-warming canister slid out of the serving port and she returned to where Susan was parked. She popped open the container and savory steam wafted out the top. Curious, she extruded a small flat section of her body out her front end and dipped it into the liquid. She shivered once, then poured the rest into Susan's fuel tank.

"Pplimz!" she said when she found them at a pay-per-watt electricity booth, a cable discreetly tucked into a port. "You'll never guess what I just did."

"Oh dear," Pplimz said with bemused trepidation.

"I tasted soup!"

"And how was it?"

Wibble rolled onto her side in thought. "Damp," she said definitively. "And… brown?"

"Well, hopefully Susan finds it more nourishing than that," Pplimz said. "And really, one of these days you're going to stick a part of yourself into something that doesn't agree with you."

"Oh, I've done that loads of times," Wibble said. "Spindly toothed petal ponds do not like it when you poke them, let me tell you."

Pplimz huffed. "Honestly, Wibble, I can't take you anywhere."

"Ooh, look, the eclipse is starting!" Wibble pointed up with a flipper.

The sky had turned a remarkable orangey green color, as a pair of disks on two separate trajectories slowly intersected with the glowing sun. In a few moments they'd converged, creating a perfect eclipse with just the corona visible. The entire valley descended into a deep twilight for a moment, everything around them appearing to be dipped in an amber-tinged luster before the moons continued their orbits and the wedges of sun slowly grew. In a few minutes it was all over and the valley was bathed in sunlight again.

"That was excellent timing," Wibble said. She always enjoyed an opportunity to see the beauty of the world on display.

"I thought I'd done the math correctly," Pplimz said with a smile. "Now that we've all had something to eat, shall we carry on?"

"Absolutely!"

It was another winding ride up to the top and exhilarating run down the other side of the northern range, until they emerged at the foothills and the entrance to Pollus Doctrian. The grand stone archway of the saurian walled city's southern opening was imposing, but it was unguarded and a carved sign proclaimed welcome in several languages. They passed several low, white-walled buildings, as well as a few grander edifices with carved columns fronting the open entrances.

"Do we have time to stop at the library?" Wibble asked, as they slowed to a stately pace along the via publica. Saurian city-states were well regulated, and reckless driving was not tolerated.

"Certainly," Pplimz said, turning off onto Via Polliasaurus, which led directly to the colonnade at the portico of the library. It was well known that the library's collection of ancient texts was second to none, and scholars and curiosity seekers alike were drawn equally to its architecture as to the knowledge the building contained.

"Breathtaking, isn't it?" Pplimz said, as they pulled into the vehicle bay.

"Hmm?" Wibble was halfway to the entrance. "Oh, yes, quite a pretty building."

"We're not here to admire the great Library of Polliasaurus?" Pplimz asked, catching up.

"No, Pplimz, it's a *library*. We're here for a book," Wibble said, shooting through the double-wide doors and into the grand foyer. She gestured for Pplimz to follow her to the reference room, then made directly for a tall set of stacks. She zoomed along the many levels of dusty tomes, then pulled one out. She hovered at its level, at least four yards above the ground, flipping through the pages.

"Aha!" she said, turning the book to face Pplimz. "Just what I thought!"

Pplimz magnified their vision to see the page, which was an index to the great works of Smaragdia Quartus, an ancient saurian who spent her entire life cataloging gemstones of the Crucible.

"You've found an entry for the Qubit Zirconium!" Pplimz said.

"Better than that," Wibble said. "I haven't."

Pplimz blinked, once, slowly. Even though, with eyes that were mere images drawn on a screen, blinking was not, strictly speaking, necessary.

"Honest Harb already said there was no record of the gem on the Crucible."

"Right, but Quartus's work is the definitive authority on gems, jewels, and precious stones," Wibble explained. "It's so thorough, that even stones that have been brought to the Crucible after her death somehow have entries in her encyclopedia. It is literally complete, but you have to actually look in the book. No database can keep up. There's a great debate about whether that's because there's something in the nature of the Crucible that transforms new matter into something already found here, or if Quartus simply used the temporal flux research method. I personally think it might be chronic paper, but–"

"Wibble."

"Right, sorry," she said. "The thing is, there's absolutely nothing in here that describes the stone we are looking for. It shouldn't be possible, but there it is. Or, you know, isn't."

"So, what we're looking for isn't a gemstone at all."

"Maybe," Wibble said. "If my theory is right, it just could be that it's so new to the Crucible that the Smaragdium hasn't updated yet. But either way, it's something special."

CHAPTER THIRTEEN
Pplimz Tries Their Luck

After a quick half-day's drive out of Pollus Doctrian, Wibble and Pplimz reluctantly returned Susan to its vending station at the transport hub at the Horizon.

"Thank you," Wibble said, patting the osteocycle's skull-lamp with a flipper. "You were a good bike."

"We should probably talk to Véronique So," Pplimz said, as they made their way back to Cynthala's.

"You think she's going to just confess?" Wibble asked, incredulous. "We don't have any proof that she was the one who traded for the MultiTool, and we also have no evidence that the MultiTool was actually used to steal the tiara. What we do have is twelve kilograms of supposition and guesswork in a nine-kilo sack."

"Exactly," Pplimz said. "So we need to start testing these theories of ours. If we can place Véronique So at Outpost Zyvax at the time of the trade, we'll finally have something solid." Pplimz unlocked the door to their rented room.

"She's a Star Alliance officer," Wibble said. "Her duty schedule is probably the place to start."

"I'll put in the request to our favorite security officer," Pplimz said, connecting to the room's desk.

"You're sure that there's no way any of these officers could have been away from the compound at this time?" Wibble asked Officer Barros, after she'd helpfully pointed them to the publicly available duty roster for Véronique So's team for the past eight days.

"Not a chance," Barros said. The holo of her face floating above the desk was the picture of certainty. "The junior engineering group was on a three-day team-building retreat over that period. And before you ask, there was no chance for any of them to sneak away for even a midnight snack. It was one of these events where they really put the *team* in team. None of them were alone for longer than it takes to shower or sh–"

"I understand," Pplimz said. "You can confirm that everyone on this list was actually in attendance at the retreat?"

"Sure," Barros said. "Here's a holo of them all on day two." The image of her face faded and was replaced with a portrait of a frankly worn-out looking group of half a dozen Star Alliance officers, each visibly looking as if they wished they were elsewhere. Véronique So was second from the left.

"Thanks for your help," Pplimz said.

"Anytime," Barros said. "Frankly, I'm hoping you can help us. The longer this whole tiara business goes unsolved, the harder it is to keep morale up, you know? No one likes to think that there's a thief in our midst – or worse, that we can't even protect ourselves from petty bandits."

"We'll do our best," Pplimz said.

"Unless someone has done a truly epic hack job on the metadata, this holo was taken when our mysterious human would have been making their trade at Outpost Zyvax," Wibble said, when the connection had been broken.

"Hmm," Pplimz said, "not So."

"It is! It's definitely the same time," Wibble argued. "See here–"

"It's not *Véronique* So," Pplimz said.

"Right, that's what I said. Make up your mind, Pplimz."

"If it wasn't Véronique So who traded for the MultiTool," Pplimz said, ignoring Wibble's almost certainly willful misunderstanding, "then who was it?"

"A very good question," Wibble said. "And if Véronique So was telling us the truth, then Zoarr did falsify the records. But why go to all that subterfuge only to officially report the tiara missing?"

"I'm starting to wonder if we've been looking at this the wrong way," Pplimz said. "What if both Zoarr and So are telling the truth?"

"You think they each put in an official request for the tiara?"

"It's a possibility. We should see if Engineer So has a requisition code of her own."

Wibble sighed. "That means another visit with Motormouth McFly at the Procurement Office."

"I'm sure Piten would be quite pleased to see us again," Pplimz said. "Let's find out."

"Two requisitions for the same item?" Piten echoed, as they scanned and recorded packages at a breakneck speed. "I suppose anything is possible in this remarkable world we've found ourselves in. Such a situation would be unlikely for a departmental request, of course, since every purchase is issued a unique product code and those are cross-referenced by the procurement order. But these would have been personal item requests, which have no such coding. I've often said that was an oversight, but personal requests can be nearly unlimited, so the coding would have to be incremental and adaptable, therefore–"

"Can you please just check to see if Junior Engineer Véronique So made any personal requests lately?" Wibble interrupted.

"Now, I can do that," Piten said, "in the sense of it being possible to search the database. However, for privacy reasons I am not able to acquiesce to your request in that matter." They paused for a moment, and looked between Wibble and Pplimz. "This is about that pretty tiara, isn't it?"

"It is," Pplimz confirmed.

"Well, that's a different matter, now isn't it?" Piten went back to their sorting. "I am unable to give you any individual's personal requests but I could look for any requests for the same item. An object can't be said to have a right to privacy, now can it? Unless it's a living object, of course, but that's an entirely different thing. Why, have you ever met a sylicate? Living rocks! Whoever would have imagined such a thing, but there they are, walking around and everything."

"Will you look for requests for a silver tiara?" Wibble said, positively vibrating with impatience. "Please?"

"Of course." Piten didn't cease their scanning, but tapped their wrist com with another hand. "Well, what do you know! There was another request for an item that's described almost exactly the same as Officer Zoarr's tiara, filed at roughly the same time. How awkward! Now, of course I can't say who made the request, since it is a personal item, but well... How many beings could possibly want this bauble?"

"Apparently more than a few," Pplimz said, "but we take your meaning."

"Oh dear. I hope I haven't spoken out of turn," Piten said. "I do have a habit of talking just a bristle more than is probably best, but it's not as if I actually told you it was Engineer S– er, Someone."

"You've been very discreet," Wibble assured them as she hovered not the least bit discreetly toward the door. "Let's go, Pplimz."

"Thank you for your help," Pplimz said.

"Do feel free to come back any time," Piten called after them as they were leaving. "It doesn't have to be for an investigation or anything, we could just have a chat. You're such excellent conversationalists!"

"I don't see how Piten would ever know if someone was a good conversationalist," Wibble grumbled once they were a reasonable distance from the Procurement Office. "They barely pause for breath."

"Do krxix breathe?" Pplimz wondered.

"Possibly not," Wibble said. "That would explain a few things."

Pplimz changed the topic. "Well, it appears that Véronique So was telling us the truth after all."

"At least about the requisition," Wibble said. "She may or may not have had anything to do with the tiara going missing."

"You're right," Pplimz said, "we shouldn't assume anything at this point. I still would like to know who traded for the martian MultiTool."

"Any chance we can just ask Elder Zaalyl?"

"Of course we can ask," Pplimz said. "But we might as well shout our request for information from the top of a mountain and expect the sky to respond. Martians who are loyal to the military system are bound by oath not to help outsiders. We can ask, but we won't get an answer. And we very well might get put on a martian watchlist, which isn't exactly something I'd like to add to our résumé."

"It's quite annoying when beings won't answer our questions," Wibble said, "or when they lie. It makes things so much harder for us."

"I'm sure if you only explained how much it inconvenienced you, they would change their behavior immediately," Pplimz said, dryly.

"I might try that sometime," Wibble said. "It couldn't hurt – if they're just going be unhelpful anyway."

They were approaching the border between the Bivouac and the Horizon when Wibble tugged at Pplimz's sleeve.

"Is that who I think it is?" She gestured toward a towering figure in a white and orange uniform ahead of them, making for the entrance to a building on the Horizon side.

"He did imply he was the only giant in the Star Alliance," Pplimz said, as they watched Zoarr enter the large complex with its flashing lights and promise of a good time. "You know, Wibble, we have been exclusively patronizing Cynthala's but perhaps it's time we availed ourselves of some of the other establishments in the Horizon."

"We wouldn't want to get stuck in a rut," Wibble agreed, as they passed one of the roadside bubbling mud pools available for hire. "Or anything else for that matter."

•••

There was no name or sigil on the building other than a generic exhortation in several languages to come in and find enjoyment. Pplimz pushed open the door to find the interior a riot of color and sound. There were easily hundreds of beings inside, most clustered in small groups around tables or the many spinning, glowing, pinging, dinging, and generally loud and obnoxious apparatus forming a veritable labyrinth in the large main hall.

Wibble shot up to the high ceiling for a skydweller's eye view, then popped back down to Pplimz's side just as quickly.

"It's a gaming parlor," she said, rippling virescently.

Pplimz nodded. "This must be Heady Burke's."

Heady Burke's Clandestine Casino was an oft-whispered about center for games enthusiasts, particularly those who found that a wager on the outcome vastly improved the player experience. There were no official restrictions against that type of activity in most of the settlements on the Crucible, but many of the powerful houses found gambling to be unseemly. And so there was an opening for such establishments in those border territories that were not controlled by any particular faction.

A loud clanging came from one of the tables, accompanied by a blinding light show and cheers from several beings. "Not terribly clandestine, is it?" Wibble observed.

"Well, we didn't know what it was until we came inside," Pplimz reminded her. "Did you see where Zoarr went?"

"He's over near the back at a table where they are playing some kind of dice game," Wibble said. "Shall we join him?"

"Let's give it a moment," Pplimz said. "I wouldn't want him to think that we were following him."

Wibble tilted to her side. "We are following him," she pointed out.

"Yes, well, he doesn't need to know that," Pplimz said, as they meandered through the maze of gaming tables. "How do you think this one works?" They pointed at a contraption of five concentric rings that were each marked with a set of glyphs. At regular intervals, the multi-limbed hydrodynamic vine wearing a blue and gray striped waistcoat would deftly spin each ring, then abruptly stop them all with a press of a button.

Wibble watched the players huddled around the spinning machine. "It looks like you bet on the outcome of the spins," she said. "These all spell out different words," she pointed at the combinations of glyphs made by the final positions of the circles.

"It's a Poetry Wheel," one of the players, a being composed of animated rock that seemed to shift in and out of phase, explained. "There are several possible wagers – as simple as a pair of glyphs coming up on the same line, all the way to the icosafecta."

"What's that?" Pplimz asked.

The semi-corporeal mineral settled into a chair with a contented grinding. "Each spin results in ten words being generated along the diameter of the circle." They extended a rocky limb to indicate the ten lines of glyphs that the stopped circle created. "You can bet on any of those coming up, of course. If you get them all, it's a very nice payday." They pointed at a complex chart showing the various wagers and odds on offer. "But the icosafecta is special. Every spin creates a single line of poetry from the results, which is recorded here." They gestured toward a screen with a few lines of verse. "Each subsequent line is added to the poem until the epic has been completed after twenty rounds."

"You have to predict the entire poem?" Pplimz asked, aghast. "The odds against that are…" They began computing, but their ersatz instructor stopped them.

"No, that's not it. Only a fool would try for that. To play an icosafecta, you write a twenty-line poem of your own before the epic begins. After the epic is completed, the poem that is the most effective response to the epic wins."

"So there's a winner every time," Wibble confirmed.

"Yes. The icosafecta is nowhere near the most lucrative wager," the rock said. "It is, however, the most satisfying."

"I think that might be beyond a novice player such as myself," Pplimz said, then put down a single Æmbit on the word "sunset." The croupier extended five branches and spun the wheels. The glyphs whizzed by each other, then abruptly the circle snapped to stillness.

"Better luck next time," their rocky neighbor said, as Pplimz's losing Æmbit was collected by the croupier.

"And you were so close! Look, 'gearshift' came up on the vertical. That's only one glyph out," Wibble said, surprised by her own disappointment. She was starting to see the appeal of gambling.

"Oh well. The house always wins," Pplimz said with equanimity as they left the table.

The layout of the tables was such that there was no direct way to get to the back of the room, and they had to pass dozens of different games, each with flashing lights, clanging bells, and whooping players. It was clearly designed to keep a being playing. Wibble and Pplimz were determined, however, and found the table with its many sets of sparkly dice soon enough.

What they did not find, however, was a giant in a Star Alliance uniform.

"There he is," Wibble said, after taking an aerial view of the room. "At the bar talking with a human."

"Anyone we know?" Pplimz asked, as they began navigating their way to the bar.

"No one I recognize," Wibble said. "I think they work here. They're wearing a gray and blue vest like the other staff."

They approached the bar, and the crowd was thick enough that they could get close without being right next to Zoarr and his companion. It wasn't anyone that either Wibble or Pplimz had met, a solidly built human of indeterminate gender with a shock of pale-yellow hair tied back in a complicated knot at the back of their head.

"Can you hear them?" Wibble asked.

Pplimz shook their head. "Too much ambient noise. I could filter out some of it, but in a place like this they have an expectation of auditory privacy, so I don't think that would be right." The two were seated well away from any other beings, and would reasonably assume that no one would be able to overhear them.

Wibble shimmered a brief flash of orangey-purple, but didn't complain.

"Does that look like casual chit chat?" she asked, after they'd observed the conversation for a moment.

"Not entirely," Pplimz said. The two had serious expressions on their faces and their discussion was continuous, but not terribly animated.

"If I had to guess," Wibble guessed, "I'd say it has a business-like feel to it."

At that they both stood, and the human reached under the bar for something. Zoarr nodded once politely, then turned and walked toward the winding path back to the exit. The human hefted a bulky bag onto their shoulder and made for the door to the staff area.

"Do you see that?" Wibble asked.

"I do indeed," Pplimz said, taking a holo of the retreating human's form and the backpack they were wearing with its faded Star Alliance logo clearly visible.

CHAPTER FOURTEEN
Wibble Discusses Literature

"It doesn't prove anything," Wibble said, as they made their way to the casino's exit.

"No, it doesn't," Pplimz agreed, "but if it were a game of chance, the odds on that being the individual who made the trade for the martian MultiTool would be strongly in our favor."

As they passed the Poetry Wheel, the mineral being was still at the table, and waved them over.

"Can I tempt you to another spin?" they enquired.

"Not today," Pplimz said. "Say, you seem like you're familiar with this establishment. Do you happen to know a human who works here? About this tall, long golden hair?"

"Oh, that's Skybrook. They run the Generalayala table."

"Have they worked here long?" Wibble asked.

"As long as I've been coming," the rock being said, "but that's not really all that long. I'm new to the area. Sorry I can't be more help."

"You've been a great deal of help," Pplimz said. "Come on, Wibble, let's see if we can talk to Skybrook."

They finally made it to the exit and went around to the side of the building in search of a staff entrance. They found the door at the back, and Pplimz was about to try the handle when the door opened and the blond human came out.

"Excuse me, Skybrook?"

The human stopped and grinned. "It's Skye Brooke. Two words. If you tell me your name, you can call me Skye. Otherwise, it's Mx Brooke and … also, kind of rude."

"I'm Pplimz and this is Wibble."

"Pleased to know you," Skye said. "I don't recall seeing either of you around Heady Burke's. I think I'd remember a dandy cyborg and …" they looked at Wibble, "your friend here."

"We aren't regular denizens of gambling houses," Wibble said, "though there were plenty of interesting diversions inside, I must say."

Skye laughed. "I sure hope so. I'd be out of work otherwise. So, to what do I owe the pleasure?"

"We saw you speaking with Zoarr," Pplimz admitted. "We are helping him with a personal matter."

"Oh, you're the detectives he mentioned," Skye said. "Why didn't you say so? I can't imagine there's anything I can tell you about the stolen tiara but I'm happy to help in any way I can."

The door opened and another casino staff member exited, nearly running into the three of them.

"Come on," Skye said, laughing. "Let's get out of the way." They led Wibble and Pplimz to a nearby clearing that had a rough-hewn bench table. "What do you want to know?"

"How do you know Zoarr?" Wibble asked.

"We were in the same induction group," Skye said. "At the Star Alliance," they added in response to Pplimz's confused expression.

"You're a Star Alliance officer?"

Skye shook their head. "Not any more. I thought I needed the discipline, the camaraderie, and maybe even the company of other humans. But it turned out that I really only needed a job." They shrugged. "We weren't a good fit, me and the Alliance. And when I saw an opening here, I figured that playing games all day that I was guaranteed to win was a better place for me."

"Were you right?" Wibble asked.

"The novelty wears off after a while," they admitted, "but it's still the best job I've ever had. I'm good at it, I like meeting new people all the time, and they've never missed a payday yet. I'm sure I'll tire of it sooner or later, but for now I'm happy here."

"And your friendship with Zoarr?" Pplimz asked. "That survived your change in career?"

"Sure," Skye said. "Zoarr had his fill of the wild life with his Brobnar family. For him, the regimentation of life in the Star Alliance is new and exciting. He understood that it was the opposite for me. We aren't that different from each other, really. We're both looking for something new, something that will take us away from the expectations of our lives in the past."

"You're lucky to have found someone who understands you so well," Pplimz said, glancing briefly at Wibble. "Who accepts your differences as well as the things you have in common."

Skye laughed. "That's true. But I don't want you to get the wrong impression. Zoarr and I are former work buddies who still hang out. We both have lots of other friends."

"Of course," Pplimz said. "I don't mean to imply anything else."

"Say, have you read any good books lately?" Wibble asked, trying to catch Brooke off guard.

"What?"

"You know, books. Those leafy paper things filled with words? Surely you're familiar with them. Didn't you trade a bunch of books to the martians recently?"

"I..." Skye swallowed hard. "How do you know about that?"

"We are detectives," Wibble said, pinking.

"There's no law against trading," Skye said. "Not here."

"No," Pplimz agreed. "But there is a law against using a martian transportation device to steal things. At least, there is in Star Alliance territory." They gestured in the direction of the Bivouac.

"You don't think I stole Zoarr's tiara?" Skye looked genuinely shocked.

"A matter discombobulator-recombinator was used in Zoarr's quarters," Pplimz said, holding out one hand, palm up. "And there happens to be an MDR-2000X in that completely legal martian MultiTool you acquired." They lifted up their other hand in a mirror gesture to the first, then shrugged. "You're an expert in probabilities. What do you think the odds are that it's a coincidence?"

Skye stood abruptly. "There isn't anything I can say that will make you believe me, but I didn't take the tiara. Zoarr is my friend. And just because I work here," they pointed at the casino, "that doesn't make me a thief."

They turned to walk away, and Wibble called after them. "So if it wasn't the tiara, what were you using the MDR for?"

"If you're such great detectives, you figure it out," they said, then marched off into the Horizon.

"That went well," Wibble said brightly, as she and Pplimz watched Skye Brooke go.

"It is long odds indeed that anyone will come right out and admit they stole the tiara," Pplimz said.

"You think the culprit was Skye Brooke with the MultiTool in Zoarr's quarters?" Wibble asked.

"They seemed truly surprised at the insinuation," Pplimz said, "but plenty of thieves are also fine liars. Honestly, I don't think we can rule out anyone yet. Véronique So is the only person we know of who definitely had designs on the tiara. That has to make her a solid suspect."

"I'm not convinced that Zoarr has been telling us everything either," Wibble said. "He was awfully quick to point the finger at Tailor, for no good reason at all."

"Poor Tailor," Pplimz said.

"Still no word?"

"I'd tell you if I heard anything from him," Pplimz assured her. "It really doesn't look good."

"That's been bothering me for a while," Wibble mused.

"I would hope so! You should be bothered by the prospect of a being going missing and, well, who knows what else."

"I am," Wibble said in a slightly hurt tone, "but that's not what I meant. If something has happened to Tailor, I find it hard to believe that the Star Alliance would be behind it. A quiet disappearing act does not seem to be their style. But they are the ones Tailor is running away from. So, why would anyone else want to hurt him? Unless he really does have the tiara, and that was the only way to get it away from him."

Pplimz was silent for a long moment. "I haven't wanted to contemplate that possibility," they said eventually. "I still don't. But I have to admit that it fits the evidence, inasmuch as we have any evidence." They stood and brushed invisible lint from the front of their suit.

"We need more data," they proclaimed.

"Back to the Bivouac?" Wibble suggested.

"Back to the Bivouac."

They were passing the main entrance to the casino, when the rock being who had been playing the Poetry Wheel burst out the front door in a grinding of pebbles.

"I did it!" they said as they nearly ran into Wibble. "Finally, after months of trying, I did it! I won the icosafecta!"

"Congratulations," Wibble said. "How much did you win?"

They held up a clear purse with eleven Æmbits jangling inside.

"It's a one Æmbit minimum bet per play, isn't it?" Pplimz asked.

"It is."

"And you've been playing for months?" they confirmed.

A rocky head bobbed up and down in the affirmative.

"Sounds like quite a lot of effort for a small reward," Wibble observed.

"But they liked my poem!" the rock being said, sounding utterly delighted. "That's what really matters." They jiggled the purse once more, then phased into another dimension without so much as another word.

"There's no rationalizing with poets and gamblers," Pplimz said, with a shake of their head. They spent the entire trip back to the Bivouac calculating the various odds for the games they'd observed while Wibble recited every limerick she'd ever heard. She'd gotten to "There was a timehog from Salt City..." when they entered the Bivouac.

The training grounds were quiet this late into the evening, although several automated drones and other robots still scurried about the Bivouac, transporting materiel and scanning the perimeter.

"I'm starting to think that we might have been talking to the wrong beings," Wibble said, as she watched the mechanical crew of the Star Alliance hard at work. "Or at least, not talking to everyone we could be. If data is what we need, then perhaps beings who thrive on acquiring data are who we should consult."

"Yes, it might be wise to get a machine perspective on the situation," Pplimz agreed.

"That nice robot who first welcomed us might be a good place to start," Wibble said. "I bet they have a lot of free time at that border crossing. We might be able to have a conversation."

There was no activity at all as they approached the checkpoint.

"Well, it appears that we won't be interrupting anything," Pplimz said, before they knocked on the small hut where the robot had been stationed. There was no response.

"Is there some kind of call button or intercom?" Wibble asked, hovering around the box.

"I don't see anything like that," Pplimz said. "When we were here before, the robot seemed to sense our presence."

"I wonder if it's ignoring us because we already have badges," Wibble said, thrusting the Star Alliance badge still solidly affixed to her side in Pplimz's face.

"Easy enough to test," Pplimz said, walking to the Horizon

side of the force fence. They removed their badge and set it on the ground, then walked forward.

"Ow!" They bounced off the force fence and nearly lost their balance. Wibble failed to stifle a laugh.

"Hello?" Pplimz called from the other side of the border. "PR0T3K-TR? Are you there?"

Nothing happened. No little robot rolled out of the small hut, asking for designations. A moment later, though, a tripedal drone clanked over from another part of the training ground.

"Do you require assistance?" the drone asked in a low voice.

Pplimz retrieved their badge and walked through the force fence. "Do you know what happened to the robot who usually works here? PR0T3K-TR, serial number 5649819874? Are they off duty right now?"

The robot looked away, nervously, Pplimz thought.

"I am not certain I am authorized to discuss this with outsiders."

"Scan us," Wibble said, turning so her badge faced the robot. "We're detectives. If there's a problem, we might be able to help."

The drone paused for a moment, as if in thought, then did as Wibble suggested. "I understand that PR0T3K-TR, serial number 5649819874 has not been in its hutch for 76683546 milliseconds."

"That's not too long," Pplimz said. "Is it just their day off?"

"AI drones do not have duty rotations," the new robot said. "We may suspend our duty to repower whenever it is required and then continue to perform our function."

"So, PR0T3K-TR should be here?" Wibble asked.

"Correct."

"Does the force fence prevent you from leaving?" Pplimz asked, concerned.

"No." The drone stepped across the border, then back again. "We are able to travel as freely as an officer."

"So PR0T3K-TR could have simply rolled away?" Wibble asked.

"It has that ability, yes," the drone said. "But why? PR0T3K-TR units are not designated for transportation or reconnaissance. They are for security and welcome. There is no reason for this unit to have left its hutch."

"I see," Pplimz said, processing the information the drone had provided and reevaluating the role of machine life in the Alliance. "You said you are as free to travel as an officer. Does that mean that you are not an officer? Are there other ranks for the crew of the Star Alliance?"

"Drones are not crew," the robot said. "Drones are drones."

"Aha," Wibble said. "I think I understand what's going on here."

"Will you investigate the current location of PR0T3K-TR, serial number 5649819874?" the drone asked quietly, as if concerned that they might be overheard. "It is illogical for it to be missing from its hutch."

"We'll look into it," Pplimz assured the robot. "Thank you for your help."

They watched as the drone clanked away to whatever its regular duty entailed.

"I am starting to think that the Star Alliance doesn't think of mechanical beings like we do," Pplimz said, only the barest hint of judgment in their voice.

Wibble flushed between pale blue and light cerise. "Many

societies take some time to enshrine rights for machines. The Star Alliance is new here, I suppose we should give them some time to adapt."

Pplimz thought back to their encounters with the various robots and drones they'd met in the Star Alliance. "No one appears to have been mistreated," they said.

"Lack of abuse isn't quite enough," Wibble said, softly.

Pplimz shrugged. "The drone we just spoke with did not appear to be dissatisfied with their role. Certainly I would not be comfortable with this life, but I wouldn't wish to be a Star Alliance officer, either."

"It's a very small sample size," Wibble pointed out. "Just because one drone is content that does not mean they all are."

"True. But it also doesn't mean that they are not. And given everything else that is going on here, I have to wonder if perhaps PR0T3K-TR learned something that put them in danger."

"Their role is in surveillance and security," Wibble said. "They'd probably know quite a lot about what goes on here in the Bivouac, and maybe even beyond."

Pplimz bent down and took a closer look at PR0T3K-TR's hutch. "This is a network node," they said, pointing at a small circle on the back of the box. "I bet that PR0T3K-TR would be connected to the entire Star Alliance security network. There was probably very little that went on here that they didn't know about."

"Well, I don't know about you," Wibble said, "but I feel like we now have several reasons to see if we can't find out what happened to that nice little robot."

"Their colleague asking us for help would be both necessary and sufficient," Pplimz reminded her.

"Sure," Wibble said, "but potentially helping us with our case doesn't hurt!"

"Sometimes I forget which of us has the cybernetic implant that prioritizes for efficiency," Pplimz said, archly. "There are more important things than solving a case, Wibble."

"Of course," she replied. "But why not both?"

CHAPTER FIFTEEN
Pplimz Overdoes It

Pplimz was down on their knees, scrutinizing the security drone's hutch, looking for any signs of tampering.

"We might not be the only ones who want to learn what PR0T3K-TR knew," they said, carefully aiming a beam emanating from an extrusion of their finger over every inch of the casing.

"You think someone stole the drone?"

"If they did, it's not obvious," Pplimz said, turning off the scanning beam and standing up. "There's no sign of forced entry to the hutch, and it's so well locked down that even I can't open it. Either PR0T3K-TR left under their own power or someone with a command override removed them."

"Unless the drone was snatched while they were out and about," Wibble said. "They came out of their hutch when we first arrived here. Someone could have approached the border, and when the drone came out to greet them, whoever it was grabbed them."

"Maybe," Pplimz said. "But I don't recall ever seeing them come out of their hutch when we crossed the border once we received our badges. And just now, the drone who is obviously covering for PR0T3K-TR didn't come over until I tried to enter without my credentials. The evidence indicates that the hutch opens only when there's an unauthorized individual at the checkpoint. PR0T3K-TR would be safe on this side of the force fence in an instance like that."

"Maybe," Wibble echoed. "But they could have talked their way in, like we did. Or they had an accomplice on this side. Or maybe whoever took PR0T3K-TR did have a command code. There are plenty of possibilities."

"Agreed," Pplimz said. "Far too many. We should talk to our friend in Star Alliance security."

Wibble looked up at the now star-pocked sky. "We should. But in the morning. Humans do not like being disturbed in the middle of the night."

"Surely they don't like being disturbed at all," Pplimz countered with a smirk, but didn't wait for Wibble's response before they began walking back to Cynthala's to pass the evening.

"I'd ask how it is you came to learn about our missing drone," Officer Barros said with a resigned sigh the next morning when they found her in the security office, "but I know. You're detectives."

"Is this a common occurrence?" Wibble asked.

"Drones going missing?" Barros said.

"Anything or anyone going missing," Wibble said. "The tiara, Tailor the Taupe, now PR0T3K-TR. Is everything and everyone else accounted for?"

Barros shook her head and defensively pulled up a crew and equipment manifest. "No, nothing and no one else is missing. Sure, when we first arrived we were raided fairly regularly by some of the more aggressive factions on the Crucible, but while the Star Alliance is not a military organization, we are well trained to defend ourselves. Most of the raiders got away with nothing more than scrapes and bruises. Word got around. It has been a long time since there has been a significant attack on our base."

"Perhaps your enemies have simply become more subtle and their tactics more precise," Pplimz suggested.

Barros frowned. "I don't think 'enemies' is useful terminology," she chided. "I admit that there seems to be a culture of animosity among some of the societies here on the Crucible, but the Star Alliance believes in trying to forge alliances – or at the very least, peaceful coexistence."

"A noble position," Pplimz said, "that is most certainly not universally shared among everyone on this world. Attacks on anyone who might have valuable items are unfortunately commonplace, and it's well known that the Star Alliance has excellent technology."

"Obviously, it's possible that there have been incursions of which we are unaware," Barros admitted, "but I can't imagine that Zoarr's tiara is something that would inspire a brilliant heist. As far as I understand it, the jewel in the piece isn't particularly rich in Æmber, and we have a much greater cache of it undergoing tests in the labs at Crash's Cliff. It couldn't possibly have been a worthwhile target."

"The labs are under heavy guard, aren't they?" Wibble asked.

"They are," Barros confirmed. "I just don't think anyone

capable of orchestrating a perfectly executed locked room theft would have stolen that tiara for its Æmber when there is such a better objective nearby."

"Hmmm. I agree that it's unlikely," Pplimz said.

"On the other hand, stealing a PR0T3K-TR drone would give someone access to our technology," Barros mused. "They are programmed to shut down in the case of unauthorized access, though. I can't imagine anyone would get much out of a dead drone."

"They are disabled permanently if they are stolen?" Wibble asked, deep blue flashing across her body.

"If they aren't on our network," Barros said.

"So if they leave the network they are deactivated?" Pplimz asked, horrified.

"No, no," Barros assured them. "They need to be disconnected and an unauthorized party has to attempt to access their programming in order for the shutdown protocol to be triggered. The drones are all fully autonomous and need to be able to operate even in the case of a network outage. If one falls off the back of a transport or something, they need to be functional."

"Well, that's certainly a relief," Wibble said.

"I take it that PR0T3K-TR serial number 5649819874 is no longer connected to the Star Alliance network," Pplimz said.

"If it was, we'd know where it is," Barros said. "All we have is the last backup of its hard drive. But the artificial intelligence installed in each drone is too complex for our technology to allow us to read the contents." She looked at Pplimz. "Perhaps you might be able to access something?"

"It might be possible," they said, frowning.

"I'm sure we could find a way for you to connect…" Barros

said, rummaging through a crate filled with a tangle of cables.

"No," Pplimz said abruptly. "I… I will have to think about it." Without another word they turned and walked briskly away from the security outpost.

"Ah, we'll be in touch, I guess?" Wibble said to the Star Alliance officer, then hurried to catch up to Pplimz.

"What was that all about?"

"There are many variables I need to process," Pplimz said, not slowing down. Wibble hovered just off to their left, keeping up but giving them space. She waited for a while, but Pplimz chose not to elaborate.

"You don't want invade PR0T3K-TR's privacy," she guessed.

"I do not," Pplimz agreed. "But if they have been taken by some being who hopes to access their technology, and if that process will cause their destruction, accessing their backup data would be by far the lesser violation."

"I see the conundrum."

"This is not a thought experiment, Wibble!" Pplimz stopped and wheeled around to face their partner. "We are talking about a sentient being here. Even if the Star Alliance doesn't perceive their drones the same as they do their other officers, they are autonomous, sensate individuals."

"I know," she said, softly, "I know. Perhaps we can find some other way." She shimmered briefly. "You know, maybe Officer Barros was on the right track, after all."

"Wibble–"

"Not about the backup, but about your ability to potentially interface with the drones in ways that the other Star Alliance crew can't. Do you think you might be able join their network?

Maybe you'd be able to communicate with the other drones, on their terms. It's possible that one of them might know something they'd be willing to tell you."

"Just like talking to any other being," Pplimz said after a moment's thought.

"Exactly like that!"

Pplimz did not have a cable which had the appropriate connection to attach to the network node on PR0T3K-TR's hutch, but they hadn't expected to. While there were many common technologies among the various civilizations that had found their way to the Crucible, every society had created its own versions with their own unique interfaces. Technicians from nearly every community had developed countless adapters and there was a roaring trade in these useful little tools in every marketplace. But Pplimz didn't bother seeking out a prefabricated solution.

They squatted down next to the hutch and slowly extruded three exquisitely thin bare wires from their right hand. The shielding and plugs on a proper cable were only there for ease of use and safety – they were, technically speaking, surplus to requirements.

"I know you'd think I'm the last being to say this," Wibble said, "but safety is not surplus to requirements, actually."

"I know what I'm doing," Pplimz said, carefully ensuring that each filament of wire was kept separate from the others as they snaked them closer to the small triangular opening of the hutch's socket. "I'm not some child shoving a fork into a socket, Wibble. I have complete sensation in each of these wires, so I'll be able to guide them each to the correct terminal. Besides, this type of socket is rated for no more than 550 volts. For me, that's barely even spicy."

"I'm not worried about you being electrocuted," Wibble said dismissively, though she had indeed been worried about Pplimz being electrocuted and was still not entirely convinced that "spicy" meant safe. "And what's a fork?"

"That's not important," Pplimz said. "Now please be quiet so I can concentrate."

Wibble struggled to keep her concern for their safety to herself, but managed to stay silent as Pplimz carefully inserted their wires into the drone's hutch. She even managed to hardly squeal at all when Pplimz's entire body jolted when they made the final connection.

"It's fine," they said, very slowly, their screen face now a scrolling list of alien sigils. "I'm asking if I might join their collective for a conversation. This may take some time."

The Star Alliance drone network immediately detected Pplimz's consciousness, and the individual who had spoken to them about PR0T3K-TR explained who Pplimz was and that they were here to help. A buffer space was instantly created to allow Pplimz to communicate with any of the drones who wished to speak with them, while keeping their usual free flow of communication separate and private.

Several minds entered the buffer zone, some clearly there out of curiosity, but a few individuals approached Pplimz with data.

"The PR0T3K-TR who is no longer connected was very interested in transportation," a mind who identified themself as a R0-V3R fed into the thoughtstream. "We shared data about our duties."

"PR0T3K-TR abandoned its post," another drone mind contributed to the stream. "Its fate is no longer our responsibility."

Several other minds, likely drones who never left Star Alliance territory, enquired about whether Pplimz could share any data from elsewhere on the Crucible.

It was like being in a room with several conversations happening simultaneously, each one expecting Pplimz to participate fully. The organic components of their mind were immediately overwhelmed, and they had to work to focus their mechanical brain to keep up.

"Is there any data showing someone tampering with PR0T3K-TR's hutch?" Pplimz asked the group. "Could a raider from another organization have stolen PR0T3K-TR?"

A cacophony of thoughts bombarded the stream, but while they all were individual and unique, they each indicated that there was no such data. Pplimz was barely able to cope with the onslaught of thoughts, reaching the very limit of their ability to multithread, and was forced to limit their data flow. They focused on the one mind who had mentioned sharing data with PR0T3K-TR.

"Is there any facility in the Star Alliance for drones to change their specified tasks?" Pplimz asked the R0-V3R.

"Negative," the mind replied. "Our intelligences and our casings are too closely integrated. We are, in that way, similar to organic life." There was a minute pause. "You have organic components?"

"I do," Pplimz said.

"PR0T3K-TR was interested in organic life," the R0-V3R thought. Other thoughts from other minds intruded into the conversation, offering opinions and asking questions about biological processes. Pplimz had to work to ignore them, hoping that their rudeness would be excused, or at least tolerated.

"Do you think PR0T3K-TR left of their own accord?" Pplimz queried.

"It is consistent with the data," the R0-V3R thought, then shared data they had once received from PR0T3K-TR, an image which filled the stream. Swirling clouds, through which verdant green leaves rustled, the background resolving into the texture of wood bark – an enormous trunk supporting a myriad of organic and machine life.

"The World Tree," Pplimz thought, as a sense of agreement from the thoughtstream flooded over them in a wave.

"I choose to calculate that the most probable outcome is that PR0T3K-TR is functional and free," the R0-V3R thought. "Should you be able to provide confirmation, it would be appreciated."

"I hope to be able to have good news for you," Pplimz thought, sending thanks to the entire drone collective for allowing them to share their thoughtstream, then, with a deliberate effort, physically disconnected.

"Pplimz? Pplimz!"

Wibble hovered anxiously over the body of her partner, who had collapsed into an unresponsive heap almost immediately after they had uttered the word "time." She peered at the network node on the hutch and saw that only two of the wires were still inside the socket. Pplimz was no longer connected. She floated back to their screen face, and saw that it had gone back to displaying the usual eyes and mouth, but the resolution was low, and the screen was alarmingly dim.

She laid a flipper on Pplimz's chest, where the tie-clip she'd given them was affixed, and extruded several fine force fingers to unbutton their shirt. She wriggled her flipper inside to touch the circuit and skin center of their chest, and opened up her body's pores to extract as much energy as she could from the gasses in the air around them. Then she generated a slight electrical charge from her skin and let it flow carefully into one of the machine sections of Pplimz's bare body.

Their screen face flickered and their eyes opened.

"We need to get you to a power point," Wibble said. "Can you move?"

"Nggh." Pplimz slowly sat up, extracting the final two wires from the Star Alliance network node.

"I've got you," Wibble said, extending her body's force as far as she could, looping under Pplimz's arm and around their body. With a great deal more effort that it really should have taken her, she lifted them up off the ground and cradled their limp body. The electrical charge she'd generated must have taken more out of her than she'd thought, but she managed to carry Pplimz back to Cynthala's and connect them to the high wattage power point before floating up to the ceiling and losing consciousness.

CHAPTER SIXTEEN
Wibble Catches Up on Sports

"... and you're always telling me not stick parts of myself into strange things I don't know anything about!" Wibble shouted.

"Perhaps you'll remember this and listen next time," Pplimz said with a weak smile.

"It's not funny! You were nearly completely drained of power!" She was circling around the room just above Pplimz's head, as she'd been doing non-stop since she'd regained consciousness.

"All right, Wibble, I know it was a foolish thing to have done," Pplimz admitted. "I've run a complete diagnostic on all my systems and there is no sign of any lasting untoward effects."

"This time!" Wibble said.

"Yes, I was lucky," Pplimz said. "Lucky you were there. Thank you for bringing me back here." They didn't remember anything between the end of the conversation in the thoughtstream and coming back to full power a few hours later in the Green Circle room at Cynthala's to find Wibble floating sound asleep in the corner. "I don't know what you had to do–"

"It was nothing," Wibble snapped, then softened, floating down to hover at Pplimz's level. "You scared me, Pplimz. It turns out that I don't like being frightened like that."

"I'm sorry," they said, and they meant it. They had never seen Wibble this upset before.

She tipped her front end slightly, flushed an unusual turquoise color, then said, "Fine. At least tell me all this was worth it."

"I think it may have been," Pplimz said and projected a copy of the image they'd received from the R0-V3R.

"That looks like Ilmapuu," Wibble said, recognizing the holo.

"Yes, the World Tree. PR0T3K-TR shared this image with one of the other drones, a friend. I think it's possible that they have gone on a pilgrimage."

"Well," Wibble said, settling under the ceiling above the holo-image. "That's unexpected."

The World Tree was at the center of a great forest far to the south, beyond the Great Glass Desert. Larger than some cities, with what many believed to be an awesome but incomprehensible intelligence, it was possibly the most massive being on the Crucible. An econoflyer bound for the Tree had left the Quantum City transport hub just around the time PR0T3K-TR had gone missing, but there wouldn't be another one for a ten-day. It would halve that time to reach it on the osteocycle, but while it would have been a lovely journey, they didn't have time for the scenic route. Finding PR0T3K-TR – if they even did find the drone at the World Tree – was only very tenuously related to their investigation. Pplimz felt a responsibility now to the other Star Alliance drones, but they couldn't justify taking so much time to chase after a side case. And so Wibble and

Pplimz found themselves hunting for a ride – again.

"I'll get us tickets," Wibble offered, and Pplimz was about to argue, citing Wibble's terrible track record with finding reliable and secure transport options, but after a wave of something not dissimilar to guilt came over them, thought better of it. Who were they to advocate for safety at this exact moment?

Wibble returned from the vendor stands waving a pair of shiny chits. "I got us a couple of spots on the *Mahoganaire*."

"That's the luxury liner that caters to acolytes and pilgrims, isn't it?"

"Yup. It's a direct flight to Werewitch, leaving right away." Wibble began hovering toward the loading ramp of the sleek, russet-colored skyliner.

"Wibble, I hate to say it, but that must have cost a fortune."

"You get what you pay for," Wibble said, "and they charge based on weight, so my ticket was practically free!" She did a flip in midair. "Sometimes it pays to be mainly gas."

"Well, you certainly can be full of hot air," Pplimz said, the barb slipping out without thought, and they immediately wished they could take it back. Wibble was nearly glowing green, though, so it had obviously amused her. Pplimz surreptitiously hefted the suitcase, wondering if it had been worth bringing their extra suits. It was too late to take them back to Cynthala's, though, as the flight was already boarding.

The similarities between the *Mahoganaire* and the SkyBounder airship they'd previously flown were nearly nonexistent. The couches, pools, and seats were plush and comfortable, with a range of different accommodations for the various body types among the passengers. The crew were efficient and friendly, without a single sign of upselling to be found. Pplimz was shown to a private table and chair next to a window, under a mesh hammock that would stop Wibble from floating around when they were underway.

"There is power and a holo port here," the large crablike steward said as he pointed out the amenities with a precisely manicured claw. "This button engages the privacy screen, should you wish to rest or meditate. If you need anything else in flight, please don't hesitate to call on the staff. We are here to make your journey as pleasant and refreshing as possible."

"Thank you," Pplimz said, and as soon as the steward had moved on, Wibble pressed the privacy screen button, engaging an opaque net which cordoned off their berths from the rest of the passengers. She pressed the button again and again, the screen appearing and disappearing instantly at each press.

"Having fun?" Pplimz asked, settling back into the extremely comfortable chair.

"We paid for all this stuff," Wibble said, flipping the overhead sonic diffuser on, "we might as well use it!"

Soon the passengers were all aboard and the liner began to rise up out of the transportation hub. It ascended well above the top of the mooring mast for the dirigibles, then once it had reached its cruising altitude it accelerated smoothly to a supersonic speed, crossing the land far below visibly quickly.

Wibble reclined lazily against the upper bulkhead, her hammock keeping her from rolling away.

"I'll give you this one, Pplimz," she said. "Traveling in style does have its appeal."

The flight was so quick that Wibble only had time to watch a single episode of highlights from the recent Spiretown Free-

Climb Invitational before they landed at a private airpark near the town of Werewitch. The town was nestled at the base of the enormous World Tree, and was home to many beings who worshipped or tended the great tree. It was also a tourist village, catering to the constant stream of pilgrims, sightseers, nature-lovers, and curiosity-seekers who visited the area.

Like on the liner, there were no hard sells found here. Accommodation, refreshment, supplies, and tours were offered, but never pushed. The overall atmosphere of the place was tranquil, even the queues for tours to the upper branches were calm and orderly. Which was a relief since there were beings absolutely everywhere.

Goblins, phylls, slithering reptilians, even the odd giant or two all mixed together in equanimity as they moved about the town. Some believed that the tree had psionic powers which calmed all who came near to it, while others simply expected that any being who would be interested in encountering the World Tree would do so respectfully. Whether you spent your days as a thief or a caretaker, all were welcome at the World Tree and all were accorded the same courtesy.

"Excuse me." Pplimz approached a goblin witch who was offering information according to his rough-hewn sign fashioned from naturally fallen branches.

"Welcome to the Forest, travelers," the witch said. "How can I help you?"

"We are looking for a friend of ours," Wibble said. "A Star Alliance robot called PR0T3K-TR. They would have arrived no earlier than two days ago."

"There hasn't been a group from the Star Alliance here in a long time," the witch said.

"PR0T3K-TR would have been alone," Pplimz explained.

"I do not recognize the name," the witch said, "but that sounds like Tiama's holo friend. I don't believe I've ever seen a Star Alliance robot here on their own, but there are so many visitors. Unfortunately, I do not have the good fortune to be able to greet them all."

"Can you tell us where to find Tiama?" Wibble asked.

The witch nodded. "She is a monk of the Opened Eye. At this time she can usually be found in the Sanctum Sanctorum." The witch gestured toward a modest hut not far down a narrow lane. Above the door the sigil of the Church of the Opened Eye, more commonly known as the Sanctum, radiated an otherworldly glow.

"Thank you for your help," Pplimz said.

"I hope you find your friend," the witch said, "and perhaps you will also find peace and harmony with all."

"An outcome which is devoutly to be wished," Wibble said, "but not all that likely in our line of work."

The witch appeared confused, but didn't press the issue.

"Come on, Wibble, let's not bother this nice goblin any longer," Pplimz said, ushering her toward the Sanctum temple.

"You think PR0T3K-TR befriended a being from Werewitch on the social holos?" Wibble wondered.

"That doesn't seem so unlikely," Pplimz said. "Social holos are a good way to meet beings from across the Crucible. And for the Star Alliance drones, it's one of very few options available to them, especially drones like PR0T3K-TR who are stationed in the base."

They approached the temple, which was clearly designed to appear welcoming, with its wide-open door and shallow ramp up to the entrance. Colored smart glass adorned the lintel and the doorway was ringed with carved images of enlightened knights. Pplimz stopped well before the door however, fidgeting with their hat.

"Something wrong?" Wibble asked.

"Beings from the Sanctum don't always react well to me," they confessed.

Wibble pulled back and gave Pplimz the once over. Members of the Sanctum were nearly universally peaceful and kind, but they did have a thing about the cyborg demons of Dis. A kind of instinctual revulsion thing.

"No, you don't look demony at all!" she said, after a thorough perusal. "I mean, you can do an amazing Dis demon disguise, but I've never met a demon who could pull off a three-piece silver pinstripe suit. Come on, let's go see a monk about a robot."

The interior of the sanctuary was as lush as an arboretum, vines and greenery covering the walls and spilling over into the main space. In contrast to the bustling streets outside, it was completely still as they entered, Pplimz's hand-tooled wingtip shoes tapping on the hardwood floor the only sound.

"It's quiet," Pplimz whispered.

"Too quiet?"

Pplimz shook their head. "No, this is pretty normal for a Sanctum church."

"Hello?" Wibble called loudly.

"Shhh!"

"It's a church, not a library, Pplimz," Wibble retorted. "Hello? We're looking for Monk Tiama."

A tall, willowy phyll stepped out from a side office on

muscular roots, the branches of her body blending in with the verdant surroundings. If it weren't for the shining white and azure robes she wore, she might have been functionally invisible.

"Well, you've found her," the monk said, with a surprisingly light and cheery tone. "Don't mind the weeds, come on in. The Sanctorum is open to all." She waved a budding tendril to indicate that they should follow her, and they did, Pplimz being extra careful not to crush any of the living plants underfoot.

Tiama's office was just as full of plant life as the main sanctuary, but there were a few sops to animal comforts, such a couple of chairs, a small mud pool, and a well-maintained holodesk.

"Thank you for your hospitality," Pplimz said, less to be polite and more to prove that they, unlike a Dis demon, were capable of communication.

"It's nothing," Tiama said. "Quite literally. The pursuit of enlightenment belongs to all beings and so that means the Sanctorum does, too. But I sense that enlightenment of the spirit is not all that you seek."

"We are detectives," Wibble explained, "and we've just come from Quantum City."

"I see," Tiama said, her voice growing hard. "I must inform you that the Sanctorum is a literal sanctuary. Any being who wishes to remain here is under the protection of not only me, but the entire Church of the Opened Eye. We can have an order of knights here at a moment's notice if necessary."

Pplimz put up their hands in supplication. "You misunderstand us. We are not here to bring any being back to Quantum City if they do not wish to return. We just want to know that PR0T3K-TR is safe. And, if they are, we'd like to talk. There's something we hope they can help us with."

"There is an elf who's missing and we're afraid something may have happened to him," Wibble said. "And there's a stolen jewel as well," she added.

Tiama looked at them both, the flowers around her face trembling as she appraised them. Before she could reply, though, there was a soft whirring from under a hedgerow. PR0T3K-TR rolled out, the lights on their upper casing blinking.

"I know these beings," they said, "you can trust them."

"PR0T3K-TR!" Wibble said. "I'm so pleased to see you, functional and apparently un-tampered with."

"I am intact," PR0T3K-TR confirmed. "I am here out of choice. I wish to learn more about existence than is possible at a Star Alliance checkpoint."

"Fair enough," Pplimz said. "May we ask you about the tiara that was taken from Officer Zoarr? And if you know anything about Tailor the Taupe, Véronique So, and Skye Brooke?"

"You may."

PR0T3K-TR confirmed that Skye Brooke had been a recruit for a short time, but had left the Star Alliance voluntarily. There was no record of misconduct, but their access credentials had been revoked when they left the service, as per standard procedure. The little robot couldn't give them any information about Véronique So or Tailor the Taupe that they didn't already know, but did confirm that Tailor the Taupe's visitor's badge was still operational – and still returning no life signs.

"I scanned the Qubit Zirconium tiara when it was being delivered to the Procurement Office," PR0T3K-TR said, "but I did not record any object with its signature leaving Star Alliance territory."

"You think it might still be on the base?" Wibble asked.

"I can only say that I have no record of it crossing the force fence," PR0T3K-TR said. "I cannot say what is possible."

"Can you show us your scan?" Pplimz asked and PR0T3K-TR projected an image of the data they had retrieved into the middle of the room.

Tiama gasped.

"The Sanctum has heard of this object," she said, pointing at the image of the tiara.

"Is it something special?" Wibble asked. "A weapon? Some kind of Æmbercrafted artifact?"

"I cannot say," Tiama said, making a religious gesture with her tendrils. "It is forbidden."

"The object? Or talking about it?" Pplimz asked, concerned they'd already caused offense.

Tiama shivered, and only repeated, "It is forbidden."

"Please, this might have something to do with a being going missing," Wibble said. "Anything you can tell us that might help, please. For Tailor's sake."

"I..." Tiama was shaking so hard now that her leaves were rustling loudly. "If you wish to know the secret of the artifact, you must seek the light among the shadows."

"What does that mean?" Wibble demanded.

"Please, do not ask me to say anything more." Tiama rustled and made for the door with shaking roots. "I cannot." She left for the sanctuary of her temple.

"Do you understand what any of that was about?" Pplimz asked PR0T3K-TR. It sounded serious. Pplimz had never seen a member of the Sanctum so distraught before.

"I do not," they said. "However, I do know that there is an

outpost of the Guilds in the Shadows near here. It is called Shaded Camp."

"Ooh," Wibble said, pinking, "she meant seek the light among *the Shadows*."

PR0T3K-TR beeped.

"Thank you very much for your help," Pplimz said. "And please thank Monk Tiama for us."

"I shall."

"When we return to Quantum City, may I inform your drone thoughtstream that you are well?"

PR0T3K-TR's lights blinked. "You shared in the stream?"

"Only a small part of it," Pplimz said. "A R0-V3R helped us find you."

"R0-V3R 6546763 and I have shared much data," PR0T3K-TR said. "Yes, you may tell them."

"I'm sure all the drones will be happy to know that you are pursuing your own dreams," Pplimz said.

"Happiness is not a function of a drone," PR0T3K-TR said, then added, "but I hope they will."

CHAPTER SEVENTEEN
Pplimz Gets Tied Up

Shaded Camp was likely a literal description of the Shadows encampment, but given that they were located at the base of a tree larger than the tallest spirecity, that didn't exactly narrow down the search.

"This isn't going to be easy," Wibble said. "I don't know of any beings who are better at not being found."

"Tiama seemed to think we'd be able to find them," Pplimz pointed out.

"Well, of course," Wibble said. "We are world famous detectives after all. She has faith in us!"

"I suspect it is not exactly *us* in which she has faith," Pplimz said.

"Perhaps the Tree's influence has extended all the way to our shadowy quarry," Wibble suggested. "Maybe they've become more forthcoming than usual after living here."

"It's the Crucible, so stranger things must have happened than members of the Shadows becoming hospitable," Pplimz said, "though I've not heard of any."

They found the witch, who was still staffing the information booth, and who gave them both a jaunty wave of his Æmbersap wand.

"Did you locate your friend?" he asked.

"We did, thank you so much for your help!" Wibble enthused. "I'm hoping we can prevail upon you one more time."

"I am here to help."

"Have you heard of a Shadows guild called Shaded Camp near here?" Pplimz asked.

The witch's face clouded. "All are welcome at the Tree of Life," he said, with a hint of bitterness, "even those who abuse the privilege."

"The beings living at the Shaded Camp don't abide by your code of peace and tranquility?"

"I can't say that," the witch admitted. "No one has ever caught any of them breaking the rules. But their members seem to receive a much higher bounty from the Tree than appears fair."

"Perhaps the Tree just likes them," Wibble suggested.

The witch snorted but said, "I would never presume to understand the Tree's choices. It is possible."

"You think they're rigging the game somehow," Wibble said. "Maybe even stealing the Tree's boons from others?"

"It is what Shadows are known to do," the witch said.

"There are thieves," Pplimz said enigmatically, "and then there are *thieves*."

"Yes, yes, there's a difference between a skill and a behavior. We know," Wibble said. "But they do go together a fair amount of the time. Can you point us in the direction of their camp?" she asked the witch.

He shook his head. "Hiding in plain sight is also what Shadows are known for," he said. "But there are several Svarr elves who are known to regularly partake of the libations at Fuzzy Gruen Inn." The witch aimed his wand toward a walking track leading out of the town. "If you can convince them to talk to you, you might get lucky. Or, possibly, quite the opposite."

"Well, that's not ominous at all!" Wibble said happily. "I guess it's off to the Fuzzy, then!"

Contrary to the impression the witch had given them, Fuzzy Gruen Inn was a comfortable, friendly establishment that catered to the many visitors who frequented the area. Like they had at Werewitch, a vast assortment of individuals mingled peacefully amid tankards of ale, steaming pies, and bowls of root stew. No one gave Pplimz or Wibble a second glance as they entered the busy taproom, aside from a genial bartender who waved a welcoming fin in their direction before going back to mixing a foaming concoction for a patron.

"I don't see anyone in a Shadows cloak," Wibble said, after giving the room a glance.

"Neither do I," Pplimz said, "but I believe there is a group of beings who are using an image generator. I can sense the field the device emits in that corner over there." They subtly gestured to a table where four individuals sat in deep conversation. They appeared to be a mixed party – a small saurian next to a tiny skyborn flitter moth, across from a pair of furry fox-faced creatures wearing matching peaked caps. An utterly nondescript group if ever there was one.

"You're right," Wibble said, after focusing a discreet sonic pulse at the group. "Their density doesn't match their shapes at all."

"Shall we go over and say hello?" Pplimz suggested, but Wibble laid a flipper on their shoulder to stop them.

"I have a better idea." She directed Pplimz to a small table in the corner where they could keep an eye on the group. They settled in, accepting a couple of steaming tankards from a passing server, which they then ignored. "Shadows aren't the only beings who know how to be sneaky. If we wait until they leave, we can follow them. Maybe they'll lead us to the rest of their guild."

"We aren't exactly dressed for subtlety at the moment," Pplimz said, pointedly looking over at their silver fedora lying on the table.

"You aren't, maybe," Wibble said, "but that's a feature. You're going to be the decoy!" She shimmered briefly then turned nearly transparent. "We'll do it just like that time in the Fire Canyons."

"If I remember that correctly, you got singed terribly. Those niffle apes smelled you a mile away."

"Sure," Wibble said, "but they didn't *see* me, did they?"

When the group they were watching rose to leave, Pplimz got up too. They made for the door just in time to run smack into the saurian.

"I'm so sorry," they said effusively, as Wibble hovered out the door to float up to a high vantage point while everyone was staring at Pplimz. "New feet." They pointed down at their shoes.

"No harm done," the saurian said, gesturing for Pplimz to go ahead and giving them a wide berth as they stumbled out the door.

Pplimz tottered off up the road, turning in behind a large root and crouching down. The party of erstwhile Shadows took off in the other direction, with Wibble in close pursuit high above them. If one didn't know to look for the slight disturbance in the air, and the tiny communication bud she'd attached to her body, she'd be completely invisible.

Pplimz didn't have long to wait before Wibble, mercifully quietly, called with a set of directions. They dusted off their suit and made for the location Wibble had given them to meet.

"There's nothing here," Pplimz said when they met Wibble a few minutes down the road.

"Untrue!" she said. "I see a patch of grass, some loose rocks, and look! There's at least three dried leaves right there."

"Wibble."

She glimmered a deep pink. "Come on." She headed directly for a dull rock sitting in the midst of a clearing, when the air around her seemed to vibrate and she disappeared.

"Oh, well done," Pplimz whispered. They'd encountered Shadows technology before and were always impressed with their camouflage. They followed in the direction Wibble had gone and in an instant found themself seemingly transported from the bare meadow to a large encampment, complete with huts, vehicles, and tents. Not to mention several dozen angry elves, all of whom were wearing the ubiquitous dark cloak of the Shadows Guild, which could conceal any manner of weapons.

Pplimz couldn't tell anything in particular about each individual from their cloak, although they knew that to followers of the guild the cloak was a distinguishing symbol of each member's standing and skill. Pplimz did recognize a series of the Shadows' famous stealth emitters set up in a perimeter around the area, the small gray badges with three dark dots creating the illusion of nothing which hid the existence of Shaded Camp.

"Seize them!" a small, golden-eyed elf covered nearly completely by their cloak shouted, pointing at Wibble and Pplimz. A pair of their comrades jumped at the command, and Pplimz found their arms pinned behind their back in a strong grip. At least there were no blades involved. Yet.

The elves were having a harder time getting a hold of Wibble, as she flattened her flippers to her round, smooth body. The harder they squeezed, the easier it was for her to pop free from their clutches.

"Get back here, you greased cyber rat," the tall, mauve-skinned elf shouted, as she lost hold of Wibble for a second time.

"It's like trying to hang on to a gurgle pool," her partner panted, worn out from several attempts. Wibble could easily have fled the camp, but she remained hovering near Pplimz, even as she resisted all efforts at restraining her.

"We're sorry to drop by unannounced," she said, as she squeezed out of yet another elf's failed attempt at capturing her, "but we're hoping you can help us. We're detectives – I'm Wibble, and this is Pplimz. We were hired by an elf called Tailor the Taupe, perhaps you know him?"

The elf in charge waved an arm, and the others gave up trying to restrain Wibble. The ones holding Pplimz didn't let go, but they relaxed their grip. Slightly.

"I don't know what he told you but Tailor the Taupe is not a member of our guild," the leader said. "Why have you come to us?"

"Tailor is missing," Pplimz said. "We think it has something to do with a stolen jewel." They projected an image of the Qubit

Zirconium into the air between them. "We showed this to a monk of the Sanctum, and she told us to seek the light among the shadows."

"We think she meant you," Wibble added. "Get it? *Shadows*." She waggled a flipper as if to more clearly indicate the connection.

Pplimz sighed heavily. "Wibble, it's bad enough that I'm being held prisoner without you pointing out the obvious in such a... gleeful manner."

No one else was paying either of them the least bit of attention, though. All eyes were on the holo-image.

"Who has control of this artifact?" the leader demanded.

"We don't know," Wibble answered. "As we said, it was stolen."

"You're familiar with this item?" Pplimz asked.

The elves ignored them, and abruptly turned toward each other with their backs to Wibble and Pplimz, with the exception of the one who was still holding Pplimz's arms. A low hum came from the group, obscuring their voices and making their conversation impossible to discern.

"What are they talking about?" Wibble asked the elf standing guard duty on Pplimz.

"If they wanted you to know what they were saying, they wouldn't be using a Cloak of Silence, would they?" the guard said in a surly tone.

"Oh, I see. You can't hear either," Wibble said. "I'm sorry they left you out of the secret conversation. It must be annoying."

"Wibble, please," Pplimz said.

"Is she always like this?" the guard asked.

"Pretty much," Pplimz replied.

The hum stopped and the elves turned back toward Wibble and Pplimz.

"You can let them go," the leader said to the guard, who did as instructed, then stepped away. "You helped our guild in the Floating Colossus of Sulphur once."

"Ooh, I remember that!" Wibble bobbed up and down. "Mistaken identity, a counterfeit Archon's key, and a pack of clones, if I'm not mistaken."

"Yes, well," the leader cleared their throat, "I understand our debt was paid in full at the time. However, our guild mates assure us that you are trustworthy, inasmuch as any outsider can ever be trusted." She dropped the hood to reveal a pale mauve face with a jagged scar running all the way from her left temple to her mouth. One of her pointed ears was missing a chunk, and she wore a golden earring which accented the wound. "I am Dree the Lucky. Please, come sit at our fire. We have much to talk about."

The Shaded Camp was rustic to look at, but its subtle technological augments made for a comfortable and well-equipped base of operations. A roaring fire glowed in a sunken pit in the center of the open-air common space where Dree led Wibble and Pplimz. Chairs and couches surrounded the bonfire, many with integrated data ports and holo projectors. Dree herself wore what looked like a heavily modified Star Alliance wrist com, although it might have instead begun life as a Logos nanoscope, and the other elves who had revealed themselves held similarly impressive tech accessories.

"What do you know about the Qubit Zirconium?" Dree asked, once they were all seated.

"We know that the jewel has been seen all over the Crucible," Pplimz said. "But no one seems to hang on to it for very long."

"Some beings think it's cursed," Wibble said. "But it's also highly sought after. Or at least it has been since it was set into a silver crown."

"At least two Star Alliance officers were trying to acquire the tiara," Pplimz explained, "and it was stolen from one of them. At least, that's what we were told."

"Have you ever encountered it?" Dree asked. "Physically, I mean, not just in holos?"

Pplimz shook their head. "We got involved after it had been stolen. All we know of it is what we've heard from other beings."

Dree nodded thoughtfully, then accepted a steaming cup from an elf bearing a tray of refreshments. Wibble reached a flipper out toward a cup, but thought better of it when Pplimz shot her a warning glance.

"Right. No more poking at mysterious substances," she said.

Dree narrowed her eyes at them, but ignored the interruption. "What you've heard is true," she said. "The Qubit Zirconium is sought after by many beings. And, one might argue, it is also cursed."

"What is it?" Pplimz asked.

"Its very nature is its curse," Dree said, then sipped her tea. "Have you ever heard of the Cult of the Architects?"

"Are they some new offshoot of the Inspired?" Wibble asked, referring to the sect of mystics that traveled the Crucible in search of enlightenment. "Following the Path to Completion through building design or something like that?"

"Quite the opposite," Dree said. "This is about the Architects, with a capital A."

A hush came over the assembled group, and even Wibble couldn't find it within her to offer a quip. The silence was broken by the pop of a damp log on the fire, and sparks shot up, illuminating the elves around the circle. Every face appeared solemn, and, if one was being completely honest, afraid.

"You mean the Architects of the Crucible," Pplimz said, finally. "I've heard that some beings believe they were the ancient makers of this impossible world, who designed it to be a magnet for civilizations and individuals from across the universe."

"And if they did, they also created the impenetrable Boundary that prevents any of us from ever leaving the world they made," Dree said.

"No one knows who – or what – the Architects are," Wibble said. "And regardless, if they even existed at all, they are almost certainly long gone. No one has ever seen even the hint of an Architect in the history of life on the Crucible."

"Perhaps," Dree said. "But perhaps there is something of them that remains. Something that would confer their unlimited power on its wielder. Something that would be of unimaginable value to the right – or wrong – being."

"You think the Qubit Zirconium is an Architect's tool?" Pplimz asked.

"If it is, it could give its bearer the power to completely remake the Crucible," Dree said. "It would be the most powerful tool in the world, maybe even in the universe."

CHAPTER EIGHTEEN
Wibble States the Obvious

"I have no idea if the Qubit Zirconium tiara is truly an artifact of the Architects," Dree said, "but the Cult of the Architects believe that it is. And they are desperate to take control of it."

"Can you imagine?" Wibble said, her body shifting through a rainbow of colors. "With the power of the Architects a being could make an entire continent disappear. Or turn land into sea. Or inside out."

"Or even make the Boundary disappear," Pplimz said, thinking about Mars and the Star Alliance, and their shared determination to find a way to leave the confines of the Crucible.

"That such power would be useful to many of us on this world, there is no doubt. But it is too much power for one group of beings to possess," Dree said. "There are some who are working to stop the Cult from attaining this artifact. I am not a member of that group, though I share their concerns. Tailor the Taupe, however, *was* working for them. I think that was why he was involved with the Star Alliance in the first place."

"If Tailor isn't part of the Guilds and you aren't part of this group, how do you know so much about this?" Wibble asked. There was obviously something that Dree wasn't telling them. "What's your involvement here?"

Dree looked down into her mug as if the answers were located in the floating leaves. When she looked back up, the glow in her eyes had softened ever so slightly.

"Tailor the Taupe is my brother," she said.

"He was never interested in guild life," Dree explained. "Even as a child he preferred games where he alone competed against the rest of us. But while we all have our clans and teams, ultimately the Guilds in the Shadows are collectives. Working alone is not our way."

"From what we know of him, Tailor usually had partners or co-conspirators," Pplimz said, confused.

Dree nodded. "Sure. He's perfectly capable of being part of a team. But he always wanted to pursue his own projects, live where he wanted, run his own schemes." She gestured with her teacup. "Don't misunderstand me – there was no great falling out among our clan over Tailor the Taupe leaving us. It's not as if he was thrown out of the family or anything like that. He simply wanted to walk his own path. I know I would have preferred if he'd stayed in the guild, but it wasn't my decision to make, and I greatly prefer that he was happy on his own rather than miserable in the guild. I am still close to my brother. Obviously, that's why I know about the work he was doing to stop the Cult."

"Have you heard from him recently?" Wibble asked. "In the last few days?"

Dree shook her head.

"I know you're not going to want to hear this, but I'm afraid that it's possible that something may have happened to your brother," Pplimz said delicately, and explained about the lack of data being sent from his Star Alliance badge.

"It was dangerous work," Dree said, keeping her composure. "And Tailor knew what he was getting into. But he's astoundingly resourceful, even compared to members of my clan. If anyone could stay ahead of trouble, it's him. And nothing puts the scent off one's trail more than … not being worth finding any more."

Dree buried her face in her teacup, the steam condensing on her cheeks. Maybe she was hiding tears, maybe she was just taking comfort from the soothing herbs.

"This wasn't the first time he's needed our assistance," Pplimz said softly, after giving her a moment.

Dree smiled. "As I said, Tailor the Taupe was resourceful. Sometimes that means being clever yourself, and sometimes it means knowing when to ask for help. He was always good at both."

"Those are useful and complimentary skills," Wibble said. "He would have made an excellent guilder."

"I always thought so," Dree said, then took a deep draught of her tea. She swallowed then sighed, a slight pink plume escaping with her breath.

"Is that magnaflower tea?" Pplimz asked, gesturing to the cup.

"Yes, would you like some? We grow our own here."

"No, thank you. Wibble, do you remember someone else who drank magnaflower tea?"

"You know, I do," she said. "And I thought it was an unusual choice for a human."

"My clan has always grown magnaflowers," Dree said. "Tailor

the Taupe took several cuttings with him when he left. But it's a popular infusion. Dozens of blends can be purchased in the Melting Pot in Hub City."

"I do not consume liquid," Pplimz said, "but I understand that for beings other than elves it is what they call an acquired taste."

Dree said, "I've heard that as well, but to me it tastes of home." She frowned. "Why are we talking about tea?"

"I think we may have encountered someone who was working with Tailor much more closely than we initially suspected," Pplimz said. "And it's time we had another talk with her."

"Do you think she knows what has happened to my brother?" Dree asked, not bothering to conceal the worry in her voice any more. Pplimz shook their head.

"If they were working together," Wibble said, "I get the feeling that she would have told us if she knew where he was hiding. But I do think she knows a lot more about the Qubit Zirconium than she let on. And the only lead we have to find Tailor is finding that tiara."

Dree reached out and put her gloved hand on Pplimz's arm. "I love my brother. I want you to find him. But if you have to decide whether to look for him or look for the jewel, you need to find that artifact. If it falls into the wrong hands, we all are in terrible danger. Whatever has happened to Tailor the Taupe, he was trying to stop that. For his sake, for all our sakes, you have to stop the Cult from getting the Qubit Zirconium."

"We will do our best," Pplimz said.

"That's all any of us can ask," Dree said, then added, "let's just hope that it's enough."

The return trip on the *Mahoganaire* was no less luxurious than it had been on their way to the World Tree, but neither Wibble nor Pplimz found the trip comfortable. This case had started as a simple jewel theft but now the safety of hundreds of civilizations and billions of beings might depend on who had control of this artifact.

It was a lot to absorb.

"Do you really think there's such a thing as a Cult of the Architects?" Wibble asked.

Pplimz nodded. "I've heard rumors of a group like that, but I always thought they were powered by wishful thinking more than anything. An artifact like Dree described is somewhat unlikely."

Wibble pondered for a moment. "Everywhere you turn on this world there's something unlikely," she said. "I think we have to act as if it is real, just in case it is."

Pplimz spent the rest of the trip going over all their notes from the case, replaying their memory files of every conversation and observation. Wibble tried to rest in her plush hammock, but she spent the voyage rolling in circles, her skin taking on deeper shades of blue as she worried about their situation. By the time they arrived at the Quantum City terminus late in the day, she was more tired than she had been when they'd boarded the airship.

"How do you think we should handle Véronique So?" Pplimz asked, as they walked back to Cynthala's to regroup.

"If she's part of the Cult, we risk tipping our hand if we ask her straight out about it," Wibble said, "but that might force her to reveal something or make a mistake to cover her tracks. And if she was working with Tailor, I think she will help us if she knows that we are on the same side."

"You're going with honesty?" Pplimz asked, feigning surprise.

"I can't come up with a story that's likely to give us the result we want," Wibble confessed. "Besides, I'm not convinced that keeping this Cult of the Architects business a secret is helping anyone except them."

Pplimz was quiet as they approached Cynthala's. They waited until they were both inside their room with the door closed before saying, "Are you absolutely certain that stopping the Cult is the right thing to do?"

Wibble wheeled around to face her partner. "You heard what Dree said! If the Qubit Zirconium can give a being the power of the Architects, they could destroy everything. Wipe out entire civilizations in the swish of a tail. It's the ultimate weapon. No one can be trusted with power like that."

"But the Architects didn't use their power to destroy," Pplimz pointed out. "What if these beings want to use the artifact to create new parts of the world? And you have to admit that removing the Boundary would be something that many beings here dream about. Having the freedom to leave would change everyone's lives."

"I know that. I am as aware of the Boundary as anyone, Pplimz." Wibble was completely still for a moment. "Have you ever met any other being even remotely like me on the Crucible?"

This was the closest Wibble had ever come to talking about her past, and Pplimz knew it was an important moment. "I haven't," they said, gently.

"Well, neither have I," she answered, letting the implication sink in. "I made my peace with the fact that no one is able to leave this place a long time ago, Pplimz, but sometimes even I wish it were different. And if all the Qubit Zirconium could do was punch a hole in that Boundary, well, fine. Why not give us a few more choices? But that's not all it can do, if the stories are right. Even if the Cult only wants to use the artifact to open the Boundary, and there's no indication that this is their goal, the temptation to do more is too high. I'm not willing to pay for my freedom with other beings' lives."

"All right," Pplimz said after a moment. "Let's get some rest and we'll talk to Véronique So in the morning, then see if we can find this artifact before anyone else does."

Véronique So was on duty the next day, but they found a few minutes to talk when she was on a break.

"Is there somewhere private we can speak?" Pplimz asked, as So wiped the sweat from her brow after she'd crawled out of a maintenance tunnel deep within the base of the mountain into which the *Quantum* had originally crashed.

"Sure," So said, and led them to a rest area in the shade of some trees. "Have you found the tiara?"

"No," Wibble said. "And it's more than just a piece of jewelry, isn't it?"

So looked at the two detectives warily. "You told me you were hired by Tailor the Taupe," she said. "But that could be a lie. How do I know you aren't working for someone else?"

Pplimz projected a copy of Tailor's initial call to them and played it for Véronique to watch. When it was done, they said, "Obviously, we could have faked this transmission. If you don't want to believe us, there's nothing we can show you that will prove our loyalties. But there comes a point when the only way forward is with a little trust. We're here to trust you, now. I hope you will do the same for us."

"Tailor was trying to keep the Qubit Zirconium away from the beings who are part of the Cult of the Architects," Wibble said.

So nodded, her shoulders relaxing but her face pinched. "I was helping him. We met long ago in Hub City and I'd helped him get on with the Alliance as a broker in the first place. When he discovered that the stone he sold that jeweler in the Horizon was really part of an artifact the Cult was trying to find, he needed some way to get it back. Simply buying it back himself would have drawn too much attention, so he asked if I could put in a procurement order for it. Of course I agreed."

"Are you really working for the group trying to stop the Cult of the Architects?" Wibble asked. "Is that why you came to the Star Alliance? As a spy?"

So shook her head. "I mean, I suppose I'm part of the group now, but that's only because of this. I had no idea what Tailor was really doing here when I connected him with the Star Alliance. Everything I told you before was true." She looked away, then said quietly, "I just didn't tell you all of it."

"And what about Zoarr?" Pplimz asked. "Is he a member of this Cult?"

"Tailor thought so. That's why he wanted access to the Bivouac. His networks had traced agents of the Cult to the SAV *Quantum,* and his mission was to infiltrate and try to gain their trust. He wasn't ever expecting to see the actual Qubit Zirconium himself, which is why he missed it when the jewel first passed through his hands." Véronique looked off into the distance. "He was so angry with himself. He'd been so focused on trying to learn about Zoarr and find his accomplice, that he hadn't even seen what was right in front of him until it was too late. And then to have Zoarr get his hands on the tiara in the end anyway…"

"Do you think Tailor stole the tiara from Zoarr after all?" Wibble asked.

"Honestly, I hope he did," So said. "But I don't think so. He wouldn't have contacted the two of you if he did have the artifact. He would have done everything he could to take it to the Guardian."

"Who is the Guardian?" Pplimz asked.

"Not who. What. The Guardian was built by Nassas, a logotarian machinist who is working to stop the Cult. He developed a special dimensional containment field to lock the artifact away from anyone who would try to use it."

"So it's a fancy safe," Wibble said.

"Yes," Véronique said. "Apparently unbreakable. Tailor would have done anything to make sure that the Qubit Zirconium made it to the Guardian."

"Perhaps he did," Pplimz said. "Do you know how to reach Nassas?"

So shook her head. "All of Tailor's contact with the network was done using dead drops or face-to-face meetings. Tailor was sure that Zoarr was working with someone else here at the Star Alliance and he couldn't risk their communications being intercepted."

"Tailor didn't know who Zoarr's accomplice is?" Wibble asked.

"No," So said. "That's why he had to run when the Star Alliance put out that writ of detainment on him. It could be anyone in the Alliance, and the entire network would have been in jeopardy if Tailor had been caught by a member of the Cult.

Of course, it's much worse if they are the ones in possession of the tiara."

"Well, at least we know that the Cult don't have the artifact yet," Wibble said, brightening.

"How?" So asked.

Wibble waved a flipper. "Because the world is still here."

CHAPTER NINETEEN
Pplimz Calls Around

"This is an altogether disconcerting sensation," Wibble said, when they'd returned to their base at Cynthala's.

"What is?" Pplimz enquired, scrutinizing Wibble to see if she'd managed to get herself caught in something again.

"Not knowing exactly how angry I should be at Tailor the Taupe," she said.

"Hmm," Pplimz mused. "It would have been much simpler if he'd told us what was really going on at the beginning of all this," they said. "But I also understand his need for secrecy."

"Do you believe Véronique So?" Wibble asked. "I mean, we still don't necessarily really know what's going on."

"True," Pplimz said, "but she's given us something solid to go on – Nassas, the Logos machinist. I think she's decided to trust us. Finally."

Wibble puffed up, her body a shimmer of different colors. "Do you think *Tailor* doesn't trust us?" she asked, eventually. "It's not as if our conversations were likely to have been monitored.

We were using an encrypted communicator, after all."

"There are more ways to spy on a being than intercepting communications," Pplimz reminded her. "If I were in Tailor's position, I'd assume that the Cult had planted a tracker on him." Pplimz's screen face lit up. "Which they probably did!"

Pplimz looked down at the orange and blue badge affixed to their lapel.

"They may have been tracking us too," Wibble said, peeling her own badge off with a slurp.

Pplimz took their badges and set them on the desktop, then extruded a set of fine precision tools from their hands. They set about carefully disassembling the badges and inspecting each component individually. When they were done, they reassembled the badges, but neither of them put them back on.

"From what I can tell, these do just what Officer Barros said they do: they're passive tags for basic identification and authorization data, and the broadcasting function is limited to life signs and location data."

"Exactly," Wibble said. "Trackers."

"Yes, but there are hard-coded blocks in place to restrict location to within Star Alliance boundaries," Pplimz said. "And I've confirmed that they are working properly."

"It's a data block?" Wibble confirmed, and Pplimz nodded. "So someone could theoretically have removed that part of the system, right? And used his badge to locate Tailor?"

"I think it would be possible," Pplimz said. "But there's no technology in here that would allow someone to overhear a conversation or anything like that."

"It wouldn't be hard to add such a device, though," Wibble said. "Bugs are small."

"Right. So, while I'm confident that our badges are stock issue, that's no guarantee that Tailor's was."

Wibble floated onto her back, her body shimmering a light gold. "I think that means we can rule out Officer Barros as Zoarr's accomplice. She'd have had plenty of opportunity to use our badges to track us if she were."

"Maybe," Pplimz said. "Maybe not. We don't know that Tailor's badge was modified. We only know that he was acting as if it was."

"Or I was right and he just didn't trust us," Wibble said, bitterly.

"It's not paranoia when they are out to get you," Pplimz reminded her. "And being angry at Tailor isn't going to help us find him or the artifact."

"I can't just turn off my feelings, Pplimz," Wibble said in frustration.

"I know," Pplimz said. "Contrary to appearances, neither can I. But I can choose to focus on finding a way to speak with Nassas, so that's what I'm going to do."

After another call to the Logos spirit who'd previously helped them track down the history of the Qubit Zirconium, Pplimz was directed to speak with Fingle, an unlikely goblin assistant in the research facility.

"I never met Nassas myself," she said, blinking behind thick goggles and brandishing a set of fine lock picks in one hand and a welding torch in the other, "but the lab that took me on as an apprentice when I first joined Logos had an inter-departmental agreement with the facility that designed micro-enhancements for the machinist workshop which manufactured orthogonal nanotools used by the theorists in the enclave which used to be next door to the restaurant where Nassas ate lunch sometimes."

Pplimz didn't miss a beat. "Can you put me in touch with him?"

"Of course," Fingle said, as if it were a ridiculous question. "I'll send you a communications link to Macro-Research Facility 82Φ. The lab Nassas runs is located there."

"Thank you," Pplimz said, sighing deeply once the connection was cut.

"For beings who value logic, they aren't terribly good at getting to the point, are they?" Wibble said.

"I never have met a logotarian who wasn't rather fond of the sound of their own voice," Pplimz said, while making the connection to 82Φ. "Here's hoping Nassas is not the exception."

"Thank you for contacting Logos Macro-Research Facility 82Φ," the reception algorithm that answered the call intoned. "If you know the extension of the party you wish to contact, please enter it now. Otherwise, please press Σ for accounting or Ω for facilities. Press ∞ to hear the options again."

"It's almost as if they don't actually want to talk to you," Wibble said.

"Not a problem. I'm familiar with this brand of gatekeeper receptionist. It's not hard to bypass when you know how." Pplimz entered a long string of characters into the input field.

"I'm sorry. That is not a valid extension codezzzzzzzz..." There was a crackle and a beep, then a real living voice came over the line, along with the fuzzy image of a tiny, grumpy, fanged face.

"Hello? Yes, what do you want?"

"I am trying to reach Machinist Nassas on a matter of some

urgency," Pplimz said to the confused pterotos at the other end of the call. "Can you put me through?"

"Do I look like a call routing manipulator?!"

"Uh… no? But if you could simply patch me through, I'd greatly appreciate it."

"Ack! Can't you see I'm in the middle of something?" The being's feathery wings flapped in annoyance as they wriggled their serpentine body away from a jittering cube that was bouncing across the lab's benchtop. They mashed a button with the tip of their tail and the screen blanked out.

"Did they just hang up on us?" Wibble asked, but after a brief moment the image brightened and the face of a grizzled old niffle ape with nearly as many cybernetic augments as Pplimz filled the screen.

"This is Nassas," his languid and sonorous voice said. "To whom do I have the pleasure of speaking?"

"My name is Pplimz and this is my partner, Wibble. We are detectives working on behalf of the elf Tailor the Taupe. I believe we all have some interests in common."

Nassas's big brown eyes grew even larger, and his silver beard trembled. "I shall contact you on an encrypted channel," he said, then broke the connection.

"Well, Nassas is not exactly what I was expecting," Wibble said. There were some on the Crucible who thought that niffle apes were no more than animals, though Wibble had encountered several with evident intelligence. Nassas, however, was clearly not a baseline niffle ape. His many technological enhancements had obviously changed him into something else entirely. She wondered exactly how much he had in common with her own partner.

For their part, though, Pplimz was unfazed. "I do hope that wasn't just a ruse to get us off the line," they said as they waited. "I was sure that mentioning Tailor's name would have made our interests evident."

"He's probably checking up on us," Wibble said. "Making sure we aren't impostors."

"As if there were any being in the universe who could ever hope to impersonate you," Pplimz said.

"Aw. Flattery will get you everywhere," Wibble said.

"It's not flattery, it's a fact," Pplimz said. "One Wibble is about as much as reality can stand." Wibble didn't have an opportunity to return the banter as an incoming transmission popped up on the holodisplay.

"Thank you for getting back to us," Pplimz said, when Nassas reappeared on the display.

"You have been working with Tailor the Taupe," Nassas said. "Can I ask you the context?"

"It's related to the Qubit Zirconium," Wibble said, hoping to avoid unnecessary circumlocution.

"As I suspected," Nassas said. "Are you in possession of the device?"

"I'm afraid not," Pplimz said, and briefly explained what they knew so far.

Nassas listened without comment, then said, "You believe that the Star Alliance Officer Zoarr was seeking the device on behalf of the Cult of the Architects?"

"He may have had an accomplice," Wibble said, and Nassas nodded.

"Our intelligence indicated that there were two individuals from the Cult dispatched to Quantum City," Nassas confirmed.

"Do you think that Officer Zoarr has control of the device?"

"We believe that he did, but only briefly," Pplimz said. "He engaged Star Alliance security when it was apparently stolen from his quarters."

"Could the accomplice be responsible?" Nassas asked. "A *double-cross,* if I have used the felonious vernacular correctly."

"Possible, but there's no evidence of that," Wibble said. "No one other than Tailor has disappeared from the Quantum City area, and I can't imagine an agent who had acquired the jewel would remain there any longer than was absolutely necessary. Besides, there's no indication that it has been used, so we're working on the assumption that a third party has taken the device."

"Word of the power of this artifact has clearly spread much further than I understood," Nassas said, unhappily.

"Not necessarily," Wibble said. "Whoever took it might have just thought it was a pretty piece of jewelry. It is, after all, quite a pretty piece of jewelry."

Nassas snorted, but did not dispute Wibble's hypothesis.

"How many beings did you think were aware of the potential power of the artifact?" Pplimz asked.

"I had understood that it was only known to the Cult of the Architects, and a select few of my own colleagues," Nassas said, "but you know about it. Tailor the Taupe told you, I presume."

"He did not," Wibble said, trying to conceal the bitterness in her voice.

"I see," Nassas said, stroking his beard with a paw. "I suppose I should be pleased that he was in fact as discreet as he claimed to be."

"Well," Wibble said, apologetically, "he did tell his sister. And she told us. So, you know, not that discreet." Nassas grunted.

"I have to ask," Pplimz said, "have you heard from Tailor recently? His friend seemed to think that he would do anything to bring the Qubit Zirconium to you if he had it."

"I have not heard from Tailor the Taupe," Nassas said. "As you can see, The Guardian is still awaiting its charge." He turned away from the screen to reveal a small spherical object with several vertical locking mechanisms extending from its exterior. A hatch was open in its side, revealing an empty compartment within. The interior was inlaid with metallic rings that were etched with cryptic patterns and it emitted a hum that was partly organic and partly mechanical.

"That's the uncrackable safe?" Wibble asked, slightly incredulous.

"The Guardian is not technically a safe," Nassas said, slipping into the speech cadence of a lecturer. "A safe is a containment system which permits the locking and unlocking of an opening, which allows items to be kept secure when necessary and retrieved when its controller chooses. The Guardian, on the other hand, performs only half of those functions. Once it is locked, it cannot be opened. By anyone."

"Not even you?" Pplimz asked.

"I am a subset of the beings encapsulated by the term *anyone*," Nassas replied. Wibble chuckled, but the niffle ape made no indication that he'd intended it as a joke.

"You're taking this all very seriously," Wibble said. "You must really think that the Qubit Zirconium has incredible power."

"If the device's capabilities have been exaggerated, locking it away does no one any harm. However, if it is able to bestow the power of the Architects, then allowing it to fall into any being's control has a potentially catastrophic outcome. Therefore, the only logical course of action is to contain it, regardless of its actual abilities."

"Surely you'd want to study it first?" Pplimz said.

"Of course I would," Nassas said, haughtily. "But my desire to learn about the artifact and its power must be mitigated by its potential for harm. Just because we have the ability do a thing, does not mean we should pursue it."

"That's an unusual position for a logotarian," Wibble said.

"Perhaps," Nassas said. "But keeping the artifact safe from the control of any being was what I, and what Tailor the Taupe, were trying to achieve. I hope that you will agree with my analysis, and deliver the device here if you should locate it."

Pplimz nodded, but didn't actually commit to anything. "One last question," they said. "How did you come to hear of the device in the first place?"

"I have been part of a group that has been monitoring the Cult of the Architects for some time. They did not arise in response to the appearance of the Qubit Zirconium, but have been a silent presence on the Crucible for longer than I have been alive. Mostly their activities have been concerning but ineffectual, but when the rumors of such a powerful artifact appeared, we were forced to take more direct action."

"Why now?" Wibble asked. "Surely if this jewel has such incredible powers, someone would have used it ages ago."

Nassas shook his head. "We understand the artifact has only recently been assembled, and the jewel itself was discovered not long ago," he said. "A new shaft had been opened on the outskirts of the Kettle Bottom Mine, tapping into what some believe is the site of an ancient architect ruin. The Qubit Zirconium was thought to have been one of the gems excavated at that site."

"One of the gems?" Pplimz said with alarm.

"The mine is a commercial operation," Nassas said, "many minerals, gems, and Æmber are taken from the ground there every day."

"So, the Qubit Zirconium may not be unique," Pplimz said. "Other artifacts might have been uncovered there."

"We have heard of no such rumors," Nassas said.

"Perhaps not, but a group that is searching for architect tools would be foolish not to investigate it further," Pplimz said.

"If I were a member of the Cult, I'd want to know if there was anything else useful in that mine," Wibble agreed. "What do you say, Pplimz? I'm sure we can find some ropes and pickaxes around here somewhere. Shall we go spelunking?"

CHAPTER TWENTY
Wibble Sniffs Around

“Spelunking is exploring caves, Wibble,” Pplimz said, as they climbed aboard the passenger compartment. “My understanding is that there are no natural caves at Kettle Bottom Mine.”

“But it’s such a fun word,” Wibble protested. “Spelunking!”

“Defenestration is a fun word as well,” Pplimz said, “but you don’t see me throwing you out a window.”

“Never say never,” Wibble said. “Who knows what we might yet accomplish?!” She settled in next to Pplimz in the rather crowded seating area of the passenger compartment strapped to the giant beast’s back. “I mean, look at us now! It’s not exactly the *Mahoganaire,* but riding a mastodonus isn’t a bad second choice.”

“It was the only conveyance available to Kettle Bottom today,” Pplimz said. “And there’s nothing wrong with traveling the way the locals do. Mastodoni are strong enough to carry the mining equipment they need and agile enough to handle the rough terrain. Six legs really help with that.”

"Oh, I'm not complaining," Wibble said, bobbing up and down. "This is all terribly exciting! The sounds, the *smells* – it's almost as good as riding a verpy."

"I'm glad you're enjoying yourself, Wibble. It's going to be a long journey."

It was, indeed, a long journey from the eastern end of the Local Group to the Photic Ocean in the West, but the mastodonus was swift, tireless, and surprisingly comfortable once one got used to the smell. At first the other beings on board kept to themselves, watching entertainments, sleeping, or talking to their companions. However, partway through the trip a group of small, multi-limbed scuttling hivebears set up a cookpot near the cargo compartment, and sold plates of spicy paste on flatbread to hungry passengers. After lunch a few of the travelers got a rousing game of demondice going, and by the time they arrived at the townsite at Kettle Bottom most of the passengers had become fast friends.

"Most of these beings are going to be here for some time," Pplimz said. "Almost everyone aboard is coming here to work, either in the mines or the town."

"It's hard labor," Wibble said. "There must be quite a lot of valuable ore underground."

"There's an incredibly rich seam of Æmber," Pplimz said. "Not to mention gems and precious metals."

"And other things that some beings find valuable, at least," Wibble said.

"Indeed. Let's see if we can track down someone who remembers the Qubit Zirconium and find out where it came from."

The town of Kettle Bottom was bustling with the new arrivals and the daily activity from the business of the mines. Aside from the usual ramshackle boarding houses, taverns, and recruitment stations, there were several Æmber valuers, gem merchants, and assorted scouts for various factions looking for specific base materials for their research or engineering needs. A few shiny new buildings were dotted among the older wooden relics as new factions set up large mining operations in the nearby wilderness. It was part frontier village and part auction house as sellers from the mining consortiums sought the best prices for their quarries, and new workers looked for lodging and positions.

"There have to be nearly a dozen different operations going on here," Wibble noted, as she took stock of the many different uniforms, insignia, and languages among the townsfolk. "Tracking down the particular mine where the Qubit Zirconium was found might take some doing."

"Then we'd best get started," Pplimz said, making for a set of swinging doors under a sign that read "Æmberdust Arms."

Raucous music spilled out of the bar, along with a rather intoxicated pair of krxix in dirty miners' coveralls.

"And don't come back in here until you've got the 'bits to pay your tab, you freeloading axehandles!" The gruff voice belonged to a tiny skeletal barkeep, dressed in a stained leather apron over a floral dress. "Now get along, you two," she added with finality, aiming a bony finger at the pair of giggling krxix.

"See you tomorrow, Kell," the smaller krxix called back, using three limbs to steady himself as he helped his companion up with his fourth.

"Yeah, yeah," the barkeep said, shaking her skull-head. "Just remember to pay your bar bill, will you? I'm not running a charity here." She turned her back on the pair and stomped off toward the bar.

The tavern was packed with beings spending their hard-won gains on food, drink, and games of chance. A four-piece band caterwauled on a makeshift stage at one end, and a group of giants nearly drowned them out as they sang along tunelessly. The sound was nearly deafening as Wibble and Pplimz made their way toward the bar.

"What can I get you?" Kell asked, standing on an upturned barrel so she could lean over the bar.

Pplimz set a handful of Æmbits on the counter. "Information." They projected an image of the Qubit Zirconium tiara over the bar and enlarged it to show off the stone in the center of the setting. "We're looking for the mine where this jewel was found."

The bartender leaned in further, a dim light glowing deep within her eye sockets as she inspected the image. "Can't say I've ever seen anything like this before," she said. "You know how many stones they pulled up like this?"

"As far as we know, only the one," Wibble said.

"Ngh," she grunted. "Most folks sell on their uniques before they ever make it in here. You probably want to talk to Tannalay. Xe brokers most of the trades for the more unusual items." She extended a bony arm toward a table where a scaly mammalian dressed in last year's Hub City fashions sat, and who appeared to be exuding an orange miasma of gas.

"Thanks," Pplimz said, and walked over to the table. "Excuse me, I'm looking for someone called Tannalay?"

The being stood up sharply, leaving a bulging coin purse

behind on the table. "It's all right, we were just finished," he said in a squeaky voice. "Thank you for your help." He loped away, the red and gold train of his trouser skirt making a trail across the bar's filthy floor. The gas remained floating about the table.

"I am Tannalay." Pplimz's translator indicated that a nearby being was using pheromones to communicate, and it rendered the words as text on Pplimz's screen. The fog coalesced into a dense ball on one side of the table and extended a tendril indicating the two chairs opposite. "How can I help you?"

"I speak Sogrulothis," Wibble said aloud, while also emitting a pheromone burst for Tannalay's benefit. "Your translator doesn't handle the nuances well."

"Go ahead," Pplimz said.

"We're looking for information about where this stone was found," Wibble asked the broker in a fine chemical mist while Pplimz showed xir the image of the Qubit Zirconium.

"A fine specimen," Tannalay replied. "And popular, it seems."

Wibble shimmered a rust color. "Have there been other beings enquiring about this stone?"

Tannalay answered in the affirmative, with just a hint of a smell of avarice. Xe was not likely to tell them more without a little something for xir trouble. Wibble turned to Pplimz and gestured to the pocket where they kept their bribe money.

Pplimz pulled out a stack of Æmbits and separated them into two piles, covering them both with their hands. "The location," they uncovered the pile under their left hand briefly, then made the same gesture with their right hand, saying, "and the other interested parties."

Tannalay expanded and contracted, xir gaseous form rippling

in the bar's air currents. A tendril reached out toward Pplimz's left hand. "The gem was found at Eremore's Pit, to the north of here." Pplimz retracted their hand and Tannalay swept the 'bits into xir coin purse with a swirl.

"Can you describe the other beings who have been asking after the stone?" Wibble asked. "And when were they here?"

"It was a lone being," Tannalay said. "Not long ago. They were–"

A crash interrupted them – and everyone else in the tavern – as an ethereal spirit riding an enormous beast burst into the bar, shooting bolts of blue plasma at their unseen pursuers. Patrons scurried out of the way, diving for cover under tables or fleeing out windows and back exits.

A group of axe-wielding Brobnar charged in after the spirit, flailing wildly as they sought to take out the legs of the poor creature the spirit was riding. Pplimz grabbed the edge of the table and flipped it toward the fight, creating a makeshift barrier between them and the mayhem.

"Just what we need," they said grumpily. "A pair of Archons sending their minions to fight over æmber while there's real work to be done. Wibble, will you get down here!" They reached up and grabbed Wibble by the flipper to pull her down to the relative safety of the space behind the table.

"But I want to see an Archon!" she complained.

"You can watch from here," Pplimz hissed. Wibble's echolocation meant that the table was no impediment to her following the action. So she stayed behind the table as they heard screams and whinnies, and several plasma bolts, then finally a deadly silence.

"Can you see what's going on?" Pplimz whispered.

"The fight's over," she said. "Brobnar won. Hang on – here comes the loser." Wibble popped up to get a proper view of the mysterious Archon.

"No need to be rude," Pplimz said, cautiously peering around the edge of the table.

"Just a statement of fact," Wibble said, as the being who commanded the spirit rider strode into the midst of the carnage. The spirit and their mount were laid out on the floor, unmoving after falling to the blows of the two Brobnar warriors. Their Archon leader approached, looked down at the carnage, then gave a wave of their mighty hand. The two bodies twitched, then struggled to their feet, spent but with all wounds healed. They followed their leader out of the tavern, leaving a trail of broken glass, busted chairs, and gouged tables in their wake.

"Huh," Wibble said, watching the Archon leave. "I've never seen anything like that before. But I think I expected something just a little more magnificent."

"Archons," Pplimz said with distaste as they righted the table. "They act like the whole world is here only for them."

"It was a good fight, though," Wibble said. "Very slicey."

Pplimz surveyed the tavern, as the remaining patrons picked up their tables and chairs, then carried on as if nothing had happened. The bartender wiped an arm over the bar, sweeping broken glass and spilled drink onto the floor, then went back to serving.

"Where's Tannalay?" Wibble asked.

"Oh no." Pplimz looked around, but the gas had obviously slipped out a crack when the vault battle had distracted them. And xie'd taken the second pile of Æmbits with them. "Archons," Pplimz said, then uttered an ancient cyborg curse.

"Well, at least we've got half a lead," Wibble said, hoping to take Pplimz's mind off the battle. "Next stop: Eremore's Pit."

There were signs of the vault battle all over Kettle Bottom, but the miners and townsfolk mostly ignored the destruction. The victorious Archon was magnanimously cleaning up after the fight, touching a broken crate to miraculously mend it here, healing grazes from flying debris there.

"It's the least they can do," Pplimz muttered, as they passed the Archon reattaching the broken branch of a spindlespine tree.

"Beings love a good vault battle, Pplimz," Wibble said, gently. "It's fine work for a warrior."

"That's all well and good for everyone who chooses to be involved," Pplimz said, glowering at the Archon, who bestowed a beatific smile on them. "But these beings have nothing to do with it, and they're supposed to just accept all this disruption? And what if neither of the Archons bothers to clean up after themselves? They don't have to do it, after all. The rest of us just have to hope that in the goodness of their hearts they restore what they've destroyed."

The Archon had stopped shoring up the wall of a building that had a hole neatly punched in its side, and was clearly listening to Pplimz as they complained.

"Pplimz, you are as brave and principled as any being I've ever encountered," Wibble said, "but this is not a fight we need to undertake at this particular moment in time." She shooed her partner along, away from the Archon, who shrugged and went back to cleaning up after their warriors. "Let's concentrate on finding out more about this jewel – and hopefully finding Tailor. We can work on fixing the inequities of the world after that, all right?" Pplimz grumbled but allowed themself to be steered through the town toward the working mines.

There were several different sites in the area, each controlled by different groups but all delving deep into the ground in search of riches or powerful artifacts. They passed one of the oldest mines, a large operation involving mechanized carts on rails bringing up a seemingly endless supply of raw ore to be processed onsite, extracting Æmber for the nearby forge. An imp in a Shadows cloak was collecting pure Æmber, flanked on either side by the Brobnar warriors they'd recently seen fighting in the tavern.

"I bet they see more than their fair share of raids here," Wibble said, "with all this Æmber."

"We all need Æmber," Pplimz said, "not just the Archons." The naturally occurring substance was the source of power for most everything on the Crucible, so extracting it, refining it, and finding new uses for it were the among the most lucrative pursuits.

They had to pass several other mining sites before they got to Eremore's Pit, and they were all as individual as the beings running them. There was a fully automated mine, staffed entirely by drones and robots, next to a group of rough-looking solo miners attacking the ground manually with pickaxes and shovels. A team of martians ran a boring operation with a hovering saucer and modified ray guns, while a group of insectoid beings created a giant hill with honeycomb holes as they crawled through looking for treasures.

Eremore's Pit was well named – it wasn't much more than a hole in the ground. Wibble and Pplimz nearly missed it as they left the more industrialized sites. From a distance the only thing that indicated that there was anything in that area was a small hut with a communications antenna on its roof, and half a dozen large piles of dirt.

"Not much to look at," Pplimz said as they approached.

"It certainly doesn't scream, 'Look at me, I'm the source of an artifact of unparalleled power,' does it?" Wibble said. "I suppose that bodes well for us getting here before an armed gang of cultists."

"Maybe," Pplimz said, warily. "I hate to say it, but doesn't it seem a bit too quiet to you? Nassas said this site was a going concern, bringing up Æmber and gems every day." Pplimz looked around. "Where are all the miners? The assayers? The rovers to bring the takings into town?"

"Perhaps they're all done for the day?" Wibble said, half-heartedly.

"Hello?" Pplimz called loudly as they approached the pit. "Anyone here?"

The silence was eerie after the clang of machinery and shouts of beings working at the other mine sites. They went up to the edge of the pit and peered into it. There were no signs of activity, but the hole was deep and they couldn't see all the way to the bottom. A rickety rope lift was affixed to the side of the pit, a counterweighted basket swaying in the breeze at the top.

"What do you say, Wibble?" Pplimz asked, gesturing to the basket. "It's not spelunking, but it will be descending into a dark, potentially dangerous hole in the ground, with no idea what we're going to find down there."

"Aw, Pplimz," Wibble said, "you sure do know how to show someone a good time."

CHAPTER TWENTY-ONE
Pplimz Finds a Body

The lift car was more solid than it first appeared, and a mechanism rang out a warning klaxon when they shut the safety cage doors around them. The lift was manually operated on a four-to-one pulley system, which, with the counterweight of the ascending basket, made hand-over-handing the rope on their way down easy enough. Pplimz increased the brightness on their screen to cast a blueish glow over the pit's walls as they descended and Wibble emanated a pale turquoise gleam. They were the only sources of light aside from the diminishing circle of the opening at the surface.

The lift finally clanged to a stop at the bottom of the pit, many yards below the surface. Pplimz opened the door and gingerly exited the cage, stepping carefully on the loose dirt at the base of the pit. Wibble hovered nearby, turning in a slow circle.

"What can you see?" Pplimz asked, the light from their screen barely illuminating more than a few inches in front of them.

"There's a bunch of hand tools lying on the ground over to

the left," Wibble said, "a drilling drone, and a couple of half-filled sacks. It looks like they were digging out the pit manually, and bringing up the spoil to sift through at the surface." She led Pplimz to the drill.

"The battery's missing," Pplimz said, peering at the open hatch on the drone.

"They must have to recharge it in the hut," Wibble suggested. "It may just be me, but I'd say they're either running a pretty lax operation here or they left in a hurry."

"There is a definite 'hastily abandoned' feel to the place," Pplimz agreed. "But they probably just left when the fighting broke out. It's not necessarily sinister."

Wibble hefted one of the sacks. "Why don't we grab these and do a little abandoning of our own?" she suggested. "There's nothing else to see down here."

Pplimz dragged the other sack into the lift basket and waited for Wibble to deposit the one she was carrying. The warning buzzer sounded again, and they made their way back up to the surface. When they reached the midpoint, Pplimz pulled on the ropes to stop their ascent.

"Can't get enough of hanging out in a hole in the ground?" Wibble asked.

"I was hoping to see if there's anything in the other car," Pplimz said, peering through the cage to the descending basket. "But it's too dark. Can you see anything?"

"There's something on the floor," Wibble said. "It's small, maybe crescent-shaped? I can't tell anything else from here." She shimmered, then stretched her body, elongating like putty.

"Wibble, what are you doing?!"

"Just going for a closer look," she said, as she squeezed herself through the gap in the cage and over to the other basket. "Well, now, isn't this interesting?!"

"Wibble, get back here!" Pplimz said, straining against the pull of the ropes. "This lift is weighted to have one of these cars at the top and one at the bottom. It's not supposed to stop halfway. I don't know how long I can hold us here."

"Almost there," she said, slowly squeezing herself back into the cage with Pplimz. "Okay, let's go." Pplimz released the rope and they jerked upward as the cars moved apart. Pplimz grabbed one of the ropes to slow their ascent but the trip back up was much quicker than safety guidelines would have mandated and the car clanged to a stop as it hit the bumper at the top of the lift.

"Well, that was exciting!" Wibble said, opening the gate and floating out to the edge of the pit. Pplimz followed on wobbly legs, eager to get out of the confining cage.

"What were you thinking?" Pplimz demanded. "You could have been trapped down there."

"Pplimz," Wibble said, gently but with a hint of laughter, "I don't think I actually could have." She floated over to the lip of the pit, then dived down into the hole, popping back up again a moment later. "I hover, remember?"

"Well," Pplimz sputtered, "forgive me for being concerned."

"Besides, it was worth it," Wibble said, holding out a dusty white and orange object to Pplimz. "Look what I found in the other car."

Pplimz eyed the item, their spat completely forgotten. "That's a Star Alliance wrist com," they said.

"Looks like we weren't the first ones here after all," Wibble said.

•••

The device was just like other arm-mounted devices they'd seen on all the Star Alliance officers they'd encountered, only simpler. Every officer they'd met had their own personal additions to the communicator, based on their roles or personal preferences. This appeared to be the base model – it didn't even have an insignia. But the shape and color scheme were all Star Alliance.

"Can you connect to it?" Wibble asked. "Find out who it belongs to?"

"I'll try." Pplimz turned the device over and located a row of data ports. They plugged in a standard connector and read the contents. They shook their head.

"It's blank."

"Broken?" Wibble asked.

"No, it's been wiped," Pplimz said. "It's still a fully functional communicator and interface to the public networks, but there's nothing personal on here any more."

"Any more," Wibble echoed. "You don't think it could be a new, unactivated unit? Maybe stolen?"

"No. There's a deactivation date in the metadata, with an official checksum. This is definitely a former Star Alliance unit."

"Maybe someone traded old surplus units at the Horizon," Wibble suggested.

"Or someone took it as a souvenir," Pplimz said. "Someone who was once with the Alliance, but then moved on." They turned the device over to show Wibble the inside, which had been etched with a human sigil: SB.

Wibble took on a lemony hue. "Skye Brooke," she said, after a moment.

"I wager so," Pplimz said. "They were unlikely friends with Zoarr and they knew an awful lot about the tiara. Maybe they are the other cult operative, and they were here looking for another gem like the Qubit Zirconium."

"It's a solid theory," Wibble said. "I'd like it a lot better if there were a little more evidence."

"Then we'd better look for some." Pplimz gestured toward the two sacks of spoil they'd brought up from the pit. "How convenient. There's a bag of dirt for each of us."

Pplimz offered to scan Wibble's bag to identify any minerals or metals within, but she just dove in tip first, burrowing into the dirt.

"I can see just fine," she said, her voice muffled and her wriggling tail throwing a spume of dust into the air behind her. "I can make out a half a dozen ingots and something that might be a gem or it might just be a rock."

"Suit yourself," Pplimz said as they carefully scanned their own sack, reaching in to precisely pluck out any items of interest. In the end, they both worked through their piles of dirt in a few minutes, each pulling out a small number of pieces potentially worth further study. The only difference was that Wibble emerged covered tip to tail in dirt.

"You happen to see a bathhouse in town?" Pplimz asked.

"No," Wibble said, "but I did see a hose coiled up behind that hut. These will all need a wash down to see what we're dealing with." She gestured to the small piles they'd excavated from the bags.

"Yes. That's absolutely what I was referring to," Pplimz said, scooping up their takings and shooing Wibble toward the hut. They turned the hose on her first, and she squealed as if surprised, then wriggled happily in the warm stream. Pplimz then carefully hosed off the piles at their feet, trapping the smaller items in a nearby sieve that was obviously used for this purpose. Once everything was clean, it was clear that mostly they'd uncovered pebbles or ordinary bits of metal, but in amongst the dross a few bright gleams shone through.

"Looks like we've got a couple of chucks of Æmber, these worthless diamonds, a nice chunk of rhodium and this." Pplimz held up a tiny, dun-colored, dodecahedral stone which glinted in the light.

"Is that a jewel?"

"No, I think it was crafted," Pplimz said, peering at it with a high magnification. "There are fittings in here." They manipulated the object with a set of extruded nano filaments until it popped open with a whir. "Well, would you look at that!" Pplimz projected a magnified image of the object so Wibble could see the minute dancing body which had sprung out from the stone. It was clearly not alive, but rather was an animated marionette made for the amusement of what must have been a very small being.

"It's a teeny tiny toy!"

"Probably worth rather a lot to the right collector," Pplimz said, closing the contraption back up and placing it in an envelope for safekeeping. "But it's nothing like the Qubit Zirconium."

"Should we take this stuff into town?" Wibble asked, gesturing to the now cleaned and shining items. "Find out what's it's all worth?"

"No," Pplimz said. "This belongs to the beings who are operating the mine. I'll just leave them in the cabin, for when they come back."

Pplimz opened the door to the hut then jumped back, a

shocked expression painted on their screen face. Wibble hovered over to peer over their shoulder into the small room, and saw what had startled Pplimz.

It appeared that not all of the miners had abandoned the site after all. There was a mechanical being inside wearing a miner's apron, and what was visible of their casing was covered in cheap gems – rubies, diamonds, sapphires. They were slumped back in a chair, their tentacles splayed out over the rough wood table and pincers out in a defensive formation over their head. It had obviously been for naught, however, as they also had a large, ragged hole in the middle of their body, and they were not moving.

Pplimz had seen more than one deactivated robot in their time, but open casings with wires and circuits visible always hit them hard. Once they'd regained their composure, Pplimz scanned the machine.

"This must have happened not long before we got here," they said, laying a hand on the mechanical's casing. "There's still has a magnetic field."

"Any idea what caused this?" Wibble gestured vaguely at the gaping wound. "Looks too deep to be a pickaxe, unless it was wielded by a giant."

"It wasn't any of the mining tools," Pplimz said. "A proper forensic engineer would be able to say for certain, but these markings here look like they were made by a sonic knife."

Wibble turned to Pplimz. "That's martian technology."

"Very common martian tech," Pplimz agreed. "The kind of thing you'd find on a MultiTool-ZX."

"Skye Brooke!" Wibble said again, this time with a distinctive deep purple tone to her body.

"This is not the kind of evidence I was hoping to find," Pplimz said, somberly.

They both stared at the body for a moment.

"Trying to destroy the world is one thing," Wibble said, "but this? It's getting out of control."

"I agree," Pplimz said. "We need to track down Skye Brooke, before they hurt anyone else."

Wibble took the high ground, hovering several feet above Pplimz, who took the road back to the township. They both kept a keen lookout for a shock of golden hair, even though they were well aware that Skye Brooke could easily be in disguise.

"If I were on the run, I'd at least put on a hat," Wibble said.

"Wibble, please," Pplimz said. "You should have a sense of gravitas at a time like this."

All of a sudden, Pplimz found themself drawn to Wibble, in a physical way. It took a real force of effort not to run right into her.

"Not like that!" they barked and things immediately returned to normal. "Gravit*as*, as in a sense of dignity and decorum. Not gravit*y*, as in you vastly increasing your mass without a moment's notice."

"Sorry," Wibble said, and she meant it. "I was just trying to lighten the mood. You know I joke when I'm nervous."

"Yes, I do," Pplimz said, then paused. "And it was more like heavying the mood, wasn't it?"

Wibble chuckled without any actual mirth. "Thanks for trying. Okay, let's get back to looking for Brooke, even though I highly doubt they're going to be walking around out in the open."

"Just because it's unlikely is no reason not to be vigilant," Pplimz countered. As it was, neither of them saw a single human on the way back to town, hat or no hat.

"They can't have got far," Pplimz said, when they entered the main square. "There's no transport leaving here until dusk and I didn't see any personal vehicles parked anywhere."

"What about that matter discombobulator-recombinator?" Wibble asked. "Can you use that on a living being? Couldn't they just have transported themself away?"

"Yes and no," Pplimz said. "My understanding is that the larger or more complex the object being transported is, the less distance it can travel. Living beings are very complex, so I'd guess that someone of Brooke's size could maybe get across this square. Possibly to the other end of town at a pinch. But they wouldn't be able to get far enough for it to be worthwhile. And the recharge time on the device after a transport like that would be significant. At least a day on solar and more than an hour on a high voltage fast charge. No, I'm convinced that Skye Brooke is still in Kettle Bottom. And we need to find them before the transports leave."

They split up, Wibble using her echolocation to check the storerooms and other likely hiding places, while Pplimz asked around at the taverns and markets. Pplimz got a promising lead at a boardinghouse run by a gregarious creeping vine in a surprisingly fashionable set of fluorescent robes, but the human in question turned out to be an ancient prospector with a false glass eye and a penchant for telling long meandering stories. None of which related the location of a young, blonde-haired former Star Alliance officer turned croupier.

For her efforts, Wibble had found not a single soul lying low in a derelict warehouse. She did encounter several beings making what appeared to be private trades in darkened backrooms, but none of them had the correct number of limbs to be Skye Brooke, so she left them to their off-the-books business dealings.

The two met up again at the Æmberdust Arms not long before the transports were due to arrive, each hoping the other had been more successful.

"Kettle Bottom is a big place," Wibble said, dejectedly. "It wouldn't be hard for a being to get lost here."

"It could take days to search everywhere," Pplimz said. "And Brooke could easily slip away while we're trying to find them."

"Too bad they lost their wrist com," Wibble said, spinning the communicator like a top on the table. "We might have been able to track them that way."

"Trying to find them here will be like searching for a faerie dart in a spineweed pile. Our best bet is to watch the transports," Pplimz said. "Whatever it was that Skye Brooke killed that miner for must be important to the Cult. I have to think that they'll be wanting to take it back to the rest of their colleagues."

"You think Brooke took something from the mine site?"

"Why else kill the miner?" Pplimz said. "Either they interrupted Brooke or tried to stop them from taking whatever they found. Maybe they'd already excavated whatever it was, and Brooke killed them for it."

"It is possible Brooke is just a killer by nature," Wibble suggested.

Pplimz shuddered. "If that's the case, it's even more important that we find them and stop them. I know it's not foolproof, but staking out the transport hub is going to be our best option."

"All right," Wibble conceded. "After all, it's not as if Skye Brooke is going to just stroll into the bar looking for a pint and a pie." And indeed, Skye Brooke did not choose that exact moment to walk into the Æmberdust Arms and ask for a pint and a pie.

It was several minutes later, and it was coffee and a sandwich.

CHAPTER TWENTY-TWO

Wibble Gets the Joke

"Yes, I was at Eremore's Pit," Brooke admitted, struggling ineffectually in their seat against Wibble's invisible but unbreakable grasp. "But I cleared out of there along with everyone else! I wasn't about to hang around while a pair of Archons and their armies tore up the joint!"

"And why should we believe you?" Pplimz demanded.

"I don't know, because it's the truth?"

None of the other patrons in the Æmberdust Arms seemed to take any notice of the interrogation happening at the table in the middle of the tavern. In fact, they all managed to find somewhere else to look, as if a visual distortion field surrounded the trio. There was no such technology being employed, however. The denizens of Kettle Bottom were simply excellent at minding their own business. Which made it particularly difficult for Skye Brooke to get the attention of a rather bedraggled-looking martian soldier a few tables over.

"Hey, you!" they shouted for the third time. "Will you please tell these two about the skirmish at that pit mine to the north? Please?"

The soldier briefly caught Pplimz's eyes, and tried to look away nonchalantly, but nonchalance had never come easily to a martian.

"Is this true?" Pplimz demanded, after storming over to the martian's table and looming over them. "Were you at Eremore's Pit?"

"I am not required to speak to you, cyborg," the soldier said, scowling. "Leave me alone."

"A being is dead," Pplimz said, projecting an image of the corpse in the hut for the soldier. "Do you know anything about that? Did you see this human kill them?"

The martian looked confused and vaguely unsettled, which was unusual for a soldier. They were no strangers to war and its consequences, after all.

"It was a mistake," the solider said quietly, looking away.

"What was?" Wibble asked, having dragged Skye Brooke over to the martian's table.

"I was aiming for the Brobnar," the soldier admitted.

"Wait," Pplimz said, "are you saying that *you* killed this miner?"

"It's not as if they're still dead!" the soldier muttered, gesturing to a group of nearby locals several tankards in and starting to get rowdy. In the midst of the group was the mechanical they'd last seen with a hole in their chest, trying valiantly to start up a round of the drinking song, "Sea, The Little Goblin."

Pplimz ran a diagnostic to ensure that their visual recognition circuits weren't acting up, but it was really the selfsame miner they'd found, gemstone casing and all.

"My Archon took care of it," the soldier said, with finality.

"Now go away. And take your human with you."

Wibble marched Skye Brooke back to their own table, relaxing her grip slightly, but still unwilling to let them go completely.

"I think it's time you tell us what's really going on," Pplimz said. "What were you and Zoarr really doing at Quantum City? And where is the Qubit Zirconium tiara?"

"Honestly, I don't know where the artifact is," Brooke said, after Wibble had finally agreed to let them have the use of their arms again. "Yes, it's true that Zoarr and I were sent to retrieve the gem, and that Zoarr had it for a few days, but it really was stolen from his quarters before I could take it… to be used. I've been trying to track it, and then finally came here to see if there was another one. But I didn't find anything at that mine other than Æmber and dirt. We're back to square one." They sounded genuinely disappointed.

"So you were supposed to take it to someone. Who? Who are you working for?" Wibble asked. "Who else is part of this conspiracy of yours?"

"I'm not going to tell you that," Brooke said, a streak of defiance in their voice. "You can detain me – and Zoarr – if you want, but we're not going to give up our friends. There's too much at stake."

"Yes, from what we've heard, there are those who believe this artifact has the potential to be a terrible weapon," Pplimz said.

"It's not a weapon," Brooke said. "It's our salvation! Don't you see? This place is a prison. Whether that's by design or by chance, it doesn't matter. Practically, we are all trapped here. If we can learn the secrets of the Architects, we can finally break free of this place. All of us." Skye looked at Wibble and Pplimz, the fervor of true belief in their face. "You should be helping us find the artifact. Once we unlock its power, it will help you, too. We will all be free."

"I think you truly believe that," Wibble said. "But it could do so much more than simply open the Boundary. And that's far too much power for any one group to hold."

"I'm sorry you think that," Skye said. "It must be hard to be so untrusting of other people that you'd rather stay locked in this prison of a world than take a chance on freedom."

The three were silent for a while, a bubble of uneasy quiet in the maelstrom of the rowdy bar.

"We're going to have to turn you in to Star Alliance security," Pplimz said, finally.

"I'm fairly confident that they've got nothing on me," Brooke said, smugly.

"Maybe not, but I think they'll probably be fine with keeping an eye on you until we sort this out," Wibble said.

"You do what you have to," Brooke said, with a shrug. "I'm already confined. Altering the scenery won't change that."

Kell, the bartender, found them a secure room at the inn in exchange for a stack of Æmbits, and Wibble got Skye Brooke settled while Pplimz had their dinner order sent up to them. They relieved Brooke of their martian MultiTool – there was no point in locking them in a room if they could just transport themself through the wall – then left to track down the resurrected miner from Eremore's Pit.

The mechanical was still carousing in the tavern, buying rounds of drinks, vapors, and herbals for anyone who wanted to help them celebrate their renewed lease on life.

"Excuse me," Pplimz said, tapping them on the upper casing.

"Hey, friend," the mechanical shouted, "come join the party!"

"Can we talk to you about Eremore's Pit?" Wibble asked.

"Aw, that doesn't sound like much fun. How about a game of dart bowls instead?"

"Maybe after," Pplimz said. "Please, it's important."

The mechanical sighed, and took a long hit off an electrical transformer, finishing off the pack. "Fine, but you'll owe me a jolt."

Pplimz nodded and led the robot to a quiet table away from the crowd.

"What's your name and pronouns?" Wibble asked, after she and Pplimz had introduced themselves.

"You can call me Bracer, it/its." Bracer smacked Pplimz on the shoulder. "Mech liberation, am I right, comrade?"

"Uh, sure," Pplimz said. "Before the Archon battle, did you see a human sneaking around the mine? About two-thirds as tall as me, golden hair?"

"Yeah," Bracer said, its tone suddenly sober. "I caught them on the surveillance feed, poking around in the spoil. I would have had Grackle and Florp, the two biggest beings on our team, help me run them off, but then, you know…" It mimed a battle with its tentacles and pincers, making *pew pew* noises.

"Do you have a copy of that surveillance data?" Wibble asked.

"Of course. You want a transfer?" it asked Pplimz, who nodded. Bracer sent the file to Pplimz, who re-encoded it for a visual display and projected it for Wibble. Knowing what to look for, they could just make out Skye Brooke hiding behind one of the piles of dirt, watching the pit closely until the miners came out of the lift and went into the hut. Then Skye Brooke disappeared and the image blanked out.

"It's a motion sensor drone," Bracer explained. "Doesn't record if there's nothing moving."

"Brooke must have used their transporter," Wibble said. "Probably to get down into the pit."

"They'd have to have taken the lift back up," Pplimz said. "Not enough charge for a two-way trip."

"That's probably when they lost their wrist com." Wibble turned to Bracer. "About how long after this did the Archons show up?"

"Pretty quick," Bracer said. "Probably while that hominid was down the mine, if your timeline's right."

"That tracks with what Brooke told us," Wibble said.

"So, what's this all about, anyway?" Bracer asked. "Every mine loses a little bit to theft, we just work it into the profit and loss calculation. And make sure we've got beings like Grackle and Florp around to scare off the amateurs."

"We think Skye Brooke was looking for something in particular," Pplimz said, changing the projected image to one of the Qubit Zirconium. "Do you remember pulling this gem out of the mine?"

"Oh, yeah!" Bracer lit up, the blinking lights on its shell glinting off the gems embedded in its casing. "This was unique, as far as we can tell. The only one we've ever had, anyway. Oh, and finding it was a funny story, too. Larae will never live that down!"

"We'd love to hear it," Wibble said.

"No problem, but, you know, telling stories is power-draining work," Bracer said, slyly. "I'll take that jolt pack now, if you don't mind."

Pplimz sighed, but signaled to a passing server and ordered a transformer pack for Bracer. It arrived, and Bracer took a couple of quick hits of fermented electricity before settling back on its tentacles.

"So we're a crew of four – me, Grackle and Florp, and Larae. She's the brains behind the operation, been in and out of mines since she was a pouchling. She's got the eye for the high value deposits, it's like she can see the merest glint of a gem even when it's totally covered in a crust of spoil. Twelve times out of thirteen she'd have identified some raw chunk correctly before we can get the nanoscan on it. She's a natural. So that's why it was quite a day when Florp dug this one out of the boney pile after Larae had already gone over the takings." Bracer laughed, as if it were the funniest thing it'd ever encountered.

"Can you explain the joke just a little more?" Wibble asked.

"Larae missed it! She completely and utterly failed to see this gem in the sluice, and just threw... it... away! It wasn't even small. I don't know how she could have missed seeing it. None of us let her forget it, either." Bracer took another hit from the transformer. "Maybe she's losing her touch," it said, pensively. "That would be bad."

"Thanks for your help," Pplimz said, but the mechanical was slipping into an electricity induced haze and didn't even seem to notice them as they left the table.

"Skye Brooke's story checks out," Wibble said, as they made their way into the back of the tavern where the rooms for hire were located. "And if Bracer can be believed, they didn't find anything else like the Qubit Zirconium at that site."

"I suspect that Bracer is not at its best today," Pplimz observed, "but even so, I think it knows what it's taken from that mine. I think the Qubit Zirconium is unique, and I'm starting to understand why so many beings think it's special."

Pplimz entered the 986-character code on the entry lock to the room they'd rented, and opened the door to find Skye Brooke stretched out on the narrow cot, an empty coffee cup and balled up sandwich wrapper on the table next to them.

"Come on," Wibble said, gesturing for Brooke to get up. "We've got a train to catch."

She kept a hold of Brooke as they walked to the transport hub where the Neutron Express was waiting. The cross-continent train generated its own rails, making it the favored form of transport through the shifting landscape of the northern wilderness, and they were lucky that it happened to be the day the Express stopped at Kettle Bottom.

"We'll need a compartment," Pplimz told the attendant at the ticketing car.

"Storage, charging, or sleeping?" he asked, not looking up from the seating chart rendered by the bioluminescent pigment on the clipboard he held by a sucker.

"A bit of each," Wibble said. "It's overnight to Quantum City, isn't it?"

The attendant glanced at them, taking in the three passengers. "I'll put you in Sleeper ThetaFive," he said, handing them tickets in exchange for a rather hefty pile of Æmbits. "You can go ahead and board now. We'll be leaving soon. Next!" He waved them on efficiently, taking the next being in line.

They awkwardly climbed the steps to the sleeper car, Wibble keeping Brooke in a strong grip. The train was a long line of gleaming bronze cars, the interiors all velveteen plush and handworn smooth varnished hypertimber. They trekked down the narrow corridor until they found their cabin, the sliding door opening to the proximity of their tickets. Inside it was cramped, but beautifully appointed, with a sofa seat and a table affixed to the side bulkhead under a large window. A button on the interior wall deployed a pair of over/under beds, complete with saurian linen bedding. They stowed the beds, as they took up most of the cabin, then Pplimz set a security lock on the door.

"Not bad for a detention cell," Skye Brooke said, stretching out on the couch. "But a gilded cage is still a cage."

"Yes, we get it," Wibble said, annoyed. "The Crucible is a prison. You don't have to keep going on about it."

"Fine," Brooke said, closing their eyes. "I really am only trying to help, you know."

"I'm going to see about the meal service," Wibble said. "You need anything, Pplimz?"

"Can you ask about the network connection?" they said. "It would be good to check in if we can."

Wibble tipped her nose forward in agreement, then hovered out into the corridor, the door sliding closed behind her.

"She doesn't like me much, does she?" Brooke said.

"She doesn't like what you're trying to achieve," Pplimz said. "Separating the being from their actions doesn't come easily to her."

"You get it, though," Brooke said. "Being able to have the same kind of control over this place that the Architects did would change everything. No more weird limits on technology, no more Boundary. No one would have to leave if they don't want to, but we'd all finally get the choice."

"I do understand," Pplimz said, "and I certainly see the appeal of your group. But Wibble is right. If the power of the Architects is contained in a single artifact, then that becomes the most powerful device in the world. Think of the wars it would spark. The unutterable destruction it could wreak. Yes, I do see its positive value, the freedom it could achieve. But its potential for devastation is even greater."

"So just because some beings would use it for harm, that means no one should have it?" Brooke asked, with a sardonic tone.

Pplimz let that most fundamental question hang between them.

"Feel free to use either bed," they said eventually. "Neither Wibble nor I will need them."

CHAPTER TWENTY-THREE
Pplimz Tries the Bed

The train moved smoothly along its self-deployed tracks after a blast of its whistle. Wibble returned shortly with a fancy printed menu for Brooke, and a network key for Pplimz.

"You can order anything off here and they'll deliver it," she said, passing Brooke the menu. "The kitchen never closes, but there's only one steward for this car after dark."

Pplimz took the network key and connected to the train's comms system. "Ugh," they said. "This will teach me to ignore my messages for a few days." Their screen blinked out for a moment, then a Do Not Disturb notice flashed up, and Pplimz became as still as a sleeping sylicate.

Wibble and Skye Brooke passed a rather long, rather uneasy silence, punctuated only by Brooke's dinner order and the resulting pleasantries with the night steward. Wibble couldn't be bothered instigating small talk with someone who was trying to destroy the world. Only after they'd finished eating did Brooke break the conversational embargo.

"Are they okay?" they asked Wibble, gesturing at Pplimz, who was still eerily unmoving.

"Oh, yeah," she said. "They like to single thread sometimes to power through a backlog of data. It shouldn't be long now."

"So, what's their deal?" Brooke asked. "Are they a mechanical with biological grafts, or a really heavily augmented organic lifeform? They don't seem like Logos, but you know how they are with their cybernetic augments. Is that where they came from?"

Wibble flushed an angry purple. "Are all humans so insensitive, or is it just you? Do you ask every being intimate details about their bodies? Not everyone on the Crucible belongs to the organized houses, either, and if they did and left, do you think it might be something they don't necessarily want everyone and their sibling to know? How utterly, abominably, rude!"

Surprisingly, Skye Brooke looked abashed. "I'm sorry, you're right. I wasn't thinking. And no, it's not all humans. It's usually not even me. I'm- I'm not used to all the different kinds of people here."

Wibble wasn't about to forgive easily, but the color of her skin faded to a deep mauve. "You're a recent arrival?" she asked.

Brooke nodded. "A few years by human time, but it's still new to me." They laughed, without mirth. "And to think that I spent my whole life looking for adventure, for the chance to meet new and unique people. The really funny part is that if someone had offered me the opportunity to come here to the Crucible, I would have jumped at the chance. But instead, I was working on a maintenance crew on a starliner – a terrible job, but it let me travel – when we hit an anomaly and the next thing we knew, here we were. The starliner completely disappeared, but all of us onboard were transported to the surface, straight to what we found out later was the human enclave in Hub City. It was probably the one place that would have been the least jarring, but it was still utterly terrifying." They shook their head at the memory. "Be careful what you wish for, I guess."

They were both silent for a moment. Wibble thought about her own abrupt arrival to the impossible world so long ago, and how much she'd changed since then.

"Your desire for excitement isn't what brought you here," Wibble said, surprisingly kindly. "I don't know how it does work, but I know it doesn't work like that. It's not your fault, none of it. Not that you were brought here, not that it isn't all adventure and fun. And it's not your responsibility to find a way to leave, either. There are things in the universe we can change, and things we can't. Knowing the difference is how we manage to deal with it all."

Skye looked like they were about to argue the point, when Pplimz's screen lit up and they reanimated with vigor.

"Wibble!" they shouted.

"Pplimz!" she shouted back, startled.

"I heard from Rua the Nimble Tail."

"Is that Rua from the Shadows guild we did that sting operation with in Eastside that one time, or Rua from the firegrass-weaving collective in the Whisperwood?"

"The Shadows, obviously."

"Oh, that's a shame. The other Rua made such delightful little hats."

"Wibble, focus!" Pplimz said. "She found it!"

"She what?"

"Rua the Nimble Tail found the Qubit Zirconium tiara! She's got it in her safehouse in Hub City!"

A modest amount of pandemonium ensued. Skye Brooke shot up off the sofa and tried to open the door to the cabin. They rattled the handle, but it remained firmly locked no matter how much they tugged. However, before Wibble could manage to grab them they'd clambered back over the couch, kicking Pplimz out of the way and into the button that deployed the beds. Brooke threw open the sash window and levered themself up and out while Pplimz fell onto the lower bunk, which promptly shut itself, trapping them between the mattress and the bulkhead.

"Mmph," Pplimz said.

"Get back here!" Wibble shouted, firing herself out the window after Skye Brooke. She had no expectation of them complying, it was just what one said at the start of a chase.

Brooke had found a foothold on the bronze filigree on the side of the carriage, and had hauled themself up onto the roof. Wibble popped up to grab them, but without the containment field from the train car, she discovered that she was now moving relative to the ground, rather than the train. It was like swimming though liquid Æmber. She pushed as hard as she could, but could only manage a minuscule amount of forward movement compared to the train. Brooke looked back as they scampered along the roof, then caught a glimpse of Wibble. They stopped and sat crosslegged about six feet away.

"I'm not gloating," Brooke said, "but you have to admit, this is kind of funny." Wibble was required to concede no such thing as she barely moved toward Brooke, her body elongated in effort.

"Sorry," Brooke said, clambering down to the junction

between cars, "but I have to run." They jumped onto the small platform and wrenched open the door. They slammed the door closed behind them, and Wibble just made it to the end of the car in time to watch furiously as Brooke barred the door from the inside. Wibble lowered herself to the gangway connection, which provided enough proximity to the train proper to allow her to move more easily. She jiggled the door handle ineffectually, before realizing she could hover forward – however slowly – and try another door or window.

It took an absolutely unreasonable number of tries before she finally found an unlatched window, and the family of feathered arthropods inside the cabin were not terribly pleased with her unannounced arrival, but she made it into the car. There was no sign of Skye Brooke, however, and the door to the next car was flapping open. Her instinct told her to chase after them, but she also knew that the train was fifty-seven cars long, and she was utterly worn out. She reluctantly hovered back to the end of the car, and unbarred the door to return to her compartment. There wasn't much she could do in her current state and the odds of Brooke attempting to jump off the train were low indeed. After all, the next scheduled stop was Hub City.

Pplimz ran a diagnostic to confirm that nothing was broken. The scan came back clean; Brooke had merely knocked them off balance on the juddering train, but they were truly stuck. If there even was a release latch in the closed bed nook, they'd be unlikely to be able to reach it if even if they could see it, which they couldn't. Their visual sensors were mashed into the bed's mattress.

They should have known better than to let slip what they'd

learned while Brooke was in earshot, but they were always a bit slow after single threading. They'd completely forgotten Brooke was even there. And now they were paying for the error.

After what felt like an eternity, they heard the door to the compartment open.

"A little help?" they called, and there was a click and a whir and then the bed opened. Pplimz bounced off the mattress as it dropped, thankful for the tight quarters as they fell onto the sofa. They looked around and saw only Wibble, nearly translucent, floating against the ceiling of the compartment.

"Skye Brooke got away," Pplimz said, a statement of fact rather than a question.

"Yup," Wibble replied, barely audible.

"I'm sorry," they said. "You tried your best."

"Yup," Wibble agreed.

"Well, it's not as if we don't know where they are going," Pplimz said, "and we've got the advantage since we already know where Rua's bolthole is."

"Yup."

"I suppose there's nothing else to do but rest until we get to Hub City, then," Pplimz said, expecting to hear Wibble's new catchphrase in response, but she was already completely and utterly asleep.

Pplimz shook Wibble awake as the Neutron Express was pulling into the Hubcenter station.

"Are you all right?" they asked, concerned as she shimmered vaguely.

"Nothing two days in a nice, unmoving corner wouldn't cure," she said, "but time waits for no being." She waved her tail tentatively, then hovered down to rest at Pplimz's side. "I'll be fine. Let's get to Rua's before it's too late."

They disembarked, and jumped into a premium hovercab from the stand outside the station. Pplimz entered an address in the Lawless Zone into the cab's autocom and the vehicle pulled away from the curb and efficiently slotted into the quickly moving traffic.

"That's not–" Wibble started to say, but Pplimz shushed her, displaying a message on their screen in their shared code.

"Brooke doesn't know where Rua the Nimble Tail is, but they know we do," the message read. "Better operate under the assumption of pursuit and surveillance conditions."

"Of course," Wibble said, disappointed that she hadn't thought of it herself. She really needed a decent rest, but it would have to wait. "Hey, Pplimz," she said casually, after a moment, "remember that time we thought we'd stumbled on a multiple murder, but it turned out it was just that poor hemogoblin who'd eaten a batch of bad clams?"

"Who could forget?" Pplimz said, engaging the manual override on the autocab's door locks. "The chef at Watery Gravlax was not terribly pleased with us when we got them shut down."

That was a slight understatement, as Karn, the chef in question, had chased Wibble and Pplimz halfway across the restaurant district of Melting Pot with a LifeSeeker harpoon. They'd gotten away, of course, but it had taken a bold move which they were going to have to attempt once again.

The cab entered the northern edge of Melting Pot on its way to the arterial hoverway, and Wibble scooted over so she and Pplimz were both in the righthand seat.

"You sure you're up for this?" Pplimz asked, quietly.

"Ha!" Wibble laughed. "And to think that some beings say you have no sense of humor." She grabbed hold of Pplimz with force fingers from both flippers, while Pplimz threw open the door of the moving hovercab. "You bet I'm *up* for this!" Wibble repeated, as she threw herself – and Pplimz – bodily out of the cab. Instead of being creamed by an oncoming quadruped, Wibble hauled Pplimz upward and they rose briskly above the speeding traffic of the lower northbound hoverway and up to the westbound upper lane. She dropped them onto the top deck of a city bus, startling the few passengers as the two detectives quickly moved to the exit in time to get off at the next stop.

There was a stand of by-the-minute pedal carts for hire at the stop, and Pplimz had one out of its charging cradle and was powering down the cart lane before the bus had set off again.

"We're not entirely inconspicuous," Wibble pointed out, as Pplimz pedaled furiously, their suit coat flapping behind them.

"Surely we've lost Skye Brooke by now," they countered.

"Brooke isn't working alone," Wibble reminded them. "We have to assume they'll have contacted their friends here in Hub City, and who knows what the extent of their network is."

Pplimz uttered an oath, and brought the cart to a skittering halt at the entrance to the gardens of the Cathedral of the Opened Eye.

"Come on," they said, abandoning the cart and running into the lush and precisely manicured garden. "This way."

They stumbled briefly as they entered the dampened zone. The Cathedral employed a communications dampening field within the garden, to aid focus and reflection. The field rendered several of Pplimz's functions inoperable, but they could still run.

"Good thinking," Wibble said, keeping up. "Nanodrones and overhead cambots won't be able to see us in here."

Pplimz, of course, could say nothing under the effect of the communications blackout. They quickly reached the southern boundary of the garden and their screen lit up as they left the dampening field.

"Hold on," they said, reaching out for Wibble as they approached an enormous steaming chasm belching plasma and smoke. They didn't slow their pace at all, Wibble following like a balloon on a tether, as they dove headfirst into the Pits of Dispair.

The Dis community underneath Hub City was consistently voted the least appealing tourist destination by listeners of the popular Hub City Insider soundscape, given how unlikely it was as a location for any being other than a demon to choose to frequent. The place was dark, gloomy, and hot, but plenty of beings would find that an interesting enough experience. It was the terrifying denizens of Dis, and their penchant for making a meal of any stray emotion they encountered that made nearly everyone avoid the place. Which made it an excellent spot for a hideout, particularly as its spacial dislocation meant that it had secret entrances in nearly every district of the city.

Wibble and Pplimz, however, had used the one marked on maps – a pair of sulphurous holes in the ground, which had no discernible bottom when viewed from street level. Only fools and demons would jump into something like that – or beings who'd done it before, and knew that the Dis spacial dislocation technology created a kind of vortex in the pits. The pit ferried those who entered it like an invisible elevator terrifyingly but safely down to the base, the dead having no feelings to eat.

Rua the Nimble Tail had managed to find an abandoned cave and outfitted it with powerful stealth emitters which included emotional dampeners, making her hiding place effectively invisible to the Dis – as well as anyone else who might be so unfortunate as to stumble upon it. Wibble and Pplimz had been there before, and followed Rua's carefully planned route that avoided areas likely to have a congregation of Dis demons. That didn't mean it was impossible to encounter one on the way, however, so Wibble did her best to make herself as calm and unappetizing to a demon as possible.

Pplimz, for their part, contemplated reshaping their body into a passable Dis demon form. Many members of the Demons of the Netherworld were also cyborgs, albeit of the "electrically charged razor-sharp spinning blades for hands" variety. But while they'd pass perfectly well at a distance, Pplimz wasn't going to fool a real demon up close. They did, after all, have feelings and with Wibble there next to them, it was obvious they didn't belong.

The directions Rua had given them previously were circuitous, taking them through passages in behind the ceremonial cauldron halls that had been used in the construction of the cavernous underground district. Aside from their augments and trophies, demons held material items of little value, so storage wasn't a concern. Most of the passages were empty of both objects and beings.

But unfortunately for the detectives, only most of the passages were empty. Not all.

CHAPTER TWENTY-FOUR
Wibble Is the Soup

They'd just slipped into a narrow corridor that was hung with a stringy, viscous, organic material in a rather meaty shade of red.

"Oh, this is much less gruesome than the last passage," Wibble said, disappointed.

"Wibble, please do be quiet," Pplimz hissed for at least the forty-third time since they'd entered the Pits.

"I'm not sure the demons can hear me," she countered. "Communication is a two-way transport, and we all know they can't communicate. Even if you have faked a conversation with them once or twice."

"Who said anything about demons?" Pplimz muttered. "I'm trying to concentrate."

Wibble flashed a dull rainbow, but said nothing as they wove through the fleshy tendrils. They were nearing the final junction, a former staging ground for the excavation, when a clawing sound came from ahead of them. It was not dissimilar to the pitter-patter of a puppy's feet on hard ground, if the puppy were a giant, cybernetically enhanced hellhound with three mouths full of vicious teeth and a blowtorch for a tail.

"Just stay still," Pplimz wrote to Wibble on their screen face, but she was already well ahead of them, literally and figuratively, translucent and unmoving in a grove of gore. The footfalls came closer, and now there was a snuffling, slavering sound accompanying them. The creature rounded the corner, and it turned out that they looked nothing like a puppy at all. Instead, Wibble was greeted by a single set of jaws, made of metal and plasma, opened wide enough that she would easily fit inside along with room enough for seconds. Organic squirming appendages inside the gigantic maw reached out toward her, each one with its own gasping mouth at the end.

Pplimz watched, horrified, as the many mouths reached out toward Wibble, who remained apparently stoic. The body that was, presumably, attached to the jaws wasn't visible in the gloom, but after a moment of reaching toward Wibble it must have been startled, because then the massive mandible swung away and the creature turned back the way it had come.

Both Wibble and Pplimz stayed where they were, whether they were rooted to the spot in fear or merely taking sensible precautions, neither ever said. But a good while later, the corridor was silent and Wibble shimmered in the shadows.

"I'm not entirely certain I've ever been tasted before," Wibble said, after they set off again. "It was … strangely intimate."

"Well, I'm pleased you have another interesting experience to add to your diary, Wibble," Pplimz said. "Let's try to keep the adventures to a minimum until we get to Rua's."

After an adventure-free few moments, they turned into a familiar cavern. There was nothing there, only wetly dripping walls and bare rock. Or so it appeared. Pplimz tapped a complex pattern on a knobby piece of stone, and a section of the wall next to them shimmered ever so slightly. Wibble forged on ahead, seeming to run right into the wall, but instead passing through it. Pplimz followed and they found themselves in a tidy workroom, where a small, indigo-colored elf sat at a bench, arcs coming off her welding torch bright in the dark room.

"Took you long enough," she said, under the cover of her welder's hood, taking her time to finish her job precisely. She dialed back the torch and flipped up the face mask on her helmet, a grin on her wide face.

"We took the scenic route," Wibble explained.

"Are you sure you lost your shadow?" Rua the Nimble Tail asked, her glowing orange eyes narrowing.

"We did our best," Pplimz said.

"I'm sure you did," Rua replied. "So I suppose you want to see this little bauble now."

"Whenever it's convenient," Wibble said.

Rua chuckled. "Okay, I'll get it. Hang tight." She turned her back on them and made a sigil in the air with a device in her hand. What had previously been a holo of a popular elven opera star flickered then resolved into a small solid lockbox. Rua turned to keep herself between the detectives and the lockbox as she did whatever she needed to do to open it.

"I saw your request to keep an eye out and figured I'd check the local exchanges. This sure is a lot of trouble for a simple silver crown," she said, as she was turning back to face them, when a high-pitched wail came from the other side of the stealth field. The three beings in the workroom froze, then a terrible scream came from the same direction. The sound of heavy feet pounding the ground accompanied the caterwauling and then the fake wall seemed to flex in spacetime and a giant in a Star Alliance uniform fell through, sprawling at Pplimz's feet. He was still wailing incoherently. Pplimz diverted a few extra cycles of processing to their fight or flight subroutine.

Hot on his heels, Skye Brooke ran into the room, the apparent source of the scream.

"There's a monster – save yourselves!" they shouted. "It has teeth… and tails! And flaming sabrewings!" Brooke babbled.

The sound of something in pursuit grew closer, and Wibble hovered into a far corner while Pplimz took a step back from Zoarr writhing at their feet, but Rua remained leaning back against her workbench casually, a smirk on her face.

"You really think I'd go to all the trouble of making a hideaway in Dis territory without employing demon repellant?"

The snuffling sounds on the other side of the "wall" became more tentative, then slowly faded off into the distance. "You forgot to lock the door behind you, didn't you?" Rua asked Pplimz.

"I believe you never provided me with the lock code," they answered, still coming to terms with the scene in the now cramped space.

"No. I wouldn't have," Rua said. "Can't blame me for trying to get you to take responsibility, though. So, who are your friends here? That tail you totally lost, I presume."

Zoarr had stopped shrieking and Skye Brooke was staring into the middle distance, stunned.

"They are among the many beings who are trying acquire the Qubit Zirconium tiara," Pplimz said, "but, of course, you found it for us."

"Sure," Rua said, slyly, "but that doesn't guarantee anything. I'm always interested in a multi-party negotiation situation. Make me an offer, new arrivals!"

Skye Brooke was apparently still in shock, but Zoarr had adjusted to the new state of affairs and wasted no time.

"My organization is willing to secure a significant amount of high grade raw Æmber in exchange for the artifact," he said.

Rua eyed his uniform. "The Star Alliance is going to pay for a piece of jewelry?"

Zoarr shook his enormous head. "Another organization. I can offer this as a down payment." He reached into one of the capacious utility pockets in his uniform and extracted a glowing nugget of Æmber. Even in his sizable hand, it looked large.

"Well. Can you beat that, investigators for hire?"

Pplimz wasn't surprised at Rua's mercenary behavior, but they were disappointed. Before they could reply, however, Wibble came out of her hiding place and addressed Rua. "Surely there are more valuable things than Æmber. We have a relationship, after all." She gestured back and forth between them with a flipper. "*History*." She emphasized the last word, implying that Rua was in their debt. The elf flushed, but turned back to Zoarr.

"Exactly how significant is this amount of Æmber you're offering?"

Zoarr tapped something on his wrist com, then turned the screen so only Rua could see the sum. Her usually inscrutable expression gave away that it was substantial indeed.

"Sorry, detectives," she said, sounding at least a little bit actually apologetic. "History or no, I can't possibly pass up an offer like this. Okay, Star Alliance, you've got a deal." She pocketed the Æmber chunk Zoarr had offered her and handed him the tiara. Wibble flushed neon purple in anger, but made no move to stop the transaction.

Zoarr's face took on a rapturous expression and his fingers brushed against the silver. Even Skye Brooke was finally jolted out of their stupor, and came to Zoarr's side to gaze at the tiara.

"What's this meant to be?" they demanded after staring at it incredulously for a long time. "Some kind of funny business?"

Zoarr frowned. "I assure you that you will be paid in full. You are welcome to accompany us to the full payment right now. But we need the entire artifact, intact, in our possession before we leave here."

Rua looked confused, and the two detectives crowded in on Zoarr to get a better look. It was the tiara in his hands, of that there was no doubt. The filigree was identical, down to the scribing lines. It was, however, missing that crucial component: the gemstone.

Wibble's body was painted in a rainbow and Pplimz felt a smirk coming on, which they graciously suppressed.

Rua peered at the tiara. "Give me a moment." She turned back to her workbench and muttered, "I was sure there was a stone in there..." She leaned into the safe, her entire torso disappearing into the box. She tossed out items behind her as she searched: a remarkably genuine-looking Sanctum eye-chalice, a pair of golden feathers, a glowing light-mace, a carefully boxed length of string. She withdrew, her face giving nothing away, but her hands holding no jewels of any kind whatsoever.

"Come on now," Rua said, her eyes darting between Zoarr and Skye Brooke. "A deal's a deal. You wanted the tiara and this is the tiara. I've held up my end of the bargain. Where's my Æmber?"

"Let's go, Zoarr," Skye Brooke said, taking the tiara from his hand and tossing it on to the bench. "This is obviously a fake. There's nothing we want here." They turned to go, but the giant stopped them.

"Not quite true," he said, staring down at Rua menacingly. "I'll have my Æmber back, if you don't mind."

There was a tense moment where the elf was obviously considering not giving it up, but Zoarr was at least five times her size, and – Star Alliance uniform or not – he was a giant. She reluctantly handed the Æmber chunk back to him, and he and Skye Brooke left without another word.

"Good luck with the demons!" Rua called after them, then turned back to Wibble and Pplimz with a grin. "Looks like the tiara is back on the market after all. I'm entertaining offers once again."

"I think we'll call it a gesture of goodwill, given our history together," Pplimz said, plucking the tiara off the bench and secreting it in an inside pocket of their suit coat. "It appears that its value has significantly reduced, after all."

Rua could tell she'd been bested, and didn't even bother to haggle further.

"Fine," she said, "but I'm changing the unlock pattern on my emitters." She gestured toward the spot on the wall that formed the exit. "You'll have to knock next time."

"Of course," Pplimz said as they left, knowing that there would be no next time. Their alliance with Rua the Nimble Tail was over. Hopefully it had been worth it, but without the jewel, there was no way of knowing.

They retraced their circuitous route back to the vortex at the Pits, minute remnants of the mysterious demon repellant in

Rua's stealth field clinging to them long enough to avoid any other demonic activity. The vortex shot them up to the surface, Dis demons preferring not to have to deal with the leftovers of their meals. When they hit the ground near the Melting Pot, they caught a city steam-train to their office.

The ancient klaxxron contraption was slow and while the seats were still more or less intact, the mud pools for semiaquatics had been devoid of actual mud for as long as anyone could remember. Most were content to ignore or embrace their idiosyncrasies in favor of the fact that they ran more or less on time and to all corners of Hub City.

Pplimz clung to a fraying strap as the packed car lurched forward from the stop. There was no possibility of carrying on an audio conversation, between the whistling of the steam engine and the crush of other beings. Wibble had been crammed in a corner behind Pplimz by a trio of boarding passengers, so they couldn't even talk using their written code. They spent the journey alone with their thoughts until they disembarked at the jungle-mall station, then quickly made their way to their office.

"I don't know about you," Wibble said, once they were off the steam-train, "but I feel like I've been chasing my own tail this whole time."

"You usually rather enjoy that," Pplimz remarked.

"When it's just for fun, sure," Wibble said, "but when I'm actually trying to get somewhere, it's a bit pointless."

"This case does seem to be rather more involved than your regular jewel heist," Pplimz agreed, as they entered the building where their office was located. "Sometimes I wonder if not a single being on this entire impossible world is who they appear to be."

"Appearances are often not an accurate depiction of the full nature of reality," Wibble reminded them.

"I agree," Pplimz said, as they approached their office. "For example, it appears as if our office is just as we left it. Door locked, premises unmolested."

"And yet." Wibble said, a teal tint to her body.

Pplimz unlocked the door, and it slid open with its usual damp slurp. The office did, in fact, appear to be entirely in order. The desk was still set up to display the contents of the data chip they'd found in Tailor the Taupe's bag, which was still sitting partially disassembled on the floor next to the desk.

All the infrared and hypersonic markers they placed at the edges of drawers and doors to show if someone had been poking around while they were out were still in place, and the desk computer was powered down. There were no signs whatsoever that an unauthorized party had entered the office, except for the fact that there was an elf sound asleep on the overstuffed burgundy velveteen couch they kept in a corner for no good reason other than Pplimz thought it tied the room together.

"What's all this then?" Pplimz said, and the elf sat bolt upright, wide awake, a stunner pistol in his hand.

"Oh, thank the Archons it's you," the elf said, lowering the pistol and relaxing back into the luscious pillows of the sofa.

"It's you!" Wibble echoed.

Tailor the Taupe smiled apologetically and shrugged. "The one and only."

CHAPTER TWENTY-FIVE
Pplimz Has an Idea

"This seemed like the last place anyone would come looking for me," Tailor said, after a joyful reunion that even featured a brief hug from Pplimz.

"I suspect that a boiling lava pool in the Everfire would be somewhat less likely," Pplimz said, drily, "but it was a clever plan."

"I know it only worked because you didn't let us in on it," Wibble said, an ominous shade of purple, "but we thought you'd been killed!"

"I'm sorry about that," Tailor said, "but I couldn't take the chance. There's no way to know who's after me. I…" He looked at the two detectives, "I assume you know it's not really the Star Alliance I'm concerned about."

"Yes, we know, Tailor the Taupe," Pplimz said. "We spoke with Dree the Lucky. Which is something you should probably do as well."

Tailor flushed but shook his head. "Not yet. Until this is all over, she won't be safe if she knows anything about where I am. I'm not about to put her in any more danger."

"You can't control that," Wibble said, fading to a pale blue.

"I know," Tailor said. "But I can do the things that are in my power, and that's not giving her any information that the Cult would want so she doesn't become a target. So, no, I won't be talking to her and I'd ask that you don't either."

The detectives reluctantly agreed, even though it wasn't a terribly good plan. Whether she knew anything or not, someone could get to Tailor through Dree. But it was his choice to make.

"So, how did you pull off your fake death?" Wibble asked. "Some kind of deep hack on the Star Alliance badge?"

"Nope," Tailor laughed. "I just stuck it on a mimicvine."

Mimicvines were semi-sentient neodymium plants found in the Macis Swamp. They were harmless, but they had the singular quality of simulating the organic makeup of the being to last handle them. Technologists and spies from several factions had tried to use mimicvine cuttings to fool bio-readers, but all attempts had failed. The plant's strange property was determined to be useless, since the energy levels they emitted were so low that the forgeries always registered as if the being they were meant to impersonate was dead.

"Clever," Pplimz said. "I wish I'd thought of it."

Tailor shrugged. "I'm glad you didn't, or who knows where we'd be now."

"Well, as it is, we aren't anywhere terribly great," Wibble pointed out. "We're no closer to finding the Qubit Zirconium gem, and now there are at least two agents of the Cult of the Architects following our trail."

"That's why I'm here," Tailor said. "Not just as a place to hide, but because I was hoping you'd come back. I've had an idea that might help us track down the artifact, but it can't be me who does it – for obvious reasons."

"Which are?" Pplimz asked.

"That with who knows how many beings after me, I can't exactly go wandering around well-populated public places, which is where I think you should go next."

Wibble shimmered, her curiosity piqued. "Any particular place you had in mind?"

"If you want to track down a tool of the Architects, then you need to think like an architect. And what better place to figure out how to do that than the Memoir of the Logician and Creator."

No one spoke for a moment, then Pplimz said, "You want us to go to a museum?"

"Not just any museum," Tailor said. "The Logos museum devoted to the study of the Architects and their lore. Something in there must hold a clue to this artifact."

"Well, I do enjoy a cultural outing," Wibble said. "And museums always smell so delightfully musty!"

"Is there something in particular we should be looking for?" Pplimz asked.

Tailor shook his head. "Not that I know of. But the Cult of the Architects must have heard about the jewel and its powers somewhere, and there's nowhere else on the Crucible that has anywhere near as much data on the Architects." He shrugged. "Besides, have you got any better ideas?"

Wibble and Pplimz left Tailor in their office and caught a steam-train to the Logos Station. The Memoir of the Logician and Creator, or MLC as the few logoticians who worked there called it, was located at the edge of the Logos Macro-Research Facility at the northeast end of Hub City. They were careful to keep the public entrance to the museum just outside the boundary of the research center, ensuring that no unauthorized parties ever had access to the facility.

Not that it was a real problem – on an average day, between zero and one visitors passed through the large key-shaped gate that was the public entrance. The museum was the personal project of a strange old logotarian, and was kept up only by the volunteer efforts of her few students. Admission was free, but any visitors who did turn up were encouraged to leave their thoughts and analyses about what they learned for the logoticians to use in their research. "It's a fair trade," Wibble said, after they'd received the obligatory request speech at the sign-in kiosk.

"Maybe," Pplimz said, "but most of the so-called artifacts in here aren't much more than junk. There's no evidence whatsoever that any of the objects on display were used by the Architects, and most of them don't do anything."

"Well, they are rather old," Wibble said. "Besides, it's nice to think that something of the beings who built this place still survives. It's a connection to the past, and to the world itself."

"Even if it's all fake?" Pplimz countered.

"The sentiment is real even if the exhibits are, well…" They passed a large installation, showing a three-dimensional holo of a group of beings that were purported to be artists' impressions of what the Architects might have looked like. They appeared to be remarkably similar to a saurian in senator's robes, a human with suspiciously-Logos styled cybernetic augments, and a Brobnar giant chieftain.

"More like self-portraits?" Pplimz finished sardonically.

"There's no accounting for taste," Wibble agreed. "But they have to create these displays to fill up all the space. Not everyone is interested in glass cases filled with broken pottery." She flipped over, and changed direction, zooming ahead to a long, covered exhibit. "Ooh, look! Pottery!"

Wibble perused the items, reading about how they had been found deep underground at the site of one of the most ancient settlements in the Crucible. Nowhere did the curators explicitly claim that any of the items had actually been created or used by the Architects, but they didn't say they weren't, either.

"That's obviously a saurian wine amphora," Pplimz said, pointing at a large vessel at the center of the display. "You can buy ones just like it at half the markets in Vendus Æmbrosian."

"But this one is *old*," Wibble said, peering at the engravings.

"So are you," Pplimz said. "Should we donate you to the museum and put you on display?"

"Maybe one day," Wibble said, floating up to hover on top of an empty plinth that had a sign reading "This item temporarily removed for restoration," and striking a pose with her tail up and one flipper out. "I'd made a great exhibit!"

"Well, for now I need you helping me to find out if there's anything in this place that will help us locate that jewel," Pplimz said. "You can exhibit yourself to your heart's content when this case is solved."

Wibble gave a flick of her tail and hurried to join Pplimz as they walked into the next exhibition hall, just as the goblin security guard began striding toward her with a stern look.

They passed through several exhibits of the broken pottery

variety, as well as an interactive pavilion which offered several competing theories on the Architects' purpose in creating the Crucible. A grand experiment in diverse ecosystems, a kind of interstellar living seed vault, a home for themselves that somehow got repurposed, and no one's favorite – that the Crucible was really a prison or a zoo.

"Is there anything in this place that isn't just some fiction dreamed up to explain the unexplainable?" Pplimz complained, as they inspected a diorama of renderings of what the exterior of the Crucible might look like.

"I like this one," Wibble said, pointing a flipper at the version that depicted a giant planet encased by a solid sphere onto which the visible sky was painted on the interior.

"A bit hard to explain the *Quantum's* crash landing, isn't it?"

Wibble tilted to the side. "Not if there's a transportation mechanism that could bring a ship to the interior first," she said. "There would be plenty of space to crash between the exterior shell and the planet."

Pplimz sighed. "And this helps our investigation how?"

"Maybe the jewel is a part of the external sphere that fell off," Wibble theorized. "It could have been one of the parts that creates those twinkly lights in the night sky."

"You think the Qubit Zirconium is a falling star?"

"That would be rather nice, wouldn't it?"

"Perhaps," Pplimz said. "But a nice story isn't what we're looking for. Will you please focus, Wibble?"

"Fine," she said, only sulking a little bit. "The technology exhibition is just up ahead. Let's try there."

The room was small, and only a few items were on display. As

Pplimz had predicted, the museum's collection of Architect technology was more the result of creative speculation than historic record. Each item on display had a description of how it *might* have worked, what it *may* have been used for, and why it *could* have been deployed.

On closer inspection, none of the so-called artifacts were anything of the sort – they were all mock-ups of theorized tools, made of printed parts and assembled to look like the object in question. There was a tablet, onto which an Architect may have inscribed a plan, then deployed nanobots to assemble the finished product. Next to that was a three-fingered glove, embedded with glowing solenoids, which purported to form elemental particles into any material configuration the wearer desired. Then there was the mundane lump of rock, which was meant to illustrate the possibility of living matter that could reshape itself at will.

"Oh," Wibble exclaimed, hovering in front of a small object near the edge of the case. "Well, this explains a few things."

Pplimz joined her and peered at the prop on display. It was a metal circlet mounted on a generic bust to show that its sensors would have been connected to transmitters embedded on the Architect's head. The panel read that this object could have been used to read its operator's thoughts directly, then using an emitter mounted in its center, it would beam instructions to remote matter transmuters. Whoever had made the reproduction had used a cheap sapphire in the center to simulate the emitter.

"Does this look somewhat familiar?" Wibble asked.

"The crown is much simpler," Pplimz said, "and the jewel is obviously nothing special. But it does bear a remarkable resemblance to the Qubit Zirconium tiara."

"But this is just another nice idea," Wibble said. "You're right. There's no reason to think that any of these were real devices used by the Architects."

"No, but that doesn't stop a being from choosing to believe," Pplimz said. "You heard Zoarr and Skye Brooke talk about it. They'd want to find anything that even had a chance of being able to achieve their goals. I think they must have heard of something that remarkably resembled this device and hope got the better of them."

"It would explain why no one from the Cult was hunting for the jewel until it was set in the tiara," Wibble said. "From all accounts it had been all over half the continents of the Crucible before the Cult even started looking for it."

"And now they've decided that it's the gem itself that is the source of the power, not the tiara."

"It is a remarkable jewel," Wibble pointed out. "The combination of an exquisitely unique item, a plausible theory, and a desperate desire is enough to make even the most analytical logician bow to wishful thinking."

"It's not that they really think it's an Architect's tool," Pplimz said. "It's that they wish it were."

"Are you certain that it really isn't an artifact of the Architects?" Tailor asked, after they'd returned to the office and explained their hypothesis.

"Without having access to the gem itself, certainty is impossible," Pplimz said. "But the evidence suggests that it holds no particular power. We know that the gem had been on the Crucible before the Cult began looking for it."

"And no one has reported any sign of Architecty activity

anywhere on the Crucible in that time," Wibble added. "Either when it was set into the tiara or not. You can't prove a negative, but other than Zoarr and Skye Brooke and their friends putting so much effort into getting the jewel, there's nothing to suggest that it's got any powers at all."

"Well, that I'm not sure so about," Pplimz said. "It's definitely got some unusual properties. I just don't think they have anything to do with the Architects."

"Oh?" Tailor said, frowning.

"While we were at that sorry excuse for a museum, I analyzed everything we actually know about the Qubit Zirconium. And I've developed a new theory."

"Well," Wibble demanded, "what is it?"

"And will it help us stop the Cult of the Architects?" Tailor asked. "Even if the gem isn't the tool they are looking for, they are still out there, trying to destroy everything that keeps this world going."

"I'm not sure one theory can manage that," Pplimz admitted, "but I think it might help us round up Zoarr and Skye Brooke."

"They are the only connections to the group that we have," Wibble said. "Tracking them down is the best way we've got to stopping them all."

"All right," Tailor agreed. "Let's hear this theory of yours."

Pplimz explained well into the night, employing diagrams, mathematical formulae, and, at one particularly complex point, interpretive dance. By the time they were done, Wibble was a deep forest green in delight and Tailor rubbed at his eyes, whether in disbelief or exhaustion, they couldn't tell.

"If you're right, this would be almost as remarkable as an actual Architect's tool," Tailor said.

"In some ways, more so," Wibble said.

"But how do we prove it?" Tailor asked. "And how do we use it to lure Brooke and Zoarr?"

"We're going to need help," Pplimz said. "A very particular kind of help."

"I think I see where you're going," Wibble said.

"Well, I don't," Tailor said. "Want to fill me in?"

"I think it's time to go back to where this all started," Pplimz said. "The Star Alliance and Quantum City."

CHAPTER TWENTY-SIX
Wibble Looks on the Bright Side

"You honestly expect me to walk right back into Quantum City?" Tailor asked, incredulous.

"You said you were really more concerned about the Cult of the Architects," Wibble said. "I'm certain we can protect you en route to the Star Alliance, and they will keep you safe once we're there."

"I said more concerned, not exclusively concerned," Tailor protested. "The Star Alliance do have a writ of detainment out on me, remember?"

"If I'm right about the Qubit Zirconium, that writ won't be valid for long," Pplimz said.

"How long?" Tailor said, his pointed ears twitching.

"I'm sure a Star Alliance holding cell is relatively pleasant," Wibble said. "You know how they go on about fairness and justice. It won't be a Brobnar dungeon."

"It will still be a cell," Tailor said. "I don't do well being confined."

"Hopefully it won't come to that," Pplimz said. "But it's going to take all of us to convince them to help us. Which is more important, Tailor the Taupe – avoiding a couple of nights in custody or flushing out the Cult?"

The elf narrowed his eyes, and Wibble wondered if he was going to try to make a run for it. Instead, he sighed and nodded.

"Fine," he said. "But I'm holding you two responsible for springing me if they lock me up, got it?"

"We will do our best to help you remain a free being," Pplimz said. "Now let's get going before it gets light out."

Wibble and Pplimz hadn't chosen this building for their office only because it was affordable and aesthetically bizarre. The biologically assembled building also happened to have some additional features which were not immediately obvious to a visitor, including a completely separate underground entrance, complete with a hovercar landing platform. Pplimz popped open a secret panel in the back of the wardrobe revealing a narrow corridor set into the interior wall.

"Let's go."

They led Tailor the Taupe into the dim space, pulsing with a pale bioluminescence. This part of the building had been left undecorated, and its organic basis was readily apparent. They hurried toward the vine-like spiral which would take them to the basement, Tailor and Pplimz squishing the spongy floor with every footfall. The winding ramp was steep and narrow, but made of a slight sticky substance to facilitate climbing up or down, and they made good time descending to the underground section.

The basement was mainly used for storage by some of the other tenants, and they wove through piles of crates, past a neatly stacked heap of cleaned and varnished exoskeletons, and stopped before a gleaming high-performance street flyer.

"Please tell me that's our ride," Tailor said, eyeing the sporty vehicle with its dual Æmberæther exhausts and "go faster" racing stripes visible under the protective clear polyfilm cover.

"Sadly, no," Wibble said. "That belongs to Yassamar, the pawn broker on the first floor. And it's such a shame, e doesn't even drive it!"

"And before you ask, we aren't going to borrow it, either," Pplimz said. "That's also eirs." They gestured at the pile of bones. "I've called a hovercab."

"What?" Tailor protested. "Those are all logged by Hub Central Dispatch. We might as well walk around town with glowing signs over our heads saying 'here we are, come and get us'!"

"On the contrary, the dispatch logs will show the cab was called by Balbi Draxis of Aris Conglomerate, for a business trip with a colleague," Pplimz said, shuffling Tailor past the flyer and through the door to the underground car bay.

"Did you really think we didn't have alternate identity accounts set up?" Wibble asked. "What kind of private investigators do you think we are?"

"Okay, fine," Tailor said, "but you've only booked for two passengers?"

"If anyone is tracking us, they'll be expecting to see two beings traveling together," Pplimz said, as they began to reshape their body, increasing the bulk of their torso. When they were done, they opened a panel in their chest to reveal an empty cavity, into which Wibble – after a great deal of shimmying – successfully squished herself. "We're taking all manner of precautions, I assure you."

The hovercar arrived, its automated external menu indicating that it was, indeed, awaiting a party of two for Aris Conglomerate. Pplimz scanned a token over the reader, which flashed a yellow light, and the doors of the cab snicked open.

"Oh," Tailor said as he stepped into the roomy compartment and settled into the plush hammock seat. "This is a luxury model."

"Aris Conglomerate is a very successful operation," Pplimz said, joining him. "And it's a long ride to Quantum City."

The hovercar dropped them off at the checkpoint at the Bivouac shortly after dawn. Tailor had slept for much of the trip over, while Wibble and Pplimz planned. They waited until the automated vehicle was well out of view before Wibble squeezed out of her hiding place in Pplimz's chest.

"Thanks for the spare room," she said, stretching her body into a few different shapes before settling back into her usual ovoid.

"You're welcome," Pplimz said, reforming themself back to their usual configuration. "All right, Tailor, let's turn you in to the authorities."

Without Tailor's badge, the force fence remained in place, and PR0T3K-TR's replacement trundled out of the hutch to greet them.

"Designation?" it addressed Tailor.

"Are you sure about this?" Tailor asked Wibble, his ears fluttering nervously.

"Of course we aren't sure," she answered. "But it's our best chance. Go on and give the nice robot your designation."

Tailor sighed and gave his name to the drone, who beeped

thoughtfully and flashed a few lights on its casing. Only a few moments later, Security Officer Barros strode up at the checkpoint, and greeted Wibble and Pplimz.

"You got here quicker than I expected," she said. "So can I assume that this is the miraculously resurrected Tailor the Taupe?" She gestured toward the elf.

"Rumors of my demise were somewhat less than entirely accurate," Tailor confessed.

"Thanks to a mimicvine, according to these two," Barros said, losing the fight to keep a grin off her face. "Clever. And, thanks to that little trick, we can work out how to patch that particular security hole." She tapped at her wrist com, and the force fence flickered. "All right, come in."

Tailor glanced at Wibble and Pplimz, then tentatively took a step forward. Barros stepped aside to let him pass and he walked into Star Alliance territory proper. The detectives followed and the tiny silver robot retreated back to the hutch, its presence no longer necessary.

Barros handed Tailor a new Star Alliance badge. "Keep this on at all times," she instructed. "You are not officially under detainment, and for now I'm going to let this all play out. But if you remove the badge, you will be taken into custody. If you try to leave the Bivouac, same thing. It's the best I can offer."

"Even though we have the tiara?" Pplimz asked, producing the silver crown from inside their suit coat.

Barros took it and compared it to the holo she had on file. "It looks similar, all right," she said, "but where's the jewel?"

"Yes, that's the question, isn't it?" Wibble said. "Come on, let's go see if we can't find out."

•••

Barros escorted them across the training grounds toward the mountain that had become the SAV *Quantum*'s final resting place. Whether it had a pre-existing name or not, everyone now called it Crash's Cliff, and in its time on the Crucible the crew had built extensive laboratories in the well-guarded caverns under the mountain.

"This is highly irregular," she said, after Wibble explained what they wanted, "and I'm going have to escalate your request up the chain of command. Our research station is not open to the public, and it's rare to allow outsiders inside."

"This is a highly irregular situation," Pplimz pointed out.

"Which is why we're going to the labs, not straight to the Security Office," Barros said. "I have to admit that I'm inclined to give you two..." She glanced at Tailor. "You *three* the benefit of the doubt. Especially since it appears that Officer Zoarr failed to appear for duty this morning."

"Zoarr's missing?" Wibble asked, unsurprised.

"AWOL," Barros said, a look of distaste on her face. "When he didn't report this morning, his badge indicated that he was in his quarters, but when his training officer went to see if he was all right, he was gone. The badge was sitting on the desk next to his terminal, which had been scrubbed of all personal logs. It will take a week before he'll be officially classed as a deserter, but I can't see him being welcomed back if he does turn up. This whole business looks very bad for his future in the Star Alliance."

"I think you'll find he was never a genuine volunteer," Pplimz said. "We think he and Skye Brooke were meant to infiltrate the Alliance on behalf of another organization."

"Skye Brooke!" Barros said, "I haven't heard that name for a while. They didn't last long at all."

"Another deserter?" Wibble asked.

Barros shook her head. "No, they moved on before the end of the trial period. It happens more often than you'd think, and that's fine. Being part of the Alliance isn't just a job, it's a commitment to a set of ideals. It's not for everyone, and that's okay. Better to find out early."

"I guess Zoarr is the better spy out of the two of them," Wibble said. "No wonder he gravitated to specialize in cryptography."

Barros narrowed her eyes, but gave nothing else away. "Wait here while I talk to the research chief." She left Wibble, Pplimz, and Tailor at the entrance to the labs and disappeared through the opaque force fence in the side of the mountain.

"You think we have a chance?" Tailor asked as they waited.

"We wouldn't be here otherwise," Pplimz said.

"The Star Alliance are kind of like logotarians," Wibble said. "They're obsessed with learning new things. Only, unlike the theorists of Logos, they readily admit that others might know more than them. You can't tell me that the possibility of discovering something unique in this world isn't going to make them more than willing to help. You know, now that I think about it, we're actually helping them by letting them be a part of this."

"That's an optimistic attitude," Tailor said, skeptically.

"That's Wibble," Pplimz said, "always hoping for the best and planning for the worst."

"At the very least there's a good possibility that with half the tiara found and Zoarr missing, they'll cancel that writ of detainment," she said. "Which is, after all, what you first asked us to help you with. So I think that, no matter what, we're likely to come out of this with a win."

"There's a lot more riding on this than my writ of detainment," Tailor said. "As you pointed out yourself."

"Oh, I know," Wibble said, "I'm just highlighting the positives."

Barros returned with another human wearing a Star Alliance uniform with the image of one of the more basic models of atomic structure on a patch on the sleeve.

"This is Researcher Wilkins," she said, introducing the new officer. "She's going to help you with your little experiment."

"You don't sound like you think it's going to work, Paulie," Wilkins said with a grin.

Barros put up her hands in a sign of surrender. "I don't have the first clue whether it's even possible. That's why I'm in security not science, Joan. I'll admit that before we arrived here, I would have thought it was absurd, but…" She gestured around her. "This whole place is wonderfully preposterous. Why not add magically disappearing gemstones to the mix?"

Wilkins tilted her head. "I strongly suspect there is nothing supernatural about this phenomenon," she said, frowning, then grinned wildly. "But if there is, what an amazing discovery that would be! Come, please join me in laboratory 4." She beckoned the group to follow her.

"See you at lunch mess?" Barros called after her as they entered Crash's Cliff.

"I don't think I'll get a chance to get away today," Wilkins said.

"Well, you have to eat," Barros said, with concern. "If I don't see you at the mess, I'll get a drone to bring you something."

"Thanks, Paulie. You take good care of me." Wilkins waved and Barros smiled, then turned to go back to the security office.

"I'm sorry, but I'm afraid this is necessary," Wilkins said, as she tied a sash over Tailor's eyes. She turned to Pplimz and said, "Is there some way you can disable your visual recording system?"

"Of course," Pplimz said, and their screen face turned the image of eyes into blinking notifications that recording was off.

"And, well, what about you?" she asked Wibble.

"I echolocate," Wibble said, proudly. "I've found that sea shanties make the best blindfolds. I hope you know a good one!"

"Erm," Wilkins said, then cleared her throat and started in on a rousing rendition of "Around the Horn, a Ship Forlorn" as she led the trio through the facility.

Laboratory 4 was two levels below ground, in what had once been a naturally occurring cavern, but was now filled with gleaming instruments, arcing electrical fields, and network terminals. Two other Star Alliance crew members were in the lab, along with several drones.

"I've also got several cameras and sensor systems we can employ," Wilkins said, after removing Tailor's blindfold and telling Pplimz they could compile visual records again. "Do you think this will be sufficient?"

"No way to tell," Wibble said. "We've never done this before."

"As far as I know, no one has," Pplimz said.

Wilkins clapped her hands together. "I love breaking new scientific ground," she said, gleefully. "All right, I'm going to develop a program we can employ, using as many different observational tools as possible. Sirgle," she turned to the krxix stationed at a large device, "can you please calibrate the nano beam microscope, and Jones," she nodded at the other human officer, "please grab a particle accelerator from the rack." Each researcher barked a quick, "yes, chief" and got to their tasks.

"I'll set up the automated systems to scan continually on all frequencies, and we'll create a rota for the organic beings as well." Wilkins tapped furiously at her wrist com with one hand while gesturing at a terminal's motion interface with her other. "Will the three of you be able to take part in the experiment?"

"I wouldn't miss it for the world," Wibble said.

"If we find what we're looking for, I want to be here for it," Tailor agreed.

"Excellent!" Wilkins said. "I'll put us all on four hour overlapping rotations, so there will always be two people on watch at any given time. In your off shifts, it would be best to leave the lab…" She broke off, frowning. "Oh. That's going to be a problem for the three of you." She looked at Wibble, Tailor, and Pplimz, then she snapped her fingers. "No, it's not!" she said, and then opened a drawer in the lab bench.

She rummaged through the materials inside, which were a chaotic jumble of bits and pieces completely at odds with the otherwise extremely orderly lab. After a moment she triumphantly brandished a small, gray disc.

"We can use the PPPTs!"

"What's a PPPT?" Tailor asked.

"A point-to-point personal translocator," Wilkins said. "It's based on martian tech, but don't tell anyone I told you that. It's got a maximum range of five miles, but that's enough. I can set it so that you're molecularly transferred from the lab to a spot just outside the entrance to the Cliff. Then you can go do whatever you need to in your off shifts, come to the entrance when you need to return and – *pop!* – translocate yourselves directly back to the lab."

Tailor frowned. "Is that safe?"

"Oh, sure," Wilkins said, digging out two more of the discs, "I use them all the time. Really cuts down on the commute." She spent a moment with a set of fine probes and a magnification loupe to program the discs, then handed them out.

Wibble grabbed hers with a flipper and slapped it onto the side of her body. "How does this work? Do I just push this butto–"

Wibble shimmered in a most un-Wibble-like manner, then disappeared.

CHAPTER TWENTY-SEVEN
Pplimz Pushes Buttons

"That device had better be in full and complete working order," Pplimz said, in a dangerously cool tone of voice.

"Oh, I'm sure it will be fine," Wilkins said, frowning. "Of course, her physiology is so weird, there's no way to be absolutely completely certain until–"

The air next to Pplimz shimmered and Wibble popped back into the lab, her body a bright green with streaks of pink at the edges.

"Ooh, that was extraordinary!" she squealed. "A little bit itchy, though." She shook herself like a skyhound then bobbed up and down. "You should really give it a try, Pplimz. The in-between bit is very... amorphous."

"I'm not sure that amorphous is an experience I particularly wish to undergo," Pplimz said, but pressed the button on their own disc. With a shimmer they were gone, then, a most disconcerting moment later, they returned.

"Well," Wibble asked, hovering excitedly in front of Pplimz's face, "wasn't it something?"

"It certainly was that," Pplimz said, brushing imaginary dust off the lapels of their suit coat, then turning to Wilkins. "This will be acceptable."

"All right!" Wilkins said, then went back to her plans.

"What about me?" Tailor asked. "Don't I get a say in all this?"

"You're welcome to try it out now," Wilkins said, not looking up from her work. "All of you. There is still a great deal of work we need to do to prepare the lab, and we aren't going to be ready to begin until tomorrow. Here's the schedule." She handed a rewritable pad to Tailor, which listed each shift. Wilkins had made sure that a Star Alliance researcher was always on duty, paired along with Wibble, Pplimz, or Tailor. "See you tomorrow!" She waved at them without looking up, effectively dismissing them.

"Come on, Tailor," Wibble said. "Give it a go! What's the worst that could happen?"

"I could rematerialize inside a spiderbear web?"

"Oh really," Wibble said, dismissively. "There are far worse things that could happen than that. Let's go, already!" She pressed her button and vanished. Pplimz shrugged and did the same.

Tailor looked around the small, bustling lab. "Well, it's probably better than being cooped up in here." He pressed the button, and in an eyeblink found himself standing next to Pplimz outside the entrance to the labs.

"See," Wibble said, "that wasn't so bad, was it?"

Tailor shivered. "How many times do we have to do that, again?"

"There's no way to know," Pplimz said. "Could be two, could be a hundred and two."

Tailor's ears twitched.

"Come on," Wibble said. "Let's go find Tailor a room."

Officer Barros had arranged for the three of them to have access to an empty junior officer's quarters in the Bivouac. Not Zoarr's, as it turned out, as he was still only considered to be absent without leave, but their borrowed room was within sight of the initial heist.

"There are meals available in the mess hall for anyone who needs them," Barros said, then glanced at Pplimz. "And feel free to recharge anything that requires power." She patted the fold-down cot in the corner. "I'm afraid there's only one bed."

"Not a problem," Wibble said, floating up to the ceiling. "Pplimz and I never use the things."

The officer offered no comment, instead instructing them on how to work the electronic latch on the door before leaving.

"Well," Tailor said, pacing around the single room. "I suppose it's not technically a cell."

"Right," Wibble said, practicing with the latch and opening the door. "We can leave, for one thing."

"Well, you can," Tailor said, pouting. "It's not fair. Zoarr and Skye Brooke were the ones who actually did something wrong, but I'm the one who's stuck here."

"Could be worse," a voice from the corridor said, and then Véronique So poked her head through the doorway. "In fact, we all thought it was rather a great deal worse."

"Vee!" Tailor said excitedly, and bounded off the cot and over to the door. They smacked outstretched hands repeatedly in a complex pattern, then Tailor jumped back to look at her. "I'm sorry about the whole faking my own death business," he said, sheepishly.

"You should be," she said. "But I get it. And I'm just glad you're all right."

"For now," he said, settling back onto the cot. "If we don't manage to get the gem back, who knows what will happen?"

"With Zoarr gone AWOL, I don't see how Star Alliance security can hold you," So said.

"Not to mention that we have the tiara," Pplimz said, placing the silver crown on the desk. "At least most of it."

"It doesn't matter," Tailor said, dejectedly. "The complaint has already been lodged. The writ is in effect whether Zoarr is here or not. And the gem is still missing. They can say I stole it and no one can prove I didn't."

So shook her head. "The Star Alliance believes that all people are innocent until proven guilty. They can't hold you on this flimsy evidence."

"Oh, Vee, you're a true believer," Tailor said. "I'm afraid I don't have your faith in their system. Not until I've been cleared and the writ cancelled."

An uncomfortable silence settled upon the group until Wibble broke it.

"Well, on a brighter note, you being effectively in the custody of the Star Alliance means you're probably safe from the Cult. You should really let Dree the Lucky know that you're all right."

"I suppose Star Alliance security aren't keeping it a secret that I'm here," Tailor said. "Fine. I'll contact her." He looked at the group in the room. "Mind if I get a little privacy?"

"Of course," Pplimz said, and moved to the still-open door. It wasn't as if Tailor could get very far if he did decide to make a run for it. "Let's all go for a walk. Anything we can get for you, Tailor?"

"How about the Qubit Zirconium jewel?" the elf said, forcing a smile. "Failing that, a confession from Zoarr that he set me up?

"No guarantees," Wibble said, "but we'll do our best."

"It's really good to see you again, Tailor," Véronique said. "Really."

"You too," Tailor said, and pulled a pocket coms device from one of his many hidden pockets, then latched the door behind them.

"Do you think that Zoarr really did try to frame Tailor?" Wibble asked, as the three of them strolled along the path near the training grounds.

"No," Pplimz said, "not exactly. Zoarr truly believes that the tiara was stolen. Maybe he knew that Tailor was working against the Cult when Zoarr accused him, or maybe he was just looking for a likely suspect. But I don't think it was more than that."

"Hang on," Véronique said, stopping. "What do you mean he 'believes' the tiara was stolen. It was, wasn't it?"

"We think maybe not," Wibble said. "Not in any true sense of the word." She explained Pplimz's theory, and Véronique's mouth dropped open.

"Could that possibly be real?"

"There's a whole team from the science branch working on it," Pplimz said. "It will be quite an unprecedented experiment."

"We're helping!" Wibble said, and explained the watch rotation that Researcher Wilkins had devised.

"I've never heard of anything like this," So said. "I bet those researchers are almost as keen as Tailor is that this works. It would be a real scientific coup for the Alliance."

"I'm sure you could join us if you were interested," Pplimz said.

So shook her head. "I can't, I have duty. And besides, this is a science branch operation. I'm in engineering. There's a bit of a rivalry between the theoretical and the applied around here. I can't see them wanting some grease monkey getting her paws on their project." She grinned, then glanced at her wrist com. "Speaking of which, I need to get going. Let me know how it goes." She jogged off toward the barracks.

"I've met several niffle apes before," Wibble said after So had gone, "but I've never heard of a grease monkey."

"There are more strange lifeforms on this world than any of us could possibly imagine, Wibble," Pplimz said. "After all, there's you."

"And you," she said, fondly.

"None more strange," Pplimz agreed. "Come on, let's clear out of Cynthala's. There's no need to pay for another room when we're guests of the Star Alliance."

The Cynthala behind the desk was a small, scuttling being with six claw-like legs and a pair of glorious turquoise and magenta wings. He oozed a miasma of fog as they entered the office, his wings beating patterns into the air which shaped the mist into words.

"How can Cynthala help you today?"

"Checking out," Wibble said. "We were in the Green Circle room, but we're moving on."

"Very well," Cynthala wrote, and tapped out their invoice on a terminal. "I trust your stay has been satisfactory."

"Yes, indeed," Pplimz said, placing their suitcase down next to their feet.

"Please do rate and review us on the Local Group Guidebook

forum," Cynthala said, as he finalized their bill.

"We'd be happy to," Wibble said.

"I hope we see you again soon," Cynthala said, his front antennae wiggling courteously as he handed them the bill. "Oh, did the parties who were looking for you manage to reach you? A human and a giant, I believe, and they were dressed in rather unconvincing Sanctum knight disguises."

Wibble and Pplimz glanced at each other.

"Zoarr and Skye Brooke," Wibble said.

"They did not provide their names," Cynthala said, "but they were asking after you in the tavern. Not as subtly as they thought, I'm afraid."

"When was this?" Pplimz asked.

"Earlier today," Cynthala said. "I imagine they are still in the Horizon, if you wish to find them. None of the scheduled transports have left yet."

"We'll ask around," Wibble said.

"Thank you for your help," Pplimz said.

"You are most welcome," Cynthala said, bowing gracefully, then added, "Please feel free to mention it in your review."

"I have to admire Zoarr's commitment to the cause," Wibble said. "It's a bold move to come back here when he's not likely to be warmly welcomed back into the Star Alliance fold."

"I doubt he has any interest in rejoining the Alliance," Pplimz said. "Its utility for him has long since been exhausted."

"Sure, but he's more likely to take over Tailor's spot on the writ of detainment if he turns up there again," Wibble said. "The Star Alliance might be peaceful explorers, but I doubt they tolerate infiltrators in their midst. Not that I have any problem with that. What Zoarr hopes to accomplish cannot be allowed, and detaining him is a good start to that."

"Skye Brooke and Zoarr have worked hard to obtain the Qubit Zirconium, and I'm not surprised they aren't willing to give up now. Shall we see if they are still in the area?"

"I have a different idea," Wibble said, a golden rose color coming over her body. "Obviously, they are looking for us in the hopes that we'll lead them to the gem. Why don't we give them what they want?"

"But we don't have the gem," Pplimz pointed out.

"No, but we might. And that's not what I meant. I'm not saying we should give it to them, most definitely not. But perhaps we might lead them in a particular direction."

Pplimz's screen face lit up. "Toward where we hope the gem *will* be," they said.

"Exactly!" Wibble agreed. "One of the most heavily guarded parts of Star Alliance territory."

"That's very sneaky, Wibble," Pplimz said.

"Thank you." Wibble bounced up and down. "I do try."

They spent the rest of the day in the Horizon, talking to any being who would listen about their plans to locate the gem. Most of the merchants were only interested until it became clear that there was no opportunity for trade, but a few of the visitors to the area were fascinated by the fact that Wibble and Pplimz had gained access to the Star Alliance's underground laboratories.

"We'd heard rumors of arcing electricity shooting out of cracks in the mountain," a visiting tourist said, after overhearing Wibble talking to a bored companionship bot. The tourist was a conjoined wraith with the heads of two owls and the body of a frost wolf. The two heads swiveled toward her, their glowing red eyes betraying a hunger for gossip.

"And even the occasional small explosion," their second face added. "Is it true? Are they building a massive world-breaking weapon under there?"

"Or is it an artificial wormhole to transport large objects across the Crucible, or even beyond?"

"I couldn't say," Wibble said, enigmatically. "I have only been inside the one laboratory myself, and there were neither weapons nor wormholes anywhere to be seen. But the research complex is enormous – who knows how deep underground it goes. There could be anything down there."

The spirit's heads turned to face each other. "The Star Alliance isn't likely to be creating a super weapon," the one on the left said. "Every being knows they are not hostile."

"That's only what they want us to think," the other face argued. "If they are so peaceful, why do they carry hand weapons?"

"Look around you!" the first face said. "We can count the unarmed beings in this tavern on the toes of one paw and still have claws left over to scratch ourselves with." As if to demonstrate the point, they brought up a huge paw and swiped at the side of one neck.

Wibble left the being arguing with themselves and went to find Pplimz, who had joined a group of Vaultwarriors on a break between raids.

"So you're saying this gem isn't even Æmber," the small, wiry, mutant scorpionsnail said, confused. "Why does anyone care about it?"

Pplimz shrugged. "Not every being is only interested in Æmber."

The group broke into peals of laughter. "Did you just arrive here at dawn, pal?" the human dressed in a Shadows cloak said. "On the Crucible there's Æmber and there's survival, and that's about it. Those Star Alliance people will figure that out eventually." She took a deep draft of her ale, then banged the empty tankard down on the table. "Come on. We've got a long battle ahead of us." She rose and led the rest of her team into the back rooms of the inn, the scorpionsnail's trail leaving an acrid acid burn in their wake.

"Making friends?" Wibble asked Pplimz.

"Probably not," they admitted. "But the word is getting out. If the Cult of the Architects have even the slimmest of networks here, Skye Brooke and Zoarr will know that we're trying to find the gem at the Star Alliance labs."

"Now it's just a question of how badly they want the Qubit Zirconium," Wibble said.

"Either way, we've got a lot of work ahead of us," Pplimz said. "Let's get back to the Star Alliance barracks. I could use a charge."

CHAPTER TWENTY-EIGHT
Wibble Sees Something

The next day, Tailor had the first watch. Wibble and Pplimz joined him at the lab to get an overview of the plan – and keep an eye out for Zoarr or Skye Brooke.

"You see anyone unusual around here?" Wibble asked the security officer on duty at the entrance to Crash's Cliff. The officer blinked at her slowly, as if contemplating whether or not to say what was on her mind, when Wibble said, "Aside from us, of course."

The officer grinned. "Nope. Only you three."

Pplimz gave her the descriptions of the two agents of the Cult, and the officer nodded.

"We're already on the lookout for those two," she confirmed. "If they show up anywhere in Alliance territory, we'll find them."

"I like the confidence!" Wibble said. "Come on, let's translocate." She pressed the button on her disc to transport to the lab, and Tailor and Pplimz followed.

Wilkins herself was the Star Alliance researcher on duty and she greeted them wearing a monocular headset with wires that attached to her shaved head. The orange-tinted lens was rimmed in thick Æmbersteel with a lightweight frame that kept the goggle firmly in place.

"The machines are already calibrated and have begun their scans," she informed them. "I've created a stasis field on this workbench that contains an environment I believe will be conducive to the phenomenon. Now all we have to do is observe."

"But there's nothing there," Tailor said, staring at the empty workbench.

"Nothing that we can see at the moment," Wilkins said. "But we have to work under the assumption that there's a probability that it is there, and we simply are not yet observing it. What we have to do is find that probability, hold on to it, and hope that the observation will be strong enough."

Wilkins dragged over a pair of comfortable lab stools to the workbench, and she and Tailor settled in for the first shift.

"Hold the image of the gem in your mind," Wilkins said. "Try to concentrate on it completely. I am aware that this is not entirely possible, but the goal is that at least one of us is watching and thinking of the jewel at all times. We want to be employing all forms of observation at once, for maximum coverage." She glanced up at Wibble and Pplimz. "Can you two please leave? We don't need any distractions."

"Of course," Pplimz said. "See you in four of your hours."

Observing an object that is not technically *there* turned out to be a rather tiring task. The machines and drones had no problem, of course, and of the organic beings involved Pplimz had the easiest time of it. Before their first shift they took the time to write a subroutine to monitor the lab for any traces of the Qubit Zirconium and set that task as the highest priority item in their operating system, then single threaded themself for the duration of their shift. Pplimz had no trouble with lapses in concentration but it was, they admitted to Wibble later, frightfully boring.

Wibble and Tailor, on the other hand, were exhausted after each shift. "I can't tell if it's the mental effort involved in holding the image of the gem in my mind or the constant narrow-band high frequency clicking sound that's wearing me out," Wibble said, floating upside down in the corner of the ceiling of their Star Alliance quarters, "but this is harder than that cloudhopper marathon."

"You slept for three days after that race," Pplimz reminded her.

"Those were a good three days," she said, then turned completely translucent and fell asleep.

She was still out when Pplimz left for their next shift and Tailor returned, threw himself on to the cot, and tucked his knees up to his nose. He was still snoring when the alarm went off and Wibble hovered sleepily off to the lab for her watch.

"When I was a little scuttler," Junior Researcher Sirgle said, arranging her legs in the stirrups on her chair, "all I ever wanted to be was a scientist. Making breakthroughs, learning more about the universe, increasing the store of knowledge among all sapient beings! It was so exciting." She lowered her thorax to the padded seat. "No one told me how much of it was going to be looking for something that wasn't there."

"You've done this experiment before?" Wibble asked, surprised.

Sirgle's antennae bobbed in a negative response. "I don't mean literally looking at nothing; this is a new one for me. But it turns out that plenty of experiments don't actually prove the hypothesis. For every breakthrough, there are countless failed attempts – looking for an answer that is either false or not attainable from your methodology. Science is more about patience than brilliance. I understand that now."

"Investigation is the same," Wibble said, wedging herself under the bottom edge of a cabinet facing the workbench. "Don't tell anyone I told you that – I wouldn't want to lose the image of the genius consulting detective."

Sirgle grinned, then donned a distraction cancelling headset, and gazed intently at a spot about two centimeters above the counter of the workbench, relieving Researcher Jones, who pulled off his own headset and rubbed his eyes. He and Pplimz left the lab without a word, handing over the watch to Wibble and Sirgle.

Pplimz would have been able to say how many watches had passed if they hadn't taken all their unnecessary processing offline for each of their sessions in the lab. But as it was, time had ceased to have any meaning for the entire observation team. They put in their time in the lab, then came back to their quarters to rest (Wibble and Tailor), eat (Tailor), and recharge (Pplimz). Anything going on outside the world of the lab and their quarters might as well have been on another planet entirely. For all they knew, Zoarr and Skye Brooke had been detained, debriefed, and the entire Cult of the Architects disbanded. Alternatively, they might have tracked down the gem themselves and were setting about using it for whatever worldaltering schemes their group had planned. They assumed someone would come and tell them if their work was no longer needed, but, until then, they stuck to the program.

It had become so routine that at first neither Wibble nor Sirgle realized that what they were seeing wasn't just their own mental image of the Qubit Zirconium. In their defense, it was incredibly faint and phasing in and out of their region of spacetime, but it took one of the sensors emitting a discordant beep before they knew that it was finally happening.

Wibble kept her focus on the nascently forming gem, while Sirgle sent an urgent message to the others to join them, then went back to her own observation. It didn't take long for Wilkins, Jones, Pplimz, and Tailor the Taupe to arrive, entering the lab with quiet enthusiasm to watch the event they'd all long hoped to see.

The stasis field seemed to be holding as within it the image of an iridescent jewel appeared. It was not entirely dissimilar to a holo-image, but somehow both more and less solid. The heart of the gem sparkled like a million tiny stars, each emitting a glow and color of its own. Overall, the jewel glowed with a soft greenish light, its shape shifting between curved and angular as it became more and more solid.

"It's happening," Wilkins whispered, as they watched the gem appear to solidify. As it became more present, the stasis field itself started to become visible.

"Why is the field doing that?" Jones asked, leaning in toward it. "It's as if there isn't enough room inside, but that jewel is no more than a tenth of the volume."

"It's not the volume or the mass that's putting a strain on the field," Sirgle said, tapping on her wrist com furiously. "It's the energy! I'm reading a massive increase in joules, and it's not showing any signs of slowing."

"She's right," Wilkins said. "Increase the field size. Now!"

Jones adjusted some dials and the edges of the stasis field became invisible again. The gem pulsed with an otherworldly light, its color slightly shifting with the beats.

"The spectrum appears to be limited to about a hundred nanometers, between 475 and 575," Wilkins said, adjusting her monocle lens with one hand while making notes with the other. "And I'm reading a slow but steady increase in mass."

"It's becoming solid," Pplimz said, and Wilkins nodded.

"Not only solid," she added. "Its fluctuations are slowing down. It's transitioning from possible to probable to actual." She flipped up the lens on her headset and looked around the room. Her face was flushed and she probably needed a meal and a bath, but she was radiant in triumph.

"We did it!" she said, joyfully raising both arms in the air.

And they had. The Qubit Zirconium gem itself was floating in the stasis field on the workbench, large as life and twice as beautiful. They had observed its inherent quantum states enough that its myriad probabilities had coalesced into becoming a single solid object here, in the lab.

Because it turned out that the gem was no Architect's tool or Æmberweapon. It was a quantum crystal, always in flux, its state of being a matter of probabilities and observation. And exactly like nothing anyone had ever seen before.

Once they'd determined that the gem was stable – for now – the group took a well-deserved break, leaving only a single organic being at a time to watch the jewel along with the machine observers. Wilkins chose to stay first, telling her team that they deserved a rest.

"I think she isn't willing to let it out of her sight just yet," Wibble suggested after they'd translocated out of the lab.

"It is a career-making discovery," Pplimz said. "It's fair that she'd want to bask in the glow of success for a little while."

"Well, I want to bask in the glow of a nap," Tailor said, yawning widely. "And then I'm going straight to Star Alliance security to get that writ canceled."

"An excellent plan," Wibble said. "Although I've got more energy now than I've had in days. It must be the satisfaction of a job well done."

"Hmm," Pplimz made a noise that implied they were not convinced that Wibble should be entirely satisfied.

"What's bothering you?" she asked. "Tailor asked us to help clear his name, and we've done that. With all parts of the tiara here in Star Alliance territory, none of which were ever found in Tailor's possession, I can't imagine they could find any reason to hold him."

"No, I don't either," Pplimz said. "So I suppose that technically you are correct, that we have fulfilled our contractual obligation."

"But?"

"But there are a few things still bothering me. Who are the Cult of the Architects, and what other plans do they have? Where are Zoarr and Skye Brooke? And who really owns the Qubit Zirconium tiara?"

"Oh no," Wibble said, deflating.

"What's wrong?"

"You're going to want to visit that overly friendly quartermaster again, aren't you?"

"An excellent suggestion," Pplimz said, brightening. "I'm glad you thought of it!" They set off briskly toward the Procurement Office.

"Ugh." Wibble watched Pplimz go, then reluctantly followed.

"Well, hello! I was hoping the two of you would pop by again," Piten said, when Wibble and Pplimz entered the quartermaster's office. "I enjoyed our previous conversations so very much. Would you believe that just the other day an ice gnome from the Underfrost came by and tried to sell us cybernetic enchantments? As if anyone in the Alliance would be willing to install an unregulated hex mod. Ridiculous! The absolute nerve of the being."

"How interesting," Pplimz said. "Say, do you remember the two procurement orders we asked about the last time we were here? For the silver tiara?"

"Oh, yes." Piten nodded vigorously, their antenna bobbing wildly as they scanned packages and tapped on their terminal. "That really was most irregular, and I have to admit that I was somewhat disappointed in myself for not having noticed. I will confess that after you left, I found that could not stop thinking about how that could have occurred, so I went back to review the requisitions in my off hours. Wouldn't you know that there was, in fact, something amiss with one of the orders."

"Was there, really?" Wibble said, actually engaged in the conversation at last.

"There was!" Piten's antenna vibrated. "A cursory inspection of both orders revealed nothing untoward, of course, or I would have noticed when you asked me about them. But when I confirmed that the checksums were correct – which they were, incidentally – I noticed something odd about the timestamp. Ordinarily, it wouldn't have been anything to remark upon, but we had taken the entire inventory system offline for a short while in order to install the new Æmber-based power supply. It was not an outage that was communicated widely to staff, as any incoming orders would simply be queued in the buffer and added to the system when it was relaunched. There was no interruption to regular service standards, I assure you! But there was a period of several hours where a new procurement order could not possibly have been entered into the system. And yet . . . !"

Piten actually stopped talking for a brief moment, to Wibble's great surprise.

"And yet what?" she demanded, eventually.

"And yet one of the requisition orders for the silver tiara was timestamped for the period the system was offline. How could that be, unless it was inserted into the system at some other time, but made to look as if it had entered the queue in the normal fashion?"

"So you're saying that one of the orders was a forgery," Pplimz confirmed.

Piten's head bobbed up and down excitedly. "It was!" The quartermaster stopped scanning and tapping for a moment and leaned in toward Wibble and Pplimz. "And it was Officer Zoarr's request that was the false entry," they whispered.

The detectives looked at each other.

"Well I can't say I'm terribly surprised," Wibble said. "Zoarr was here as a spy, after all, so it makes sense that he'd be doing spy things."

"He probably made sure his requisition was higher priority than Véronique So's, to ensure that the tiara would be delivered to him," Pplimz guessed.

"It would have worked, too, if the gem hadn't decided it wanted to be somewhere else for a while," Wibble said.

Pplimz chuckled. "I don't think quantum states work that way," they said, then froze, a wild idea forming in their positronic mind. "But what if this one does?"

CHAPTER TWENTY-NINE
Pplimz Says Something

"Do you have any evidence for this hypothesis of yours?" Officer Bryn Suryamanjaya of the First Contact Branch (Finance Department) asked Pplimz, after they'd explained their request. "The Star Alliance takes the discovery of a new form of life very seriously, and they aren't likely to be very happy if it turns out to be a wild goose chase."

"I most certainly do not think that the gem is related in any way to an Earth-based waterfowl of the Anatidae extraction," Pplimz said, surprised that someone from First Contact Branch would be trying to avoid determining if the Qubit Zirconium was, in fact, a new lifeform.

Suryamanjaya stifled a chuckle. "It's just a turn of phrase… oh, never mind. What I'm saying is that no one will be terribly pleased if we spend a lot of time and energy on something that turns out to be nothing."

"I'm sure Chief Researcher Wilkins and her team would disagree with you there," Wibble said.

"Yes, the science branch does tend to try to ignore our budgetary constraints," Suryamanjaya said. "If it were up to them, we would attempt anything and everything regardless of the cost. But the reality is that we have to prioritize. So, can you convince me that this is worth prioritizing?"

"I don't know how I could possibly do that," Pplimz said. "It's a theory that could easily be wrong. And what value can you place on a life, anyway?"

"Well, without a clearer return on investment calculation, I'm not at all sure that we can proceed with this project," Suryamanjaya said, curtly.

"You do realize the incredible potential you're passing up here?" Wibble retorted. "Is that really what First Contact Branch is for – choosing not to seek out new life if it's at all inconvenient?"

"I have no doubt that the other areas of the branch would be as excited as you are to pursue investigating this possible lifeform," Suryamanjaya admitted. "But that's why everything has to go through Finance first. Someone has to be realistic around here."

"I don't believe this," Pplimz said, exasperated.

"Come on, let's go," Wibble said. "I might have an idea."

At first, Chief Researcher Wilkins was adamantly against the idea. But when Pplimz showed her the recording of their conversations with Officer Bryn Suryamanjaya, she was appalled.

"The Star Alliance I joined would never be concerned with something as mundane as the cost if there was a possibility of finding a new kind of life." She gripped her input stylus so tightly that the unbreakable alloy flexed. "'Return on investment?' The return is adding to our knowledge of the universe. The investment is our entire mission! This is what happens when a ship that is meant to be traversing the stars is stuck in one place. We lose sight of what's really important." The rage subsided and she sank into a chair, gazing at the pulsing gem in its containment field. "What a disappointment."

Wibble gave her a moment, then said gently, "We're not asking for any data other than what pertains to the Qubit Zirconium. You can firewall your system however you like, move the information to an air-gapped data crystal, whatever you need to feel secure. But with direct and complete access, Pplimz has the onboard capability to conduct the tests we need to perform. We can do this entire experiment without First Contact Branch, if you just give us access to the data you have."

Wilkins looked at Pplimz, who was quietly awaiting her decision, fiddling with the hat in their hands. "Fine," she said, nodding once. "It's not as if you couldn't have been recording all this data yourselves anyway, since you had access to the lab the entire time. Okay, here's how it's going to work."

She laid out a strict protocol for Pplimz to follow: they'd be given access to a crystal with the existing data, and from now on the lab would be isolated from the rest of the Star Alliance network, so Pplimz wouldn't be able to find their way into the rest of the system, or share their findings with any other network.

"This is an acceptable arrangement," Pplimz said. "Let's begin."

It took some time to get Pplimz set up, but then they asked to be left alone to analyze the data and try to communicate with the gem.

"You really think you'll be able to talk to it?" Sirgle asked.

"Likely not," Pplimz said, their suit coat removed and shirtsleeves rolled up, a tangled nest of wires now leading from the lab's terminal to their arms. "After all, I am capable of speaking with only some forms of sapient life. Most lifeforms are beyond my abilities. But even if the attempt is almost guaranteed to fail, it is surely worth trying."

"Besides," Wibble said, "even if they can't have an actual conversation, Pplimz might be able to communicate with the gem somehow. Like patting a squidlet on its dorsal flank or giving a robo-mite scratches under the ears."

"I promise not to pat the Qubit Zirconium," Pplimz said, in response to Wilkins's horrified expression. "On my honor, I shall leave it safe in its stasis field, unspoiled."

"All right," Wilkins said, visibly uncomfortable with the idea of leaving the gem alone in another being's care.

"You'll know if anything happens," Wibble assured her. "This lab is probably the most highly surveilled place in all of the Crucible right now." She gestured at the many devices still tasked with observing the Qubit Zirconium gem.

"But with the network connection severed, I won't know anything until after the fact," Wilkins complained.

"True," Wibble said. "But you either trust us or you don't. And if you don't, you'll never find out if what you've discovered is a fascinating new object or an incredible new being."

Wilkins sighed. "Okay. Paulie told me that the two of you have always been honest with her, and she thinks you're as good as your word. If she's going to vouch for you, there isn't much more I can ask for."

"Officer Barros said that about us?" Pplimz asked, pleasantly startled. "How lovely."

"All right, enough basking in your accolades, Pplimz," Wibble said. "The sooner you get to it the sooner you'll get out of there."

They all left Pplimz alone in the lab, Wibble translocating to the entrance to the cavern system while the others made their exit the slow way. She didn't bother to wait for them. While Pplimz was busy with the gem, she had her own theory to test.

Heady Burke's Clandestine Casino was as busy as always when Wibble floated in. There were players at most of the tables, trying their luck and losing the Æmbits they'd just won in a vain attempt to walk out the door with more than they'd had when they arrived. Somehow, though, the house always won, and Wibble wondered how much of it was the odds on the games and how much of it was Shadows technology in the mechanisms. Either way, the players knew what they were getting into, and it was all part of the appeal – trying to beat a system designed to win.

She passed a kiosk with flashing lights, aromatic mist, and a set of brightly colored balls, the gray and blue liveried staff member beckoning players over with promises of a winner on every play. Tempting as it might be, Wibble was singular in her focus to get to the bar area at the back of the casino. Her quarry was in sight, sipping a bright pink drink with a large piece of fruit sticking out of it.

"Training Officer Levesque," Wibble said, hovering next to the human's right shoulder, "how nice to see you again."

"Of course," Helene Levesque said, a tight smile on her face. "Wibble, isn't it? I heard the good news that Taupe was found unharmed. And that the tiara wasn't really stolen after all? It's all very strange."

"Yes, it is," Wibble said. "Quite strange all around. In particular, I found it especially odd that no one realized that Officer Zoarr wasn't really here to become a Star Alliance crew member."

"Wasn't he?" Levesque asked, her face a caricature of surprise.

"Come now, officer," Wibble said. "Zoarr is a good spy, but he was a Star Alliance trainee. They don't get a lot of freedom from scrutiny. It would have been hard for his direct supervisor not to notice his clandestine meetings with Skye Brooke, for example."

"I don't know what you're talking about," Officer Levesque said, glancing past Wibble as if to look for an escape route.

"Don't you?" Wibble asked, hovering to stay in Levesque's view. "You weren't aware that former trainee Brooke was using their martian MDR to bypass the Bivouac's border and transport directly to Zoarr's quarters for their meetings? You weren't aware that they were working to secure a device that they said would allow passage beyond the Crucible's boundary, which is something you've been trying to achieve since you arrived here? You weren't helping Zoarr stay undercover and you aren't helping him and Skye Brooke now?"

Training Officer Levesque's eyes were wide, and it was obvious that her specialty was not counterintelligence, as Wibble's questions were clearly getting to her. Good.

"Yes, fine, I helped them." She drained her drink, settling the glass neatly on a cocktail napkin, then tapped the tabletop menu to order another. "Of course I did, I'd have done anything to help get the *Quantum* flying again. The longer we're stuck here, the more we end up being dragged into these ridiculous Archon battles. Our mission is exploration, not getting caught up in some local skirmish over treasure in vaults. We need to find a way to get past the Boundary, and if Zoarr and Skye Brooke and their friends could help us do that, obviously I'd help them. After what I'd done, I had to."

"What you'd done?"

"I let it get away in the first place," Levesque said, miserably. "I had a component to something that could solve all our problems and because it wasn't exactly what I expected, I sold it. I had to do something to atone for my mistake. So when Zoarr asked me for help after the two of you turned up, how could I refuse?"

"But it wasn't a mistake," Wibble said. "You know the Qubit Zirconium isn't really an Architect's tool, right? It's not going to set the *Quantum* free."

"Maybe not," Levesque said, "but something else might. This whole business has made me even more certain that Zoarr and Brooke and their friends are our best hope."

"That's why you're here, passing them information so they can stay a step ahead of Star Alliance security."

She nodded. "You can turn me in if you like," she said, stoically, "but I know that even if they strip me of my rank that I was doing my duty as a Star Alliance officer."

"I don't think that will be necessary," Wibble said, "if you tell me how to find them."

Levesque shook her head. "I'd rather be detained by security and face disciplinary charges."

"I was afraid you might say that," Wibble said, genuinely disappointed in Levesque's choice, then sent a message on a modified wrist com that she wore on her right flipper. Officer Barros joined them, and looked at Levesque with sadness.

"Helene," she said. "I never would have thought it was you."

"Save the speech for someone else," Levesque said, rising to go with Officer Barros. "I did what I thought was right, and that's the most anyone can expect."

"I suspect Captain Jericho might disagree," Barros said. "But we'll find out soon enough. Okay, let's go." She led Officer Levesque out of the casino, neither the players nor the staff noticing one bit in all the clamor and din.

Wibble asked around at the casino, but no one knew anything about Skye Brooke or Zoarr. Brooke hadn't been in to work since they'd gone to Kettle Bottom, and their supervisor said he hadn't heard anything.

"We get a lot of transients around here," the manager said, licking his eyeball suggestively. "Lots of our staff leave without saying goodbye. It's annoying, but you just work around it. That's part of my job."

"And I don't suppose you've seen Zoarr around here since then either?" Wibble asked.

The manager puffed out his chest in a bulbous bubble and hopped back and forth. "I wouldn't know. I don't pay much attention to the customers. I've got my pouch full organizing the staff roster."

He showed her to the pit boss, who confirmed that she hadn't seen Zoarr in the casino since Wibble and Pplimz's first visit. Wibble was sure that Officer Levesque was here to pass a message to them, though.

"Was Skye particularly close to anyone else on the staff?" she asked. "Or a customer they were unusually friendly with?"

Neither the manager nor the pit boss knew anything.

"Like I said," Skye Brooke's supervisor darted a tongue out to catch a minute flying zephyr grub on the wing. "Staff comes and goes. No one knows much about anyone. It's part of the appeal." He chewed thoughtfully on the grub, a wing dangling out of his mouth.

Wibble left them with the usual spiel about contacting her if they learned anything useful, but she didn't expect to hear from them. Either one of them knew something but wasn't interesting in sharing, or they just didn't care that much.

Wibble was about to leave the casino, when an autobot rolled out of a hatch at the end of the bar to clean up the empties. She saw it collect Levesque's two glasses in its sanitizer bay, then sweep the damp napkin into a recycling chute.

"Oho!" Wibble said aloud to no one. "Maybe there was no other accomplice after all."

She made straight for the lid of the recycler and dove into it, following the tight tunnel down into where it emptied over a large bin full of old napkins, beak straws, and betting slips. The bin was in an underground bay that was open to the back of the casino, presumably to make it easy for whoever collected the recycling to come in and out. But anyone could get in there any time, and it made for a perfect dead drop.

Wibble dove into the bin, her flippers and tail tossing items around until she found what she was looking for. The napkin under Levesque's drink with the message she'd written on it, obviously intended for Zoarr and Skye Brooke.

It was short, only explaining that the Alliance had the gem in a secure lab in Crash's Cliff, and that they were likely under threat of detainment. Nothing planet-shattering there, but proof that the Cult of the Architects had at least one other accomplice in the Star Alliance beyond Zoarr and Brooke.

Wibble quickly hovered back to the room in the Bivouac and

rooted through Pplimz's suitcase until she found what she was looking for. She hurried back to the underground bay at the casino to install the apparatus. It wasn't a surveillance device exactly – Pplimz had an aversion to surreptitiously monitoring beings without their consent – but it would notify her if someone else entered the area. The recycling bin wasn't terribly full, so she guessed that the collection wasn't for some time. This was likely the best opportunity to track down Zoarr and Skye Brooke, assuming she hadn't missed them in her short trip to the Bivouac and back.

She hoped very much that it would pay off, as she had a couple of questions for the giant and Mx Brooke.

How many other beings in how many other organizations were helping them? And was there anywhere on the Crucible that was safe from their quest for power?

CHAPTER THIRTY
Wibble Accepts an Invitation

"It's alive!"

Researchers Jones and Sirgle smacked open hands in delight as Chief Wilkins reviewed the report Pplimz had prepared, unable to keep the grin off her face.

"Now, let's not overdo it," Pplimz said. "Yes, I have found evidence that implies that the Qubit Zirconium is a living quantum gem. But while it is not terribly plausible, it is still possible that those readings are merely fluctuations in energy, or interference from rogue particles, or a miscalibration in my sensor array, or–"

"Pplimz." Wibble put a flipper on her partner's shoulder, and spoke to them quietly. "There are more strange lifeforms on this world than any of us could possibly imagine, remember? After all, there's you."

"And you," Pplimz replied, softly, then turned back to the rest of the team. "Yes, I believe that it is alive. But I haven't been able to establish a reliable communication stream with the gem. I don't know what it wants or why it's here, why it changes its apparent composition, and why it sometimes chooses to stay in one place and at other times chooses to exist elsewhere."

"Chooses? You think it controls its own superposition?" Wilkins asked, and Pplimz nodded.

"We know that it can exist in a state of quantum flux," Pplimz said, "we saw that for ourselves as it became extant in this stasis field. And we know that it can stay coherent in a single dimension for long periods. There are plenty of reports of it behaving like a regular inert crystal until it just goes missing. I think that those moments when it disappears are when it decides to exist elsewhere."

"But isn't our containment field forcing it to stay here?" Jones asked.

"No," Wilkins said, "what the field is containing isn't the gem itself, but rather an environment I designed to be attractive to a mineral deposit. If the gem really can essentially observe itself, it could disappear any time it wants to. There's nothing forcing it to stay here."

"I certainly hope it does, though," Sirgle said. "We've got a team of linguists and mineralogists coming on board to attempt to establish true communication with it." She fluttered her antennae happily, and turned to Wibble. "I think I've finally found my life's work. Just imagine what we could learn from each other! What does the universe look like from a quantum crystal's point of view?" She wiggled her antennae in excitement. "I know it's going to be difficult. The odds are that we'll never succeed, but how could I not try? After all, it's the tunneling that matters, not the burrow at the end."

"I couldn't have said it better myself," Wibble said, glowing nearly as green as the Qubit Zirconium itself.

Tailor the Taupe and Véronique So were waiting for them by the entrance when they left Crash's Cliff.

"We heard that Zoarr's requisition order was forged," Tailor said. "That means the tiara rightfully belongs to Véronique."

"I suppose it does," Pplimz said. "But something tells me that you might not get the exact item you purchased."

"No?" she asked.

Pplimz explained that the gem might actually be a never before seen form of life. "I don't know if the Star Alliance would allow you to own a lifeform."

"It's a gray area," So said. "Of course, people own plants, some animals, and robots. But there's a line after which something is considered an independent living being in its own right."

"That sounds like a difficult call to make," Wibble said.

"Maybe," So said. "It's self-awareness, I guess. If the being can make its own choices, and articulate those somehow, then we know it's sapient, and must be free to live its own life."

"You might want to have a talk with your superiors about your robots," Wibble said, archly, "if that's the metric you're using."

"Regardless," Pplimz said, "I strongly suspect that the Qubit Zirconium gem is unlikely to be reset into the silver tiara, unless it's by its own decision."

"That sounds fair enough," Tailor said. "It's not as if we could stop it if it decided to remove itself."

"Speaking of which," Wibble said, "is it safe to assume that you are a free elf once again?"

He grinned, showing a full set of pointed teeth. "I watched a security officer nullify the writ of detainment right in front of my eyes," he said. "There isn't even a record of it any more."

"Excellent news," Pplimz said, then turned to Wibble. "Well, I suppose that means our job here is done."

"Before you leave," Tailor said, "would you join me at Cynthala's later? It feels like a celebration is in order."

"Of course," Wibble said, before Pplimz could demur. "We wouldn't miss it for anything!"

"Wonderful," Véronique said. "We'll both see you there." She and Tailor the Taupe headed back toward the Bivouac, hugged briefly, then Véronique went toward the engineering compound while Tailor very nearly ran through the checkpoint and into the Horizon.

"Odd friendship there, don't you think?" Pplimz asked. "A human and an elf."

Wibble turned bright pink and burst out laughing. "Oh, Pplimz. You'd know a little something about odd friendships, wouldn't you?"

"I suppose I would," they said, adjusting their hat. "They are the best kind, after all."

Wibble and Pplimz were clearing out of their borrowed Star Alliance room, when a notification light on Pplimz's screen began to flash.

"It's the recycling!" Wibble said, and shot out of the room at speed. Pplimz barely managed to keep up, a particular feat since they had no idea where she was going.

They sped through the Bivouac, drawing no shortage of attention. As they passed an off-duty security officer, Wibble yelled, "Heady Burke's. Recycling room. Now!" as she zoomed past. Pplimz, now understanding what they were chasing, took a detour that would be a better ground route than Wibble's flight path, and sent a message to Officer Barros in case the officer they'd just passed was as baffled as Pplimz had been.

When Pplimz made it to the underground bay, none of the Star Alliance staff had arrived at the casino yet. But Wibble held Skye Brooke tightly in her force fingers, the cultist wriggling ineffectually, still wearing their Sanctum knight disguise.

"Nice to see you again," Pplimz said, as Skye Brooke continued to struggle. "Sorry things haven't worked out as you hoped."

"I'm not sorry," Wibble said, "you've caused quite a lot of trouble."

Officer Barros and a team of three other officers then arrived on a Star Alliance R0V3R, and took custody of the prisoner.

"Looking for that artifact wasn't breaching any of your laws," Brooke said, as the officers bundled them into the back of the vehicle.

"We'll see about that," Barros said. "Perhaps we need to update the rules and regs."

"We're trying to help you," Brooke cried. "To help everyone!"

"Well, if you'd like to tell us who the rest of your colleagues are, I'm sure Captain Jericho would be happy to find out more about this assistance you're so generously offering," Barros said.

Skye Brooke barked a laugh. "Not on your life," they said. "You'll get nothing out of me, not now, not if you throw me in the brig. So just take me away and be done with it."

The R0-V3R drove off, leaving Wibble and Pplimz with nothing but a bin full of trash.

"You think Brooke will give anything up?" Wibble asked.

"I doubt it," Pplimz said. "They are a true believer."

"They are at that," Wibble said. "Come on, let's go finish packing up. There's still a party to get to!"

There was a function room at Cynthala's that Tailor the Taupe had rented for the evening, and Wibble and Pplimz found it already packed with beings when they arrived. It seemed like half the Star Alliance was in attendance, along with a small group displaying obvious Shadows insignia. The rest were a random assortment of beings, many of whom were regulars in the market stalls of the Horizon. In a corner, an enormous, augmented cyborg niffle ape held a snifter of brandy while deep in conversation with a saurian dressed in an orator's robe.

"Nassas!" Wibble said, and hovered over to the two, interrupting their discussion.

"Ah, the detectives," Nassas said, his deep voice drawing attention from half the room. "It seems that my Guardian is to remain unemployed for some time longer."

"It's pretty conclusive that the gem is not part of an Architect's tool," Pplimz said.

"So I understand," Nassas boomed.

"Is it true that it's exhibiting signs of life?" the saurian asked, breathless.

"It is," Wibble confirmed. "And the Star Alliance has put together a team of researchers to study it and try to communicate with it."

The saurian blinked her third eyelids. "Surely the Alliance will not confine this new lifeform to a lab? That's barbaric! Why, the Republic outlawed imprisoning creatures for science millennia ago. I believe it was Alvinius Sulpicius Gaius who argued before the Senate that–"

"There's no confining of anything going on, I assure you," Pplimz broke in, before an epic lecture on saurian history could break out.

"I don't think that even Nassas's Guardian could imprison the Qubit Zirconium," Wibble added. "It goes where it likes."

Pplimz explained the gem's unique abilities, and even the saurian was quiet as they spoke.

"It is no wonder that our adversaries believed they had found an artifact from the time of the Architects," Nassas said. "Such abilities are beyond even the most advanced of civilizations on this world."

"So you're continuing in your battle against the Cult of the Architects?" Wibble asked.

"Of course," the saurian replied, revealing herself as one of Nassas's colleagues. "Just because this particular item did not confer the power they desire, that does not mean there is no such object. And we know that they will never cease in their pursuit, therefore it is imperative that we do not waver in our commitment to oppose them."

"The promise of power is a great temptation," Pplimz said.

"That is true. But in this case, the consequences are potentially far too catastrophic to ignore," Nassas said.

"I'm afraid that I have to agree," Wibble said. "I'm glad you'll be continuing your vigilance. If you ever need any help, please feel free to call on me."

Pplimz glanced over at her, noticing the care she took to use the singular pronoun. She knew they did not entirely agree about the danger of the Cult, and they were both pleased and a little sad that she made sure not to include them in her offer.

It was good fun to bicker with Wibble, but it was rare that they disagreed on anything important.

Pplimz was spared thinking about it further when a strong grip took hold of their shoulder. They turned to look down into the scowling face of Dree the Lucky.

"It's good to see you again," Pplimz said, and scanned the room. "And so many of your clan."

"This isn't a social visit," she said, angrily. "You should have contacted me as soon as you knew that Tailor the Taupe was out of danger."

"As far as we know, he still is in danger," Wibble said. "Probably will be his whole life, unless he undergoes some kind of radical personality overhaul."

Dree narrowed her eyes to only a sliver of a golden glow. "You know what I mean," she said, ominously.

"He asked us specifically not to tell anyone," Pplimz said.

"I told him he should contact you," Wibble said. "But he refused."

"Ugh!" Dree groaned. "Typical Tailor the Taupe. If I weren't so happy that he's alive I'd murder him myself."

"Surely not!" Wibble said, horrified.

"Just a Shadows figure of speech," Dree said, softening. She glanced around the room, eyeing the other beings with suspicion. "So, have you disbanded the Cult of the Architects?"

Pplimz shook their head. "Not even close. The operative we've detained isn't giving the names of any of their collaborators. And the other one we do know about is still on the loose."

"I did find a Star Alliance officer who was helping them," Wibble said, "but she wasn't part of the core group and didn't know anything useful."

"So nothing has changed," Dree said, sourly.

"While that is obviously not accurate," Pplimz said, gesturing to the rousing party, "with respect to the state of the Cult, it's true that they are mainly still at large and continue to be in operation."

Dree blew a stream of air out her nose. "It's just frustrating that after everything Tailor the Taupe went through, it isn't even over."

"As long there are rumors of artifacts that confer great power, there will be beings who desire that power," Wibble said. "So much so that they could create those rumors themselves."

"They want the device to exist so badly that they talk themselves into believing that it's real," Dree suggested.

"Perhaps," Pplimz said. "It would not be the first time such a thing has occurred."

"Well, let's just hope you're right," Dree said, as Tailor caught her eye and came over to them, his arm around Véronique's waist.

"Right about what?" he asked, bright blue face flushed in the warmth of the full room.

"Right about you settling down and finding some honest work for once," Dree said. "Like being a thief. Thieves make a real good living; you could do a whole lot worse."

Véronique laughed, and both Dree and Tailor looked confused.

"Sorry," she said. "Where I come from 'honest' and 'thief' don't really go together."

"You do keep strange company," Dree said to her brother, who shrugged and grinned.

"You know I'm not cut out for the guilding life," he said to Dree. "I like my strange company too much."

"Speaking of which," Véronique said, "any sign of Zoarr?"

"Not a thing since he was in here trying to follow our trail," Wibble said. "I guess he's abandoned his fake armor and moved on."

"Armor?" Dree asked. "Is he a brobnar warrior?"

"No," Pplimz said. "Well, I suppose he might have been once, but not any more."

"Apparently he and Skye Brooke were in here asking after Pplimz and myself," Wibble said, "dressed in cheap knock-offs of a Sanctum knight's armor."

"Zoarr," Dree said, her face scrunched up in thought. "That sounds like a giant's name."

"It is," Véronique said. "And Skye Brooke is a human. Do you know them?"

Dree shook her head, but still looked deep in thought. "Never heard of them before," she said. "But I did see a rather large down-at-heel Sanctum knight on my way over here today."

"How long ago was this?" Pplimz asked.

"Not long," she said. "I only just got here."

"Tell us exactly where you saw him," Véronique said, tapping on her wrist com. "He is wanted by Star Alliance security."

"Not to mention a few other beings as well," Wibble said.

"It was by the transport hub," Dree said. "Around the personal vehicles for hire."

"Of course," Wibble said. "He's trying to make a quiet getaway now that Skye Brooke has already been detained."

"A security team is on its way," Véronique said, and indeed a few of the Star Alliance crew who were at the party were tapping on their wrist coms and making a hasty exit. "I just hope they get there before he drives off into the sunset."

CHAPTER THIRTY-ONE
Pplimz Calls Security

The transport hub at the Horizon was busier than Wibble and Pplimz had ever seen it. Beings milled about in trios and couples as well as a few larger packs.

"What's going on here?" Wibble asked.

"The Ellipticalite Grapple just pulled in," Véronique said. "It's the first time in months."

"Ah, well that explains it," Pplimz said. The Grapple was probably the cheapest method of transportation in the area, mainly because it was grossly uncomfortable for almost all beings, and unless you happened to be lucky enough to want to travel to whatever its next destination was, extremely slow. When it took off, the large carriage container shot its eponymous grapple up to the sky, latching on to *something*, one presumed.

Some believed it attached to the Boundary itself, others wondered if there were hooks on the visible stars. Perhaps it held some unusual gravitational property and managed to pull the carriage along from the force of its own trajectory. Regardless of how it worked, the process flung the carriage up into the air, then swung it high over the landscape to its next destination. Then, once unloaded and reloaded, the contraption did it all over again as it made its ponderous way around the Local Group, transporting thousands of beings and many megagrams of cargo.

Between the disembarking passengers and those waiting to board, the transportation hub at the Horizon was full to capacity.

"You'd think that looking for a giant among dwarves wouldn't be that challenging," Tailor said, as he elbowed his way through a group of dwarven minstrels who were heading for the Horizon taverns. "And yet."

"The good news is that Zoarr isn't getting out of here very quickly," Pplimz said. "That's quite the traffic jam." They pointed at the long line of private autocars and shared ride services barely crawling along the one road through the Horizon.

"What if he hired a flyer?" Wibble asked.

"There are no flyers," Véronique said. "Star Alliance airspace regulations."

"Well, I don't know anything about that," Wibble said. "We're clearly going to have to split up, and since no one informed me of any vertical restrictions, I'll be taking the high road. As I usually do." She shot upward into the air for a panoramic view of the crush of beings.

"It's only a prohibition against vehicles," Tailor said, smirking at Wibble's attempt to flout the rules.

"If anyone catches sight of Zoarr, call it in to Star Alliance security," Véronique said. "They have the ability and authority to detain him here."

"The Horizon isn't Star Alliance territory," Tailor reminded her.

"No, but we have an arrangement with the merchants' guild," she explained. "It's mutually beneficial."

"All right," Pplimz said. "Let's debate jurisdictional nuances after we find Zoarr, shall we?" They took off toward the private vehicle hire kiosks and left Tailor and Véronique to bicker or search or both.

Wibble thought that getting a skydweller's view on the problem would have made finding Zoarr easy, but her perspective from the air made all the beings below appear roughly the same size. With a knight's cowl over his head, Zoarr would be indistinguishable from half the other beings.

"I can't see anything useful from up here," she complained to Pplimz over their comm link.

"For all we know he's sitting in an idling hovercab halfway out of the Horizon," Pplimz said, as they wove through the queues of beings hoping to get something more roadworthy than a bucket of bolts. "If he got here before the Grapple, we've probably lost him."

"Wait, what in the embers of Everfire is that?" A voice came over their comms; whether it was Tailor or Véronique, Pplimz couldn't tell.

Wibble hovered over to their location, Pplimz following as quickly as they could through the crush. When they joined Tailor and Véronique, it was obvious what they were talking about.

There, at the entrance to Horizon Rent-A-Rectopod, stood a tall, imposing figure, ablaze in a golden light and completely covered in flames.

"That's definitely what a knight looks like," Pplimz said.

"I thought Zoarr's disguise was supposed to be bad," Wibble said. "That's not bad at all."

"That's not *Zoarr* at all," Tailor said, his eyes wide. "I mean, the one on fire isn't Zoarr. The other poor being probably is."

"Oof," Véronique said as the authentic Sanctum knight drew a sword and aimed it squarely at another being wearing what appeared to be a knight costume in poor condition and even poorer taste. "I almost feel sorry for him."

"WHO DARES IMPERSONATE A HOLY WARRIOR OF THE OPENED EYE?" the knight boomed, causing everyone who wasn't being directly shouted at to flee as fast as possible in the crowded marketplace. The knight reached a flaming hand forward and hauled the cowl down, revealing a terrified Zoarr.

"Should we rescue him?" Wibble asked.

"I've already called Star Alliance security," Pplimz said. "They should get here before the knight does any real damage. I think."

The knight had grabbed Zoarr by the neck of the phony armor and was now lifting the giant up so they were face to face. Zoarr's feet dangled above the ground, and it looked as if he were attempting to run away in midair. They couldn't hear whatever the giant had to say, but it was obvious that it wasn't terribly convincing to the knight.

"You dishonor yourself by donning vestments to which you are not entitled," the knight explained, loudly and angrily. "And you dishonor the Opened Eye. You will remove the offensive fabric at once."

The knight set Zoarr down surprisingly gently, but then poked the giant with the tip of the flaming sword. The cheap costume fabric smoldered where the sword touched it, and Zoarr slapped at it in a panic to stop a complete conflagration before it started.

"Remove it!" the knight intoned again. Zoarr hurried to comply and soon was standing in the middle of the Horizon transport hub in nothing but his regulation Star Alliance underwear.

The knight bent down to look Zoarr in the face.

"Here's some free advice: if you want to wear a House's regalia, try earning it first. And here's another tip: don't ever let me catch sight of you again." Then the knight swept away, trailing the scent of smoke and petrichor.

"Well, you don't see that every day," Wibble said, as a team of Star Alliance security swarmed Zoarr to take him to the brig.

"More's the pity," Véronique said wistfully, watching Zoarr being stuffed into the back of a R0-V3R. "Those are some really great tattoos."

Zoarr and Skye Brooke were reunited in adjoining cells in the *Quantum*'s brig, which was no longer aboard ship, now that the downed cruiser was among the most heavily guarded areas in Star Alliance territory. Instead, the engineering team had transported the secure cells directly from the ship to a back lot in the Bivouac, near the security office. It was probably somewhat less secure than it would have been on the *Quantum* proper, but it meant that detainees weren't marched through sensitive areas and past technologies the existence of which the Alliance would rather they kept to themselves.

Wibble and Pplimz were shown into the security office by Officer Barros.

"They both refuse to name any of their collaborators," Barros said. "They won't even admit to being helped by Officer

Levesque, although we have her sworn statement that she was secretly providing information to them since they left the area."

"I can't say I'm terribly surprised," Pplimz said. "If I were part of a secret organization, I imagine that I too would take the secret part fairly seriously."

"You'd never be involved in something like the Cult of the Architects," Wibble said.

"No, but if there was something I believed in as much as they believe in trying to attain the Architects' power, I'm sure I'd do anything to keep my confederates safe."

Barros nodded. "I can't say I disagree," she said. "I have to admit that I admire their conviction and loyalty. I just wish it were to a cause I shared."

"So what's going to happen to them?" Wibble asked.

Barros shrugged. "Brooke was right when they said the whole tiara business wasn't, technically, against any Star Alliance regulation. It's certainly not one of the few offenses on the Joint House Agreement on Behavior and Ethics."

Wibble laughed. "There's almost nothing on the JHABE, and it only applies in a small area anyway. I wonder why anyone even signed that document."

"I think it's so that no one can say the Local Group is a purely lawless sector," Pplimz said. "It's much easier for the Houses to enforce their own rules if there are at least a handful of joint mandates we can all agree on."

"Well, we'd be hard pressed to find any society that would have a law against trying to find something that may or may not even exist," Barros said. "Treasure hunting is practically mandatory around here."

"Surely Zoarr and Skye Brooke contravened some Star

Alliance regulations in the course of their hunt, though," Wibble said.

Barros nodded. "We've got Zoarr on filing a false application to join the crew, and Brooke for entering secure premises without authorization."

"Skye Brooke was breaking and entering?" Pplimz asked.

"Oh, didn't I tell you?" Wibble said. "I figured out that Skye Brooke was using their martian transporter to bypass the border checkpoints to visit Zoarr."

"Of course," Pplimz said. "What better way to meet without being seen."

"And that explains why Zoarr's quarters showed traces of xylocarbonate-zeta and zyphoric acid. No actual theft required."

Barros nodded. "Brooke did admit that much. But honestly, both of those are minor infractions. The best we can do is hold them until the security chief makes a final ruling, but I can't see it coming to anything much more than Zoarr being stripped of his rank and both of them being barred from Star Alliance territory."

"Zoarr did enter a false procurement order," Pplimz reminded her. "That is technically breaching a networked system with the intent to defraud."

"Maybe the chief will make something out of that," Barros speculated. "We'll find out in the morning."

"Can we see them?" Wibble asked.

"Knock yourselves out. I doubt you'll get anything more out of them than we did, though."

Each cell was large enough for even Zoarr to walk around comfortably, with a small private sanitary cubicle and a pull-down cot. Zoarr and Skye Brooke were asleep in adjacent pods, the translucent orange sides of their cells glowing with a soft light.

"Barros was right," Wibble whispered. "No one's talking."

"You aren't as funny as you think you are." The voice came from Skye Brooke's pod, although there was no movement within.

"And your cause isn't as righteous as you think it is," she shot back.

"Wibble," Pplimz had a warning tone to their voice.

"I know that the Qubit Zirconium wasn't what we thought it was," Skye Brooke said, the usual nonchalance entirely absent from their demeanor. "But that doesn't mean that no such artifact exists. Zoarr and I aren't alone. There are more people on this world who believe that we can change our fate than you'd possibly imagine. If there's a way to gain the power of the Architects, we'll find it. It may not be in my lifetime, even, but we'll succeed. We have to. Now, leave us alone, detectives. Surely your work here is done."

Pplimz looked at Wibble, who obviously wanted to argue, but who hovered out the door and back to the security office without another word. Brooke was right – they were done, but somehow it didn't feel like they'd been entirely victorious. Pplimz followed after Wibble, the force field rippling as they passed through with their coded Star Alliance badge. A solid Æmbermetal door closed behind them, snicking locked.

"You were right," Pplimz said to Officer Barros. "I doubt either of them will say anything further. This is a matter of principle."

"There's no reasoning with them," Wibble said, sadly. "They think they are the heroes of the story. They imagine themselves fighting for freedom from the tyranny of beings they think created this world and then abandoned it. But whether it was by a powerful architect's design or the random effects of the laws of physics, no one can fight the reality we live in."

"So there's no point in hoping for a better world?" Barros asked.

"There's nothing wrong with wishing existence were different," Wibble said. "But it's a waste of a life to fight against things that can't be changed. It's so much better to spend that energy working on making the world we do live in a better place. That's how we improve reality, by striving to create the world we want to live in. There is no magical or technological artifact on any world that can replace working together."

CHAPTER THIRTY-TWO
Wibble Has Reservations

Wibble and Pplimz found their office exactly as they'd left it, all hypersonic and infrared markers in place, no elves whatsoever sleeping on their couch. Pplimz unpacked the suitcase, hanging their suits back in the closet with the secret exit. They closed the door and set the closet to "clean and press."

Wibble gathered up the remains of Tailor's bag and said, "We should probably send this back to him."

"It's ruined." Pplimz pointed at the ripped lining.

"It's still Tailor's," Wibble said, looking for a box to pack it in. She found an old carton from Pplimz's milliner, and stuffed the torn bag into it. She hovered over to the desk to call for a courier, then set the box outside their door. As it slurped shut behind her, she turned to see Pplimz reclining on the sofa, catching up on messages.

"The Star Alliance security chief made her ruling," Pplimz informed Wibble. "Officer Barros had it right – Skye Brooke was let go, and the only sentence is that they are now barred from all Star Alliance territory."

"And Zoarr?"

"Found liable for dereliction of duty, one count of low espionage, one count of unauthorized system incursion. The chief reminded him that those charges could lead to a sentence of detention, but she couldn't find any compelling reason to limit his movements." Pplimz read directly from the ruling. "'It is the opinion of the Star Alliance that incarceration as a punitive measure is not in line with our values, and as such we avoid detention as a sentence when the offense is not likely to be repeated. As a result, we find that former Trainee Officer Zoarr, Specialization: Cryptography and Applied Communications Operations, is hereby dishonorably discharged from the Star Alliance, and no longer welcome in any Star Alliance region, facilities, or allied territories.' Essentially, the same as Skye Brooke."

Wibble rippled in several colors. "I agree that detaining a being who poses no further risk is of no practical value. But it feels like they got away with it, somehow."

"Maybe," Pplimz said, then cast a news story up on the desk holo for Wibble to see. "Maybe not."

It was one of the salacious gossip casts from a sylicate communications consortium, which was popular with beings across the entire Crucible. Any story they broadcast would be common knowledge before the show was over.

"Secret Society Seeks Superpower, Sources Say," the teaser read in thirteen different scripts. The story presented by the perfectly chiseled sylicate caster was loosely based on what had actually happened, with less focus on the specific events and more wild speculation about who the Cult of the Architects were and what nefarious schemes they might be plotting.

"I suspect it's going to be quite a bit more difficult for them to carry on their activities now that practically the entire world knows about them." Pplimz made a face at one of the more implausible speculations of the so-called news service. "Well, thinks they know about them, anyway."

The story changed to a piece on xtreme cyclerball, highlighting the controversial recent triumph of the New Photic Comets over the Bone Island Bandits and their subsequent advance to the Hranzit Grand Finals, with the implication that illegal Æmberinjectors had been employed in the victory. Pplimz switched off the cast.

"Maybe this is all for the best," Wibble said. "Getting it all out in the open."

"We'll see," Pplimz said. "If it were me, I'd just lie low for a while until the next ridiculous thing comes along and everyone forgets about the Cult of the Architects. There is no shortage of drama on the Crucible, after all."

"All of which is good news for us," Wibble said. "If life here were dull, there'd be nothing for us to do."

Pplimz made a throat-clearing noise, which was particularly noticeable since they didn't have a throat. "Speaking of that, what would you say to a little holiday?"

"Pplimz," Wibble sounded shocked. "Have you met me? You know exactly what I'd say: 'Hello, holiday!'" She hovered over to the desk and pulled up a couple of booking forms on the holo. "So what do you think? Rocket ballooning or sky surfing?"

"I was actually thinking about something a bit more relaxing," Pplimz admitted.

"Oh, I know exactly what you have in mind," Wibble said. "I'm just suggesting how we get there."

Sticky Fingered Luce's Discount Rocket Balloon Emporium wasn't anywhere near as dodgy as Pplimz had feared, and they walked out with a nearly completely intact second-hand inflatable and a low power atmo rocket for less than the cost of a round-trip first-class ticket on a skyhopper.

"Do you know how to set this up?" Pplimz asked, unfolding the instructions.

"How hard can it be?" Wibble said. "It's only rocket science."

The instructions were, indeed, straightforward enough and within a few minutes they'd packed the balloon into the payload section of the rocket, installed the required liquid Æmber fuel, and settled into the rocket's passenger compartment.

"I've input the landing coordinates into the onboard computer," Pplimz said. "Ready to go?"

"Yes I am, Pplimz!" Wibble was literally vibrating with excitement. "Start the countdown."

Pplimz chuckled. "We don't require a countdown," they said. "You just push the big purple 'Go' button."

"Pplimz. If I am riding a rocket, there will be a countdown. From six, if you please."

"Of course. Six. Five. Four. Three. Two. One." Pplimz pushed the button and with a roar the rocket took off into the sky. Wibble and Pplimz were pressed back into their seats, though the pressure was probably less than riding the Grapple. The rocket wasn't going that high, after all.

When they reached the apex of their upward journey, the nose cone of the rocket turned inside out, deploying the balloon, from which the rest of the rocket, including the passenger compartment, now hung suspended. The balloon had filled with the remaining gases from the rocket's propulsion and was now drifting gently on the breeze next to the floating island of Brighthaven.

"Hello!" Wibble called as they passed a Sanctum monk on the island, who waved courteously, then went back to their gardening.

"The view is quite breathtaking," Pplimz said. "In a manner of speaking. It's been a long time since I actually breathed."

"I told you that floating was delightful," Wibble said. "Ooh, maybe the spa can give you an antigrav upgrade. Or jet feet?"

"We don't call them 'upgrades' any more, Wibble," Pplimz said, gently. "It implies that one is lesser without them."

"Oh, you're right. I hadn't thought of that before. I'm sorry."

"It's fine. Besides, I don't want any new augments, Wibble. I'm happy to take a balloon ride if I wish to float."

"Indeed. After all, I *can* float and this is wonderful!"

It wasn't the fastest way to travel, but watching the landscape go by underneath was very soothing. A wild speckled octopter paced them for a while, riding the air currents as they approached the forest. They passed underneath a Raptrix flyer, the Skyborn inside bonded to their ship for life. A sugarcloud enveloped them in its sweet vapor before they passed through to the other side. The whole experience was a much-needed change of pace for the two detectives.

The balloon's onboard system steered them gently toward the upper landing pad at the Floating Pines Resort and Spa. They landed, disembarked, and the balloon slowly deflated as the gas dissipated. They packed it back into the rocket's nose cone and found a storage cube to stow the whole unit into until the return trip. A three-day at a remote resort was just the break they needed.

Wibble and Pplimz followed the now-familiar path toward the resort, this time turning left toward the reception chalet.

"I believe we have a reservation," Wibble said to the friendly insectoid at the front desk. "Wibble and Pplimz."

"The investigators for hire!" the receptionist said, running a tarsus down the guest list printed on a pressed wood pulp leaf. "Yes, I have you here."

"Excellent," Wibble said.

"Do you have an opening for the mechanic at the spa?" Pplimz asked. "I'd like to schedule an adjustment for one of my actuators." Pplimz flexed their fifth upper manipulator.

"Oh, not to worry, we already have you booked in for first thing tomorrow morning," the receptionist assured them.

"Wibble, you really did think of everything," Pplimz said, accepting the pressed metal-toothed fob which was used to unlock the door to their room.

The receptionist stared at them with compound eyes, as if there was more to the transaction still to come.

"Is there something else?" Wibble asked.

"You are those two detectives, aren't you?" the receptionist asked, coyly. "I saw it on The Crucible Chronicle."

Wibble glowed pinkly. "Guilty as charged," she said. "If you'd like to take a holo, I'm sure we'd be happy to oblige..." She glanced at Pplimz, who nodded and adjusted their hat.

"Oh," the receptionist said, wings flat against their thorax. "It's not that. It's... well... you see, I've got this problem. It's my brother's husband's sister's grandchild's partner, and they were on this vault run the other day. It went badly, which is not unusual for Zirckle – they're useless against Untamed – but there's a rumor going around that they deliberately sabotaged the battle. And now there's an angry Archon after them, who is going to be arriving at their burrow tomorrow!" The receptionist had now completely lost all their professional composure and was rubbing their forelegs together in worry.

"I know you're here on holiday and I hate to have to bother you, but I don't know who else to turn to. Please, can you help my hivemate?"

Pplimz thought about that fifth upper manipulator, and how much they'd been looking forward to a relaxing wrench and grease. Wibble thought about the floating forest and how lovely it would be to hover through the rustling leaves.

"Of course we'll help," Pplimz said.

Wibble flushed sunlight yellow. "Now, tell us everything you know about Zirckle."

ACKNOWLEDGMENTS

Thanks first and foremost to my editor, Lottie Llewelyn-Wells, who helped bring Wibble and Pplimz to life. To my agent, Chelsea Hensley, and her colleague Sara Megibow, for steering and cheering me along.

I'm indebted to my various online and in-person writing friends for years of advice and support. There are too many of you to name, but I owe you each a drink of choice.

Last, but the complete opposite of least, thanks to my partner Steven for everything, always.

ABOUT THE AUTHOR

M DARUSHA WEHM is the Nebula Award-nominated and Sir Julius Vogel Award-winning author of the interactive fiction game *The Martian Job,* several SF novels, and the Andersson Dexter cyberpunk detective series. They have also written the Devi Jones: Locker YA series, and the coming-of-age novel *The Home for Wayward Parrots.* Originally from Canada, Darusha lives in New Zealand after spending several years sailing the Pacific.

darusha.ca // twitter.com/darusha

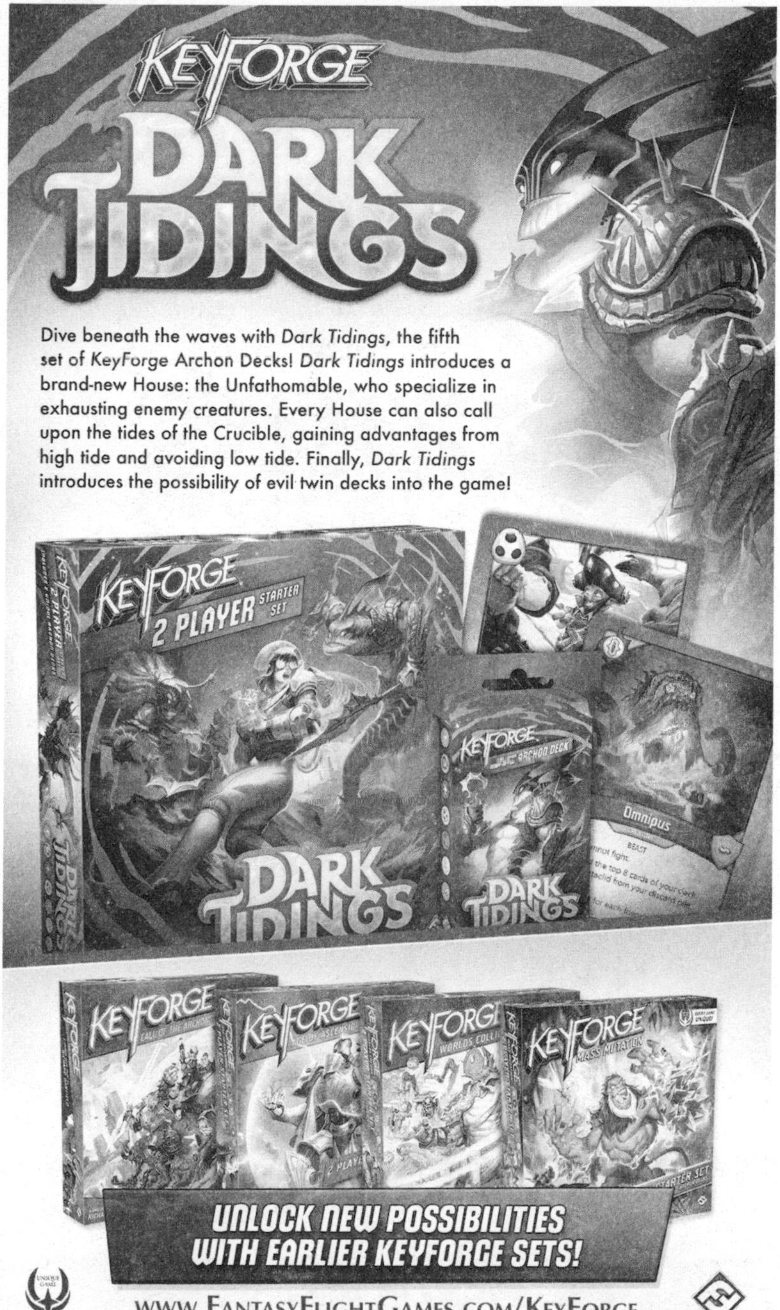
KeyForge
Dark Tidings
Dive beneath the waves with Dark Tidings, the fifth set of KeyForge Archon Decks! Dark Tidings introduces a brand-new House: the Unfathomable, who specialize in exhausting enemy creatures. Every House can also call upon the tides of the Crucible, gaining advantages from high tide and avoiding low tide. Finally, Dark Tidings introduces the possibility of evil twin decks into the game!
KeyForge
2 Player Starter Set
Dark Tidings
Omnipus
Unlock new possibilities with earlier KeyForge sets!
www.FantasyFlightGames.com/KeyForge
© 2021 Fantasy Flight Games. KeyForge, the Unique Game logo, and the FFG logo are TM/® of Fantasy Flight Games.

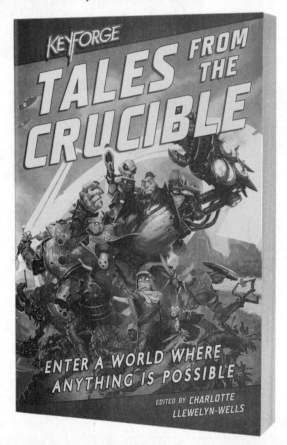

WORLD EXPANDING FICTION FROM ACONYTE BOOKS

@ACONYTEBOOKS